PRAISE FOR HEIDI CHIAVAROLI

"Chiavaroli delights with this homage to Louisa May Alcott's *Little Women*, featuring a time-slip narrative of two women connected across centuries."
PUBLISHERS WEEKLY on *The Orchard House*

"Beautifully written, this God honoring and compelling story is Heidi Chiavaroli's best yet."
CATHY GOHLKE, Bestselling, Christy Hall of Fame and Carol Award-winning author on *Hope Beyond the Waves*

"*Hope Beyond the Waves* tugged at my heart from page one, and I was totally immersed in the seemingly insurmountable challenges of both the past and present day characters. Kudos to Heidi Chiavaroli for pouring out this beautifully raw and moving story about finding love and hope in the most unexpected of places."
MELANIE DOBSON, Carol Award-winning author of *Catching the Wind*

"*The Hidden Side* is a beautiful tale that captures the timeless struggles of the human heart."
JULIE CANTRELL, *New York Times* Bestselling author of *Perennials*

"First novelist Chiavaroli's historical tapestry will provide a satisfying summer read for fans of Kristy Cambron and Lisa Wingate."
LIBRARY JOURNAL on *Freedom's Ring*

The Way Home

HEIDI CHIAVAROLI

HOPE CREEK PUBLISHERS

Also by Heidi Chiavaroli

The Orchard House

The Tea Chest

The Hidden Side

Freedom's Ring

The Edge of Mercy

Hope Beyond the Waves

The Orchard House Bed and Breakfast Series

Where Grace Appears

Where Hope Begins

Where Love Grows

Where Memories Await

Where Dreams Reside

Where Faith Belongs

Where Promises Remain

Lights of Acadia Series

The Way Back

The Way Home

Biblical Fiction

Covenant of the Heart

Chapter One

There's no life lesson you can't learn in a Walmart.

~ SCOUT SWIFT'S JOURNAL

I learned what kind of a person I wanted to be in Walmart. Right there, in between the first-aid and shampoo aisles. Past the diabetic supplies and through the half door that small children can't help pressing against despite the bold STOP sign at their eye level. In many ways, behind that pharmacy counter is where it all began.

And where it all ended.

I work my spatula over the counting tray, sweeping tiny white pills into the dish.

Five, ten, fifteen, twenty.

Lisinopril. A maintenance drug—something a patient took every day—to stabilize high blood pressure.

Most of our maintenance drugs surround the health of the

heart. A person has to take care of the heart. It's pretty important. And we all know how fragile it can be.

"Can I have some help on the register, Scout?" Sherry calls out to me from the front counter.

Yes, my name is actually Scout. As in *To Kill a Mockingbird*.

My mom was a huge fan of literature, and my dad only disagreed with her about one thing—and it wasn't my name. Though I thought about changing my name more than once, even entertained changing it to Jean Louise to appease Mom *and* give myself the semblance of a normal designation, I never did. Turns out I actually like the name Scout better than Jean Louise, and after Mom died . . . well, I didn't have the heart to change the one thing she gave me that's supposed to stick all my life.

"Be right there." I finish counting out the pills, dump the tablets from the tray into the orange prescription bottle, cap it, and peel the label from the printer to place on the bottle. I pride myself on straight labels. Those suckers can be stubborn to put on right, but I like them neat and straight. Just as much as I like my counting tray clean. And the disinfectant wipes and Purell handy. But while I *do* like neat labels on pill bottles, I don't always like them on people, which is why I don't claim the label of OCD slapped on me ten years ago by some doctor.

Yes, I like things a certain way. And no, I don't like germs. But it's a minor thing to live with—not a major inconvenience that needs a label. Pill bottles . . . now those need labels. People who like shoes in their closet lined up neatly from heel to toe—they don't.

I hang the pill bag on the rack beside Elise, the pharmacist, and walk around the worktable to the customer counter, my face warming at the sight of the next patron in line. The only patron in line.

"I am going to kill you," I whisper to Sherry as I pass.

She laughs. For a spunky single mom who's worked the pharmacy since I was a ten-year-old living blissfully on the coast of Maine, she has a wicked sense of humor.

"Hey, Tom. Picking up?"

Handsome and well-built with a curly head of dark hair, the girls often joke that he has a crush on me. I suppose the feeling is mutual. But after all these years of him coming to get his cholesterol pills, he's never asked me out. I'd long ago accepted we aren't meant to be, simply chalked it up to the "not going anywhere" relationship column, which was just about all my romantic relationships. There was another column, of course. The "stole my hope" column. But that list held only one name, and I vowed he would remain alone there forever.

Tom smiles, his dark eyes resting on me. "Sure am." He gives me his date of birth, as if I don't already know it. I punch in the information, wondering for the hundredth time why this thirty-five-year-old Greek god doesn't have a wife or girlfriend. Does he have some untreatable, horrible personality disorder that he's able to successfully hide for the five minutes I see him every month?

I grab his medicine bag from alongside the hundreds of others behind me.

"Getting nice out there. Done any hiking lately?" he asks.

"I drove out to Beavertail the other day. Walked the rocks. It was beautiful." While I'd checked the Rhode Island light off the list of lighthouses Mom and I had wanted to see a long time ago, I still enjoyed visiting a few times a year. Even if it was by myself. Even if knowing how much Mom would have liked it still caused pinpricks of bittersweet pain to trample my soul.

"It's gorgeous over there," he says.

And just as I think he's about to suggest that we go together sometime, a blonde woman in a tasteful pantsuit that accentuates her figure walks up to Tom and slides her arm through his.

He turns to her, gives her a smile I've never seen on him before. "Oh, hey, honey. Did they have our chips?"

She holds up a package of grain-free hummus crisps. "Score."

Tom grins at me, must have mistaken my look of surprise for

doubt over the credibility of hummus chips. "They're actually amazing."

I laugh, a rigid, funny thing. I look at the register. "Twelve dollars and ninety-nine cents."

He inserts his bank card into the pin pad machine while the woman beside him ignores me, rambling on about where they should go for dinner that night.

He takes the prescription bag I hand him, gives me a wink, and then they are both gone.

"Scout . . . I am so sorry," Sherry says.

Truthfully, something deep inside me has come to terms with the fact that I will be alone forever. I like to think I've made peace with it. After almost thirty years, I should have. Maybe someday, I'll believe it. Needing a man to feel complete is such an old-fashioned notion, isn't it? Besides, nursing loneliness is preferable to nursing a wounded heart.

I shake my head. "He could have at least done the courtesy of introducing me." I elbow Sherry as she gives me a look of pity. "Hey, no worries. I never thought we'd actually get together."

"I did. You should have asked him out years ago."

I shake my head. "Not my style."

She pokes me in the arm, trying to lighten the mood. "Oh, you have some of that?"

Only the presence of a familiar young man approaching the counter in a rush stops me from sticking my tongue out at her.

I know his name because I carded him the first few times. He is twenty-two years old. Skinny, with pants that hang loose on his backside, a Bruins baseball cap slightly sideways on his head, and a familiar hollow, hungry look in his eyes. His name is Jaden. Jaden Hansen.

I look behind him to his girlfriend, a dark-haired porcelain-skinned beauty. From the beginning, something didn't measure up about the two of them. She seemed to have her act together. Almost, anyway—at least she didn't show visible signs of needing a fix. And while she never approaches the counter, she often smiles timidly at me. Like now.

I return the gesture.

"Can I get a pack of 1CC needles?"

I don't like this part of my job. Initially, I wrestled with it. A lot. Massachusetts law says you don't need a prescription for needles. You only need to be eighteen. And while I don't like being an accomplice to illegal drug use, I also reason that clean needles are better than dirty needles, and I am only doing my job.

I walk to the back of the pharmacy wall, grab a single pack of needles from the box of ten, and scan them into the register. "A dollar ninety-nine."

He counts out coins in his palms while I greet his girlfriend, still a few feet away. I gesture to her middle, where an obvious bump resides beneath her sundress. "When are you due?"

She places her hands protectively over her belly. "August twenty-second."

"You know if it's a boy or a girl?"

She shakes her head. "We want to be surprised. Like it used to be way back before all the fancy ultrasounds and stuff." She looks at her boyfriend with something akin to hope painted on her features, but he doesn't notice. Instead, he transfers coins from his own shaking hands to mine.

He grabs the receipt from the printer before I can, scoops up the needles from the counter. "I don't need a bag." He shoves the purchase into the pocket of his jeans and leaves with quick steps out the door of the main entrance, beside the pharmacy.

The girl trails behind him, granting a small wave to me as she leaves.

I exhale a long breath and return to the back of the pharmacy.

"That poor baby," Sherry says. "Going to be born addicted, going to wind up in the foster system in one month. Just watch."

I scoop up my handheld scanner and grab a pharmacy bag. The drug *furosemide* pops onto my screen. A water pill that aids the body in ridding itself of excess fluid and salt, thereby relieving the heart's workload.

"I think she's clean," I say, for some reason wanting the best for the pregnant girl in the sundress, wanting to believe I am right.

"Yeah, and I'm a virgin," Sherry says, making us chuckle.

I finish filling the prescription and count a few more medications. I place a label on an inhaler, lining up the edges perfectly on the red-and-white box, when the sound of flip-flops slapping laminate comes from behind.

"Help! Please help!"

It's the girl, the pregnant one in the sundress. I place the inhaler on the counting pod.

"I called 911, but he's not breathing. It's never happened before like this . . . please, he's in the parking lot."

My breaths quicken. I turn to Elise, the only one of us with medical letters behind her name. She can't leave the pharmacy. "Can I take a Narcan?"

"Scout . . ."

"Please, Elise?"

A life is a life. Had I not just put the needles into his hands? Minutes can count. I could get there before the ambulance.

"You can't take product off the shelves. The medics will be here fast."

I plead with my eyes, unspoken words between us.

She sighs. "Go, then. But I'm in no way endorsing this."

I grab a Narcan off the shelf along with a pair of rubber gloves, pulling them on as I follow the running pregnant girl into the sunshine. She runs all the way to a beaten-down old camper on the side of the lot.

I hesitate only a moment. The camper has been parked there for days. The girl runs up the two flimsy steps and disappears inside. I follow.

It's surprisingly neat and tidy within. Terribly outdated, but clean with a scent of lemon. I peel the Narcan package open. The man I'd just given the needles to lies unconscious on the floor, his skin and lips a bluish gray, a rattling in his throat. I place the tip of the nozzle up one of his nostrils, press firmly, then stand back, waiting.

Nothing at first. The rattling weakens, then suddenly a sharp intake of breath, eyes wide open.

I slump back in relief, the whine of sirens drawing closer as the young man stares vacantly at me, groggy and sluggish, but breathing steadily.

The girl behind me is strangely quiet. She clutches her arms around her belly and hums softly to herself. I hop down the stairs of the camper and wave down the ambulance when it comes barreling into the lot. I update the EMT's on the Narcan administration, then back away so they can do their work.

When the ambulance takes him away, barely cognizant of his surroundings, I am left alone with the girl.

"Can you call someone?"

She nods. "I'll be fine."

I shift my weight. A gentle breeze tugs at my bright blue Walmart smock. I want to get back inside the building, away from this mess. "You sure?"

Her dark ponytail bobs with her nod of determination. I can practically feel the shame oozing out of her. "Thank you," she whispers.

I reach out and squeeze her arm—wanting to comfort, but unable to find the words to do so.

The muscles beneath her arm grow tight, and I snatch my hand away. "I'm sorry," I mutter. "Let me know if there's anything I can do, okay? My name's Scout." Such a paltry offering, my name —something she probably already knew from my blue and white name badge.

I go to leave, almost missing the small voice behind me. I turn. "What did you say?"

"My name is Reagan."

I force the smallest of close-lipped smiles. "I hope he's okay, Reagan. And I hope he can get some help."

I leave the camper and the girl, fighting off a strange urge to say goodbye, feeling as if I will never see her again. She'll likely be too embarrassed to show her face at the pharmacy after what happened.

Her boyfriend better be too embarrassed to show *his* face.

Just before I enter the store, I search her out again, but she's no longer in sight. Something like a prayer whispers across my heart for her and her unborn child.

"Goodbye," I whisper.

Strange how I can't ignore the need to say it.

Stranger still because goodbyes are nothing I've ever been good at.

Chapter Two

"Lighthouses are endlessly suggestive signifiers of both human isolation and our ultimate connectedness to each other."
- Virginia Woolf

~ SCOUT SWIFT'S JOURNAL

The dream haunts me for two weeks straight, beginning the night of the parking lot overdose incident with Jaden Hansen and his pregnant girlfriend.

It would be wrong to call it a nightmare, because it's quite pleasant. Me and Mom visiting our lighthouses. Taking pictures, printing them at the Walmart kiosk, and pasting them into our scrapbook. Fun times. Beautiful times.

But always, the end comes. Mom, standing in front of picturesque Bass Head Light, her eyes a sparkling blue-green that match the ocean behind her, asking me the same question always. "Why'd you give up, Scout? Why?"

We'd had a goal back when I was a young. An aim to visit every lighthouse in New England. We hadn't made it even halfway when the cancer came hard and fast.

When I started at the Walmart in Massachusetts, after I'd saved up enough for a car, I set out to finish our lighthouse task. On my days off, I'd search out Rhode Island lighthouses, even going to Block Island to take pictures and check them off my list. When that was done, I sought those on Cape Cod and then the Boston area. Driving, seeing, snapping pictures, and leaving. All very calculated.

All very empty and lonely.

It hadn't been the lighthouses that made the trips with Mom special—it was Mom.

So why now, years later, did this dream haunt me? Is it having lived nearly three decades on this earth, with seemingly nothing to show for it? Or perhaps it's the near death of Jaden Hansen and the sale of the needles that almost killed him. Maybe it's the fact that twelve years have passed since I left home, a slew of forgotten dreams trailing behind.

I had left coastal Maine expecting so much for myself. Leaving my small town, I intended to chase my art, chase success.

But the chase ended all too soon. I'd settled, my dreams never taking me farther than the doors of Walmart.

The nightly dreams continue with ferocity, and when I begin to lose hours of sleep and make a handful of mistakes counting pills—something I've never done—Elise insists I take some long overdue time off. She doesn't take no for an answer. And just like that, I have three weeks paid vacation before me, and I am considering, after all these years, returning home.

The urge has come and gone over the years. Most of the time I ignore it, but sometimes I pick up the phone and give Dad a call or send my former best friend Lexie a text message. I'd even gone back to visit once during Christmas. But Dad tried too hard, Mom's absence was a palpable reminder, and I found myself longing for my new life in Massachusetts.

Or, more accurately, to be anywhere but the place I grew up.

That had been eight years ago now. Maybe it was time.

The first day I seriously consider the trip, the night visions stop. As quickly as they came, the dreams cease. And I know.

It is time to finish what I'd started with Mom all those years ago. There is nothing left to keep me from going home.

I WOULDN'T HAVE FOUND her if not for the birds in my backyard.

I told myself I came to Walmart that morning at opening time for cream for my coffee, but that wasn't entirely true. I came for my birds. I hated to think of them scouring my backyard while I was gone, feeling betrayed that I hadn't lived up to my end of the bargain while they were entirely too eager to live up to theirs— keeping me company with their gentle whistling twitters, happy flight, and majestic colors.

Now, I wait for the doors of the superstore to open before wheeling my shopping cart over to the dairy section to grab a small container of cream. I'd be leaving for my trip north that morning. I'd given it some thought, even tried to dissuade myself, but as soon as I did, the dream returned. While I didn't dwell overly much on the ethereal, it seemed that someone—God or Mom, I couldn't be sure—wanted me to search out the lighthouses, wanted me to return home.

After grabbing cream, I head over to the Lawn and Garden section. I walk down the empty aisle, snatching up a variety of suets and seed cakes before perusing the large bottom shelf for a value pack of bird seed. A sharp intake of breath gives me pause, but I don't hear anything else, so I bend down to heft the forty-pound bag into the bottom rack of my carriage.

I am halfway into the lugging when something behind the large stacks of seed catches my attention. I let out a yelp and drop the bag, heart pounding at the form crouched in the back of the metal racks.

Black maternity dress. Pale hands. My gaze flies to her face, but I know I will see delicate porcelain features and dark hair that matches thick eyelashes. I blink, try to catch my breath.

"Reagan?"

She scrambles out from behind the seed, not an easy feat considering her belly seems to have gone from the size of a cantaloupe to the size of a watermelon since I last saw her. "I—I can explain."

I look from her to the place where she'd been tucked behind the seed. "You *slept* here?"

She doesn't answer, but her eyes remain frantic, glued to mine. "Please . . . please don't tell anyone. It was just for the night. I'll find someplace else."

I stand from my crouched position, squeeze my eyes shut, as if when I open them the pregnant girl will disappear.

She doesn't. "How . . . I mean, there's security and . . ."

She swallows. "I didn't know where else to go last night. I read this old book once, *Where the Heart Is*, that made me think . . . anyway, I'm going to figure out something today. I promise."

I rub my temples. "What about the camper?"

"I left him."

Her boyfriend. Jaden.

"I thought for sure after that day in the parking lot, he'd be done. But I was wrong. I want my baby to be raised right. He was mad when I told him last night. I can't stay with him, I just can't."

I nod. She's as skittish as Sherry's tabby cat.

I drag in a deep breath. How is this girl going to take care of a child? "There are shelters. There are people who care."

"Who will care?" Her doe-like eyes, young and lucid, stare back at me, as if begging for an answer. I claim there are people who care, but is that true? I stand right in front of her and how much do I care? Enough to direct her to a shelter, yes, but not enough for much more.

I remember what it was like to be in a situation not so unlike her own twelve years earlier. What would I have done if temps had dropped as low as they had last night? Would I have snuck into this building, hid behind stacks of birdseed?

A squeeze starts in my chest, and I recognize the pinch of a panic attack. I breathe through my nose, forcing thoughts of my own past away, refusing to succumb to these old attacks after so many years of being free of them.

"What about family?" I force out. "Or Jaden's parents? You're carrying their grandchild . . . won't they help you?"

"They blame me for—" She shakes her head, seeming to change directions. She drags in a few deep breaths. "Did you know there used to be a leper colony off the coast of Massachusetts? In the early 1900s."

My mind spins. "What? No. No, I didn't know that."

She nods, suddenly enthusiastic. "I read about it in a book called *Hope Beyond the Waves*. They sent people there who had the skin disease, even if it was barely noticeable. People were so scared of it, they would fling the diseased off as outcasts, even tear mothers from their children. It was horrible, but they didn't know what else to do, how else to control it."

"Okay . . ."

"Well, that's how Jaden's parents think of me. Like I'm a leper, an outcast."

"But why?"

"They think I poisoned their son."

I press my lips together before speaking. "Did you?"

"No." She sniffs. "But I couldn't save him from it, either."

We stare at one another, and though I feel I should have answers for her, I have none.

"Miss Scout?"

I sigh, slump against the handle of my carriage. "Yes?"

"Miss Scout, I just want a second chance. A way to start over. You know what I mean?"

The words pierce me. I open my mouth to speak, but nothing comes out.

After a moment, she ducks behind the bird seed to grab an old duffel bag and her sandals. She slides them on. "Never mind. I don't need you to understand. I'm fine, okay? And I won't come back. I promise. And I didn't take anything when I was here last night, not even a breath mint. I'm not a thief."

She begins to stalk away with waddling steps, and the gesture causes my tongue to loosen. "Wait."

She turns, defiance still hard in her features.

Someone once told me the best way through hurt is helping someone else.

A voice from my past visits the vast space between us.

"I'm leaving this morning. For Maine. I don't want to leave, knowing you need help." Even as the words drift from my mouth, I want to snatch them back.

I have plans. Plans to see lighthouses, to visit my old home. This girl will only get in the way.

"I have family in Maine," she whispers.

"Really? I'd be willing to give you a ride, if you want." Even as I speak the words, I doubt them. I like things a certain way, including my car rides. I don't know this girl, don't know her habits—does she wash her hands after she uses the bathroom? When is the last time she laundered that maternity dress? These are things that have the potential to send me over the edge.

And she might be a minor. If I don't alert the authorities, could I be held accountable?

Reagan's chest rises and falls. "You would?"

. . . the best way through hurt is helping someone else.

Was I hurting? I hadn't thought so, but my recent dreams

make me question if I haven't been hurting worse than I thought for the last dozen years.

With a sharp snag of remembrance, I think of my own family. Mom, Dad, me. Just the three of us.

Then, images of Mom in the hospital bed in our living room those agonizing weeks before she left us. The night of their horrible argument that revealed my parents' secret. The following tension with my Dad—a tension I still felt more than three hundred miles away.

We'd never made amends, not really. Sure, we were civil enough over the years. He accepted my new life in Massachusetts. I accepted that we'd never be close again. Maybe we'd never been close. Maybe that was the entire problem.

I sigh. Mom's death, my parents' secret—it had all broken something inside me. Over the years, I'd tried to piece it together with various things—a job, friends, meaningless first dates—but none of that possessed the power to hold any of the broken together.

"How old are you?"

"Eighteen."

The same age I'd been when I'd been dumped at this very Walmart. I'd had no one and probably wouldn't have survived if not for the generosity of a stranger.

"Then, yes, I can take you," I say in answer to Reagan.

"I would pay you back for gas when I could. I would—"

I shake my head. "Don't worry about any of that. I only have two conditions."

"Okay."

"First, I have to make a few stops along the coast."

"Sure, anything."

"Second, no drugs. At all."

She lifts her chin. "I know you'd think I use too because of Jaden, but I don't mess with that stuff. And I don't mess with anything that could hurt my baby."

Her words appear genuine, but the image of her boyfriend unconscious, skin like ash, on the laminated floor of that camper, makes me doubt. I don't say anything, though.

Sometimes, you just need someone to believe in you.

Chapter Three

ZACK

I consider myself a reasonable guy. I keep my cool when supplies run late, when subcontractors don't show up, when customers hold back payments, when I mess up on a job quote and lose a boatload of money. I pride myself on keeping it together.

So now, as my parents tell me this earth-shattering news, I am trying like heck to do just that—stay calm. Stay controlled.

Keep it together.

I force a smile, more for my sake than for the sake of my parents. As if to ensure myself that the words that just came out of my dad's mouth are indeed funny instead of terribly, terribly devastating. "You're joking."

Of course, they're joking. I'm still smiling, still trying to bring them along with me. It's not too late. They can take it back.

I feel like I'm seven years old again, finding out Scooby, our dog, just died. At thirty-four, even though I haven't lived beneath my parents' roof for over a decade, I'm looking to them to make the world right again.

Mom rubs her temples. I notice the new lines at the corners of her eyes and mouth for the first time. "I'm afraid we're not honey. I know this is a bit of a shock, and I'm sorry for that."

I wince. "But . . . how?" I turn to my father for answers. He's always had them, hasn't he? The best way to swing a golf club or work a math problem or build a shed. Dad knows best.

He shifts in his seat, adjusts his elbows over outspread legs. Unlike Mom, I don't see any new lines on his face. In fact, now that I look at him—really look at him—he looks great. Tan and trim. Did he lose weight around his middle? The gray smatterings at his temples give off a distinguished air to his full head of hair. I can imagine him in the corner office of his engineering firm just as well as I can on the golf course.

"Son, this isn't easy for me to say, but . . . I've met somebody."

All the air sucks itself from my body. I hear the words, but they don't make sense.

I've met somebody.

"Somebody?" I say like an idiot. Somebody *not* Mom? Is that what he means?

No, this is *Dad*, after all. Upstanding, faithful Dad. He can't possibly mean that.

I'm still looking at him, looking to him to make sense of this funnel of nonsense these two people I love most in the world have just spun up for me.

He clears his throat. "I tried not to fall in love—"

My ears ring. He's fallen in *love*?

As the words sink in, as everything slides into place—the missed family dinners, the strained look my mother possessed the last several months, Dad's choice to step down from the church's board of trustees—hot, burning anger consumes me.

I shoot up to a standing position. My father sits in the same chair he occupies when he watches *This Old House*, the television show that got me hooked on construction when I was six years old.

"I don't believe you." I aim the words at my dad, but can't

resist a glance at Mom, crumpled on the couch, looking small and weak and *old*. A protective streak races through me. "What is wrong with you?"

Dad grits his teeth. "This isn't something I planned, Zack. Believe me when I tell you the last thing I want to do is hurt your mother."

"Then don't." The words shoot out of me, like a firecracker from a tube.

"Zack . . ." Mom says.

"No, Mom. Aren't you the ones always telling me that love is work? That marriage is work. How could he just *find* someone?"

I'm throwing a tantrum. I'm thirty-four years old, and I'm throwing a tantrum, and I could not care less.

"Sometimes, things change. Your mother and I haven't been happy for some time . . ."

"Happy?" I spit out the word. He's talking like someone I don't know. Have I ever known my father? Is everything I believed about him a lie? "You made a vow. What about your word, Dad? What about 'a man's only as good as his word'?"

"I didn't plan for this, son. I know you can't understand now, but I hope in time, you'll see it's for the best."

His mouth is spewing words I can't comprehend. I want to pummel him, shake some sense into him, spit curses upon him. None of this is my normal way. None of this is keeping my head about me.

"I have to go. Mom, I'm sorry, but I can't look at him right now."

Tears spill onto Mom's cheeks. I walk over and kiss her on the head, where a thick line of gray roots show at her scalp. "If you need anything, call me, okay? I'll stop in later."

I send a scorching look to Dad. "You—you man up and fix this. *Now.*"

I turn from the room and shove open the screen door, sending it slamming against the back wall. Now, I'm a fuming teenager instead of a toddler. But as I get into my work van, I don't feel as if I've so much as graduated high school. I don't feel as if I've accomplished one blasted thing.

I turn the ignition and my stomach churns. Anger used to feel good on me, but it doesn't anymore. I thought I was a different person, above such raw, hot emotions.

I allow my head to fall back against the rest.

God, what just happened in there?

I think of my demand for my father to fix the mess he's made. I've never spoken to him like that.

I dig my phone from my pocket and vacillate between calling Charlotte, the woman who's been like a grandmother to me since I was twelve, or Jason, a guy I've come to think of as a little brother over the last year. Maybe I should just go home and hug Atticus, my mutt of a faithful dog.

I don't want to worry Charlotte or be the one to give her bad news, so I opt for Jason, but just as my thumb hovers over the button, another call comes in. I bite back a groan at the name.

Mrs. Darling.

The sweet elderly woman is one of my most faithful customers. She's also anything but low maintenance.

I swipe right. "Hello, Mrs. Darling."

"Zackary! I hate to bother you—I've told you how I hate to bother you, haven't I?"

"You have, Mrs. Darling. It's okay, though. That's what I'm here for." This slice of normal life drains a small bit of tension within me. "What can I do for you?"

"Well, I was wondering if you could clean out my gutters. It's been some time, you know."

"Mrs. Darling, I did them three weeks ago, remember?"

"Oh, I'm certain I would remember."

I'm not so certain. I've been doing work for Mrs. Darling since high school, and even I've noticed a drastic decline in her memory the last year. I'm starting to worry it's not safe for her to live alone.

"Let me check my books, okay? But if it makes you feel better, why don't I stop by tomorrow and take a look? I'll be over at Charlotte's anyway. I could swing by at four?"

"Oh, that would be wonderful, Zackary! Thank you so much. How is the lighthouse coming?"

"It's done." She'd been at the town celebration to commemorate the restoration of the historic lighthouse beside Charlotte's bed and breakfast, but I don't remind her of that. "I'm working on the guest cottage now. Hey, Mrs. Darling, do you think you could invite Laura over when I'm by tomorrow?"

"Laura? Well, certainly, but don't you think she's a bit old for you, Zackary? And she's very busy with her job. What about that nice girl from New York? Penelope, wasn't it?"

I close my eyes at the thought of the girl who broke my heart and hightailed it back to New York eighteen months ago. I think of my parents.

"Priscilla," I ground out. "And no, Mrs. Darling, I'm not interested in Laura in that way. I'd like to go over the house maintenance schedule with her." And try to find a way to tactfully bring up my concern for her mother. Does she know how fast Mrs. Darling is declining?

"Okay, dear. I'll give her a call. Thank you so much, Zackary. You are such a sweet boy."

I think of the temper tantrum I just threw in front of my parents.

I'm sweet, all right.

I say goodbye to Mrs. Darling and hang up the phone, fiddling with the AC vents. The mess with Priscilla taught me a lot about forgiveness and grace, but just the thought of my Dad sitting in his chair telling me he's in love with another woman right in front of Mom causes my blood to reach volcanic temperatures. I tap my phone and press the speaker button before turning around in the driveway of my childhood home.

"Hey, what's up?"

"You think Laney can spare you for a couple hours tonight for some burgers at the Tavern?"

"Oh, but that would take me away from the exciting prospect of picking out wedding invitations."

"So, no?"

Jason laughs. "I'm kidding, man. We don't have plans. She's helping Charlotte with something."

"Great. Meet you at five?"

"You got it."

I hang up and roll down my windows, the AC still on. The briny air swipes through the van and I throw my baseball hat on the passenger's seat, allowing the breeze to cool my head. I think of Jason and Laney. High school sweethearts with a lot of history, getting married in just four months.

Would they last? Would Jason sit in his living room thirty-five years from now and tell his son that he *found* someone else?

I pound my steering wheel with my palm. *Thirty-five* years. Didn't that count for anything? How could you throw in the towel after that long?

Of course, love could fail on the short-term, too. Priscilla was proof of that.

The only answer seems to be that love is indeed a farce, after all.

Chapter Four

Ralph Waldo Emerson wrote that life is a journey, not a destination. It makes me wonder what kind of journey I want to be living.

~ SCOUT SWIFT'S JOURNAL

"Wow, your car is . . . really clean." Reagan tosses a backpack into the rear seat and slides—as well as an immensely pregnant woman can—into the passenger seat. "It smells really clean, too."

"Thanks," I say, though for some reason her words don't sound like a compliment. I look at the inside of my Toyota Corolla, which I have lovingly named Chippy in memory of a small poodle we owned growing up. Not a speck of dust rests on the dashboard, not a crumb of dirt on the mats. Clean always wins in my book. It's how I like it, and I'll assume she means it as a compliment.

I start the car and drive out of the Walmart parking lot, past Jaden's camper. "You're sure about this, right?"

She nods, mouth in a firm line. "Absolutely." She shifts in her seat. "Um, you think I could crack a window?"

"Sure." I open mine as well and turn down the AC. "I actually prefer the open air." I glance at her. She looks a little green. "Are you okay? Tell me if you're going to be sick, all right?"

I want to help this girl. But the thought of her stomach contents spewing all over Chippy's interior is enough to send me hyperventilating. Some things stick around forever—grief and regret and what-ifs, and most definitely the scent of vomit in car carpet.

Reagan clutches the handle on the door, breathes deep of the air pouring through the windows. "Some cleaners aggravate me. I think I feel better already. Thanks."

"Oh. Okay. Well, I just need to stop home to grab a few things and feed the birds."

"Okay."

In five minutes, I make quick work of stocking the birds up on suet and seed, hauling my suitcase down the stairs, and heaving it into my trunk. I tuck the scrapbook I started with Mom alongside the backpack behind my seat. In ten minutes, we're taking the entrance onto the highway.

There. I'm doing this.

Silence envelopes the car, made more bearable by the whoosh of air coming through the open windows.

"Thanks again for this. I really appreciate it." Reagan fiddles with her seatbelt.

"I'm glad to help."

Was *glad* an accurate word? Yes, I decide. I am glad if I can help this troubled young girl, even a little bit. And if driving to her family delays me from facing my own past, then the better for it.

"What part of Maine did you say your family was from again?"

"I didn't say."

"Oh." My fingers tighten on the steering wheel. "But you do know where they are, don't you?"

She looks out the passenger window. "Not exactly . . ."

My foot slides off the gas pedal, all notions of this task being painless flying out the window. "Not *exactly*?"

She clears her throat. "I don't know where *exactly*. But I know I'll be closer to them in Maine than I will in that Walmart parking lot."

How does she not know where her family lives?

"I guess I'm just wondering where you plan on going then? I mean, I can get you to Maine, I can even bring you to whatever town your family lives in, but if you don't know where that is . . . well, don't you think that's a problem?"

She leans her head toward the open window, and I fear she's nauseated again. A truck passes us, exhaust fumes mixing with the tangerine scent of the cleaner I use. I'm about to ask if she's okay, but I don't want to let my previous question drop, either.

"I'll figure it out when we get there."

"If your figuring includes sleeping at another Walmart, I think we have a problem."

She's quiet for two exits and I'm at a loss for words myself. What have I gotten myself into? She suddenly seems so much younger than I'd been when I first traveled away from home.

"Are you really eighteen? Don't lie to me." My voice is stern and motherly, surprising even me.

"What? I look young for my age."

I almost give in. Instead, I cock an eyebrow at her. "Look, if this is going to work, you need to be one hundred percent honest with me. I don't need to know everything, but I think I should know if I'm carrying a minor across state lines."

She rolls her eyes. "Is that a crime?"

"I sure hope not," I grumble.

"Fine. I'm seventeen. I'll be eighteen in three weeks. Does that change anything? Are you going to drop me off at social services or something?"

Her tone is sarcastic and bitter, and I recognize it from my own past. She's been hurt. Deeply. This tough act is a sort of defense mechanism.

I glance at the dust-free console of my car. I know a thing or two about defense mechanisms, I suppose. I work to soften my tone. "I'm not going to drop you anywhere. I said I'd take you to Maine and to your family, and I meant it."

We fall into silence as we cruise along Route 24 at a decent clip. We pass Assonet and Berkley and Taunton without speaking.

"He didn't always use, you know."

I swallow, hoping if I stay quiet, she'll say more. I'm not disappointed.

"The first time I met him he was surfing in Newport. I was sitting on the beach, watching the sunset. He brought me a shell." She reaches in her pocket, revealing a smooth gray shell, worn from bits of sand and water brushing against it over the years. "It's all I have of him to give my baby."

I bite my lip. I want to say something deep and meaningful, that maybe she has already given her child more than she thinks possible simply by walking away from the poisonous choices of the baby's father, but I can't move the words past my lips. I can't pretend to know what I don't about this near stranger.

I remember how, after Mom died, people came up to me and said trite things—things like they were sorry. Things like at least Mom wasn't suffering anymore. Things like God needed another beautiful angel.

The thought leaves a bad taste in my mouth even now.

And so I keep my thoughts to myself. I definitely don't want to do anything to worsen Reagan's nausea.

Chapter Five

Mom used to tell me that if sunlight has the power to touch each person every day, then it's not too much of a stretch that God has that capability, too.

~ SCOUT SWIFT'S JOURNAL

"Wow. That's . . . impressive."

I glance at Reagan. "It's the only skeletal tower in New England." I hate that I feel the need to defend the site before us.

The girl must think I'm crazy. Driving miles out of our way to see the Marblehead light, nothing but hard metal poles and scaffolding holding up a lens—definitely not the kind of lighthouse people get nostalgic over.

I look at the book in my hand, remembering the day Mom brought it home. I'd been reading *Harry Potter and the Goblet of Fire* on the hammock beneath the pine trees in our backyard after school, the green army blanket Mom always used spread over my feet.

She sat beside me on the hammock, her weight causing mine to slide toward the edge in a familiar, comforting way. "Hey. How was school?"

I thought about the drama surrounding my best friend Lexie and nasty Sabrina.

I glanced at Mom's lap, where a book lay. I'd tell her about my day, but not yet. Even I understood how petty eighth grade drama could be, and I was *in* the eighth grade.

"It was good." I nodded at the book, breathed in the scent of lilacs. "Watcha got?"

"I stopped at The Beacon on the way home. Charlotte received some new books, and I wanted to check them out."

"That doesn't look like the latest Anne Tyler."

She clasped her hands around the book. "It's not. Actually, I had an idea I wanted to run by you."

I placed my bookmark in my open page. "Okay."

"With summer around the corner and Dad working so much, I thought it might be fun if we had ourselves a little adventure."

I looked at the book her hands covered.

"Lighthouses," she said.

"Lighthouses?"

"Yes. There are dozens along this coast. Beautiful beacons of light that we're not far from but we'll never see unless we make a point to see them." Her voice grew animated, full of passion and something else—a subtle sort of desperation I didn't dwell on until later. "I thought it'd be fun to make a point of it. I know lighthouses have always been more my thing than yours, but I figured we could take day trips, maybe get a bite to eat, explore some rocky beaches—just be together. You're growing up so fast, Scout." Her voice wobbled, and I reached for her arm, willing to commit to whatever would take that emotional quiver from her voice.

"That sounds great, Mom."

"Yeah? Really?"

"Really."

My assurance seemed to instill energy within her. She showed me the book, her voice growing strong. *New England Lighthouses* by Bruce Roberts and Ray Jones. "I was doing a little research and there are so many. But I figured we could just do some of the more noteworthy ones, maybe the ones in this book. We could start way north"—she showed me a map in the book, where dozens of red dots marked the lighthouses along the coast of New England—"and work our way down. Maybe Dad would even want to take a weekend trip with us to Connecticut and Rhode Island once we got there."

I sat up on the hammock, felt the first flutterings of excitement. This could be fun. Though I'd been to Boston and Plimoth Plantation and Florida once, we usually didn't travel. Adventures were expensive, and in the summer months Dad was too busy catching fish on his boat to accompany us, so we just didn't go.

"What's our first stop?" I asked.

"West Quoddy. How does Saturday sound?"

It had been cold that weekend, but we'd found a grassy spot in the sun beside the candy cane-striped lighthouse to eat our PB&Js, Mom reading the short passage in our lighthouse book regarding the historical information of West Quoddy. All of this after we snapped a picture of the two of us in front of the light.

"How's it feel to be the person farthest east in the United States?" Mom asked from her spot on the blanket.

I squinted at her, a smile tugging at my lips. "Pretty much the same."

She slapped my knee and scooted over so she was closest to the ocean. She closed her eyes and lifted her face to the sun. "No . . . no, it's different."

I studied her closed eyes, slight wrinkles around the edges. While we'd had our fair share of arguments and strife, in the end she was my best friend, although I'd never admit as much to Lexie.

"How?"

"It's in the knowing, I think. Just dwelling here. Knowing that of all the millions of people in the country, I'm closest to the sunrise—to the first touch of light."

Later, after we'd developed the picture of us in front of the candy cane-striped lighthouse, Mom pointed out a cloud behind us. "Would you look at that?"

I squinted at the cloud. "It's pretty. Kind of looks like a bird."

"A dove. A symbol of the Holy Spirit."

"What do you think it means?"

She shrugged. "It doesn't have to mean anything, but I like that it's in our picture. I like that it reminds me of God's spirit—His promise to us that we'll never be alone."

Now, I blink around wet eyelids as I stare at the spider-like structure before me—a light held over a hundred feet above the ground by eight, skeletal iron legs. It resembles a transmission tower more than the iconic, historic lighthouses one thinks of in New England. Its structure is cold, hard, empty. Quite fitting to what these trips without my mother resemble.

I hand my phone to Reagan. "Will you take my picture with it?"

"Uh, yeah, of course."

I stand before the light, the scent of ocean reminding me of home and all that's before me. My smile strains as Reagan snaps several pictures.

She hands me back my phone, and I start toward Chippy, fighting the urge to wipe the phone down. As far as I can tell, the girl's hygiene is up to par.

"That's it?" she asks.

I shrug. "Well, yeah."

She falls in step beside me. "So, all you wanted was a picture with the lighthouse?"

Yes, that's it. Something to put in the scrapbook to complete what Mom and I started all those years ago. What more is there without her? "Yes."

She nods. "Okay. It's your thing."

I grind my teeth. That's right. It is *my* thing.

Once we're in the car, Reagan takes out her phone. It's the newest iPhone, and she looks at me, sheepish. "Jaden gave it to me. I think his parents paid for it. I'm expecting them to stop the plan when they hear I left with their grandchild."

"You don't have to explain yourself to me."

"So, where to next?"

"There are two lighthouses in Salem. Derby Wharf and Bakers Island Light."

She taps on her phone as I drive away from Marblehead Light. "Bakers Island Light," she says.

"What are you doing?"

A pause. "Ah, now here's something interesting."

"What?"

"Well, I just figure if we're going to visit all these lighthouses we might as well find out some history behind them, right? I mean, Salem! One of the most historic towns in the country. Don't tell me we're going to waltz up to these lighthouses, snap a couple pictures, and call it an adventure? There has to be more, right?"

She is a precocious little teen, isn't she? How did someone with so much promise end up a pregnant runaway at eighteen?

I breathe deep through my nose. Not sure how crazy I am about the *we* part of Reagan's sentences. And yet her words prick me. Like the appliqué needles Charlotte used for her quilts, they dig in, dragging up the threads of old memories and emotions.

That's what Mom intended the lighthouse trips to be: an adventure, a meaningful experience. Why then, in my dream, did she want me to finish it?

I shake my head. Who knows if that was even her speaking to me. Maybe it was God. Maybe it was some part of my inner self. Regardless, what value did these trips have without her?

"Says here that the lighthouse keeper of Bakers Island, a Joseph Perkins, saw a couple of British warships trailing the Constitution in the War of 1812. It says the American ship was outgunned and outnumbered. The crew wanted to escape into Salem Harbor but couldn't find a channel. Seeing what was happening, this guy—Perkins—hopped into his rowboat and guided 'Old Ironsides' to safety." Reagan places her phone in her lap. "Wow, very cool. Says he resumed his duties as keeper that very afternoon."

I breathe deep, the story pulling at unwanted emotions. Mom would have been just as excited over this little piece of history. "Very neat."

"Neat? It's awesome. And now when we visit, we'll be able to imagine Joseph leaving the safety of his island to rescue Old Ironsides. Do you think he was cute? He had to be strong to row that quickly. That it happened right where we're going . . . doesn't it give you goose bumps?"

I laugh. "The part that gives me goose bumps—the scary kind, mind you—is that you're pondering poor Joseph's physical brawn as much as his bravery and intelligence."

She rolls her eyes. "I like to have a picture in my head, is all."

"We need to ferry over there, so we'll have to wait until tomorrow to visit. We'll stop by Derby Wharf and find dinner and a place to stay in Salem tonight. Sound okay?"

She doesn't answer right away, and I glance at her profile. She bites her lip.

"What is it?" I ask. "I mean, I know you're probably anxious to find your family, but I told you I had some stops to—"

"No, that's not it at all. It's just . . . ferry tickets, dinner, a hotel. Maybe this wasn't such a good idea after all."

"Reagan, I know you don't have money. Don't worry about it, okay? We'll square up eventually and if we don't, I'm okay with that, too."

"Why are you doing this for me, Miss Scout?"

"Just Scout, okay?"

"Scout. Why are you doing this?"

I shrug. I have to admit that half an hour into our journey, I was convinced I'd made the worst mistake in bringing Reagan along with me. Now though, her enthusiasm reminds me that seeing these lighthouses is about more than checking them off a list. "I haven't had many opportunities to help people out." I breathe around the lie, tight in my chest. "No, that's not true. I've been too preoccupied with my own life to take any opportunities." Too scared to venture out, too set on trying to make a life for myself, too intent on saving money so that I would never again be that helpless girl who'd been abandoned at a Walmart. "I'm glad to do this, Reagan. If I can help you reunite with your family, well, that's one good thing I did with my life."

Chapter Six

Life is a story. The part we're born into is already written for us, but everything else is a blank page.

~ SCOUT SWIFT'S JOURNAL

I stare at my current enemy, soft and deceptive with cream and rose colors.

To distract myself, I unwind the towel from my head and begin brushing out my hair. But I can't help it. My gaze goes back to the comforter on my bed, and I wrinkle my nose. The hotel I'd chosen is decent enough, and while I'm one hundred percent certain they put fresh sheets on for each new visitor, comforters always give me the heebie-jeebies. Some argue they don't need to be washed regularly. And perhaps if the same person stayed in the same bed all the time, that's true. But who knew what the hotel's policy is? How many people sat on this bed in their underwear? Or —*without* underwear? How many hair and skin follicles and questionable bodily fluids lay within the weave of fabric?

No. It simply must be done.

I look at Reagan, comfortably settled in her own bed, knees propped up, scribbling furiously in a purple memo pad. Maybe she won't comment. Maybe she'll pretend not to care.

Pinching the comforter between my thumb and forefinger, I peel back the offending specimen from the bed and fold it while holding it well away from my body. I lay it on the chair. I then do the same with the bed sheets, then the pillows. When everything is stripped bare, I dig in my suitcase for sheets I'd brought from home.

"What are you doing?" Reagan stares at me, her gaze darting from the folded hotel sheets to the ones I now pull over the bed.

"I have issues," I mumble. I pray we can just leave it at that.

"Like OCD issues?"

"If we have to put a label on it—yeah, like OCD issues."

She flings the covers back from the bed and flips her long dark hair over one shoulder. Her T-shirt stretches tight over her swollen belly. "That's okay. I get it. Can I help you? Unless you'd rather I not touch—"

"No, I don't mind." I heard her wash her hands after she used the bathroom, and I already discreetly sterilized the doorknobs. "Thank you."

She tucks the fitted sheet beneath the mattress. "So that's why your car smells like Lysol."

Heat rushes to my face.

"How bad is it?"

"Not debilitating. I don't need to clean my house ten times a day or anything like that. Just, you know, germs and stuff. I probably wash my hands too much, use too much Purell, and I'm kind of a freak about doorknobs and handles and hotels and phones."

"Gotcha. Well, I guess if you think about it, germs are kind of gross."

"And dead skin and hair follicles and possible critters . . . hence the bed sheets."

Reagan scrunches up her face. "When you put it like that, I'm not sure I'll sleep so good tonight."

We both laugh.

I point to the purple notebook on the nightstand. "What are you writing?"

Her gaze darts to the memo pad, nearly full by the looks of it. She doesn't answer right away.

"I only ask because I used to journal a lot. I was thinking maybe I should pick it back up again." Maybe cataloguing this trip —this journey to finish what I'd started with Mom—will give me more insight and meaning into why I feel compelled to do this, why I'd dreamt so intently about it.

"Part of it is a record of sorts. Like what I owe you for food and gas and the hotel. But in the back, I started a baby book."

"But you don't have your baby yet."

"Sure, I do." She sits back on her bed, cradling her belly. "And it's not a normal baby book, listing where he's born, when he lost his first tooth, you know, stuff like that. It's more of a story I'm telling him or her of its life." She bites her lip. "I thought this trip was a good place for my baby's story to start."

For some reason, the words touch me. To think that I could have a small part in the beginning of a tiny new person's story, to think I might be making a difference in helping Reagan leave harmful choices. Maybe I can write the beginning of my own story, too.

"That's really nice, Reagan. You're going to be a great mom."

Her eyes shine, and she blinks fast. "No one's ever believed in me before. Maybe that's because I haven't earned it. But I'm starting new." She looks down at the mound of her abdomen. "I promise."

I lay my head on the pillow I'd brought from home. "And you can stop tallying up prices in that pad of yours. I'm glad to have company. Maybe if you're up for waking early tomorrow, we might be able to fit in a museum or two before going to the Island."

Earlier, over a large veggie pizza at The Flying Saucer Pizza Company, Reagan had babbled on about all she knew of the Salem Witch Trials and Nathaniel Hawthorne—quite a bit, actually. Talk of Hawthorne had led to The House of the Seven Gables which had led to other book discussions. Turns out Reagan and I shared similar tastes in stories—gravitating toward Kristin Hannah, Delia Owens, Charles Martin, Toni Morrison, and Richard Paul Evans. But while I preferred contemporary authors, Reagan loved the classics as much as the latest bestseller. She said the first thing she would do once she settled back home was get a library card.

It all makes me wonder again. This educated, bright girl . . . how had things gone so terribly wrong for her?

I turn on my side to shut the light off. Reagan breathes deep, eyes closed, hand resting on her baby.

Then again, who am I to say that things were going wrong for her? Maybe this trip, finding her family, getting away from Jaden, getting away from living in a camper in a Walmart parking lot, is the first step to things going very right.

THERE IS nothing quite as exhilarating as breathing in the sea air sixty feet above ground. I close my eyes, listen to the call of gulls, the not-too-far-away swirling ocean. Like the rhythmic rocking of my childhood, it soothes in a way nothing else can. I remember the many trips to Bass Head Light with Mom. While we'd checked it off long ago, we always planned to go back again to mark the end of our journey. Could this be the beginning of a new chapter in my own life? One where I finally put the pain of grief behind me?

I look down at the rolling grass, the jutting rocks where the ocean meets land, the craggy reefs, and I feel alive for the first time in a long time. Here, I can almost taste home and unexpectedly, I long for it. I think about Charlotte and The Beacon Bed and Breakfast, wonder if she still owns it. A pinch of guilt niggles within. It's been too long since I sent her a text or an email or a birthday card. Despite my neglect, I miss her—my mother's best friend, the closest thing I had to an aunt or even a grandmother.

Behind me comes small bursts of huffing and puffing. I'd been so caught up in the moment I nearly forgot about Reagan. "Are you okay? Were the steps too much?"

She shakes her head. "I'm just out of shape is all." She places both hands on the rail, closes her eyes, and pulls in deep breaths. "There." She straightens and stretches, rubbing at a spot on her lower back. "Wow. This is amazing. Definitely better than the two disappointments of yesterday."

I try to look offended, and she rolls her eyes. Marblehead and Derby Wharf were not the most picturesque of New England Lighthouses, but the surrounding views certainly made up for them. But this . . . this is another world.

"Can you imagine Joseph up here, spotting the Constitution threatened by those British warships?"

I smile. "Actually, I can."

"And now that I've climbed those steps, I can appreciate how difficult it was to get down them *then* row a boat out to sea. He was definitely strong. And probably cute, too."

I shake my head, at ease for the first time since embarking on our trip. The overwhelming feeling that all is going to be okay swells in my soul. I think of Mom, wonder if she can see me from heaven, if she can see me doing this thing we'd started so long ago, if she can see me trying to do something good with my life by helping Reagan. I hope to heaven we find Reagan's family. And I hope when we do, they will prove a good family, a family where this young girl can thrive.

We don't speak for a long time, just take in the majestic sight before us—the sailboats dotting the skyline, the faint crescent moon already high above the horizon, the green land across the bay.

"I feel like, looking at all of this, it's hard *not* to believe in God," Reagan says.

I nod, understanding, but reluctant to add anything.

"Like, sometimes, I wish so hard I could feel Him or understand Him, only I can't. But right now, with all this beauty and light around, it seems so obvious. Like, how did I not know it all along?" She shrugs. "Who knows, probably pregnancy hormones."

"My mother used to tell me that it's during our darkest moments when the light shines brightest."

"That makes sense. And somehow it makes me feel less lonely." She glances at me quick, shakes her head. "Sorry, I talk too much."

"Don't be sorry. And you're talking to the woman who brings her own set of bed sheets to hotels, so no judgment here."

We laugh.

"I bet you're anxious to see her, huh? Your mom?"

I press my lips together. "I won't be seeing her."

"Oh, I'm sorry. I didn't realize—"

"It's okay. She died when I was eighteen. Cancer. This lighthouse trip is kind of in her honor."

"That's . . . nice. Really. You're finding that light she was talking about, right?"

"Hmm. I never thought of it like that." But maybe I should. "What about your mom? Is she in Maine?"

A big sigh. "No. She died, too."

"I'm so sorry." The fact that we share this bond only endears the girl to me more.

"We weren't close."

I wait for more, but Reagan offers nothing. Apparently, this is not one of those moments where she feels compelled to talk.

Pain is pain. No doubt Reagan's past contains hurts, too. They may be of a different kind and color, but in the end, hurt is hurt.

I look north. Tomorrow, we'd see two New Hampshire lighthouses, and by evening, we'd be in Maine. I think of the events that took me from my home, and for the first time I try not to let bitterness overtake me, try to believe that a new beginning lay somewhere north, a light in the dark, a beacon bringing me home—if not to a physical one, then perhaps an emotional one.

40

Chapter Seven

LILLIAN

Fourteen Years Earlier

The church takes a different shape on the weekdays than it does on Sunday morning. Somehow, it seems more sacred, which does not make sense since part of the sacredness of the church is the worshippers that occupy it.

Hands folded, I lean over the back of the pew in front of me and stare at the wooden cross hanging above the simple altar, a reminder of the anchor of my faith. I empty my heart out to God.

There is a lot troubling me today. Scout's uncertainty over her future and whether to attend college. The mysterious deduction from Bud's paystub that I noticed last night but that has been coming out for as far back as I've kept records. The obvious lump on my right breast.

I sigh, try to envision handing each of these worries over to the Lord, casting every anxiety upon Him.

Scout and I are to visit Owl's Head Light tomorrow. Bud will be out on the boat, as he has been for most of the season. I don't know when I'll get to ask him about the paycheck. Or, if I should.

I pray for a long time. I pray for wisdom and strength. I shed tears for my husband, who has not darkened the door of this church since we married.

We will celebrate twenty years of marriage next week and yet sometimes, I'm not sure I even know the man I call my husband.

"Lillian?"

I know that voice. Maybe I'd even hoped he'd be here.

"Doug, hi." The widowed accountant stands a few feet away, his tie loose at his neck, curls a bit tussled as they tend to be at the end of the day. "What are you doing here?"

"I was driving home and saw your car. I hope it's okay that I stopped."

No . . . no, it wasn't okay. And in some ways, it was more than okay.

God, forgive me, I needed to bat these feelings right out of the park—and most certainly right out of the church.

Doug had moved to Bar Harbor last year with his eleven-year-old daughter. He told me they both needed a fresh start after the death of his wife two years earlier. He never missed a Sunday at church, a prayer meeting, a Bible study, a barbecue. He led the youth group, and we got to know one another better the year before while co-directing the Christmas play.

Charlotte's voice during that time comes to me. "Be careful, Lillian. That one is a temptation waiting to happen."

I'd brushed her off. I'd never be unfaithful to my husband.

And I never had.

Doug tilts his head. "Have you been crying?" He sits in the pew in front of me, turning to face me. Always observant, always respectful. He must feel this forbidden force of attraction between us, just as I did.

I swipe at my eyes and laugh. "I always cry when I pray, don't you?"

He raises his eyebrow. "Need to talk? I have to kill some time before picking Gretchen up from softball practice."

It would be easy to pour my heart out to this man. To feel cared for, listened to. He'd probably even offer to pray for me, something Bud had never done.

For the hundredth time, I question my decision to marry a wandering soul like my husband and then, feeling instantly guilty, slash the thought from my head. If nothing else, he gave me the best gift in the world—our daughter.

I stand and gather my purse. "Thank you, Doug, that's very kind of you, but I should get home."

His look of disappointment is obvious. He stands alongside me. "Well, I'm here if you ever need me."

I smile. "Thank you." I shimmy out of the pew and into the aisle. I'm almost to the door when he calls my name. It echoes into the high ceilings of the church sanctuary.

I turn.

"You deserve to be listened to." He sticks his hands in his pockets as he says it.

I press my lips together, heart aching. He may be right, but I couldn't underestimate the slippery slope such a talk might lead us down. Not with the palpable attraction between us. It would only take me stepping toward him to send us both sledding down a hill I couldn't come back from.

"Have a good night, Doug."

I drive home, replaying the what-ifs of having a real conversation with Doug. I pull into my empty house. Scout has a shift at the Terrace Grille, and Bud won't be home until nightfall. I'm alone, again.

I put the key in the door but find it unlocked. The scent of grilled chicken meets my nostrils, and I enter the kitchen to see Bud taking a bottle of barbecue sauce out of the refrigerator. A beer is cradled in the crook of his elbow.

"Bud, what are you doing home?" Had I been so dazed I'd missed his truck in the driveway?

He smiles at me in that rare but disarming way of his. He's showered, in a gray T-shirt, bare feet beneath faded jeans. He's tanned and fit from being on the boat.

"Got a great catch early in the day so I decided to come home to surprise my woman."

I hang my purse. "And with food, no less."

"Grilling some chicken and vegetables. Picked up a quart of ice cream from Jordan's on the way home."

"Wow, what's the occasion?"

He comes over and wraps his arms around me. The scent of aftershave and coconut soap cling to him. "Twenty years married isn't occasion enough?"

I pull back. "But our anniversary's not until next week."

His brow crinkles. "No, it's today. The sixteenth."

This isn't funny. "Bud, our anniversary's the twenty-fourth."

The smile dissolves from his face. He squeezes his eyes shut. "I'm an idiot."

I place a hand on his cheek. "Hey, it's okay. It's not a big deal. We can celebrate early." I'd been hoping to go out, maybe walk to Bar Island on our anniversary, but this works, too.

"I'll probably have to work late next week. I don't know why I thought it was the sixteenth in my head. You think I'm getting early onset dementia or something?"

I laugh. "I doubt it." I rack my brain for why the sixteenth stuck in his brain. It's not the date of anyone's birthday—not me or Scout or his parents. It's not even the day he asked me to marry him. I push the niggling thought aside. "Let's just enjoy tonight."

Two hours later, we're lying in our bed, content in one another's arms. It really was a lovely anniversary celebration with lots of laughter, talking, and yes, passion. Now, Bud breathes heavy, but that same niggling feeling I had at church causes me to speak my thoughts. Surely, Bud will be able to clear things up for me and I can rest easy on one thing at least.

"I noticed something funny on your paystub yesterday. Maybe it's been there all along, but I think it might be a mistake."

I know from the change in his breaths that he's come fully awake. "Yeah, what it'd say?"

I swallow. "Child support."

The muscles of his chest tense. "Must be a mistake. I'll clear it up with HR tomorrow."

But I can tell from his response he knows about it. It's not a mistake.

He rolls away from me and reaches for his pants. "Would be nice to have some money coming back to us soon, wouldn't it?"

I clutch the covers to my naked body, suddenly chilled and alone. "Yeah," I squeak out, a lump forming tight in my throat.

Happy anniversary to me.

<h1 style="text-align:center">Chapter Eight</h1>

ZACK

"That sucks, man. I'm really sorry." Jason takes a swig of his drink and places it on the countertop of the bar. Above us, a television illuminates the Red Sox scoring a run over the Mets.

"I could strangle him for what this is doing to my mom."

The bartender places burgers in front of each of us but the sight of it, cheese and caramelized onions oozing out the sides, churns my stomach. I pick up a fry and half-heartedly dip it in the paper container of ketchup on my plate.

"I'd say you have every right to be disappointed in him."

"I mean, this is the guy who never forgot a birthday or anniversary, who brought home flowers, who went to church every week, faithful as a dog. I don't get it."

Jason lifts his burger and takes a hefty bite. Even now, in the middle of my mess, I can recognize how grateful I am that Charlotte's granddaughter Laney brought him into my life—okay, *our* lives. Though more than ten years younger than me, we'd spent hours working on restoring the Beacon Lighthouse together. His work ethic and integrity are top notch, and he treats Laney and Charlotte like gold.

He is also the only guy on Mount Desert Island who can hold his own against me in a game of one-on-one basketball.

Jason chews slowly, then swallows. "I feel for you. I know what it's like to have a less than perfect dad."

I snort. "Less than perfect is being late for a baseball game or never helping with homework, not screwing around on your mom."

Across from us, the bartender sprays orange soda into a glass. Beside him, two women in their twenties are making eyes at me and Jason. I wonder if this is how my dad *met* someone else. At a bar, having dinner. Or was it someone he worked with? A woman on the golf course? A younger woman? Did she realize all she ruined by throwing herself at my father?

"What are you looking at?" I snap at the blonde woman who can't seem to take her eyes off me.

She leans back. "Apparently not much."

Jason slaps me on the chest. "Never mind him, ladies. Rough day. Apologies."

I push Jason's hand away and dig in my wallet for enough cash to pay for both of us. I throw it on the table next to my uneaten meal. "I probably shouldn't be out in public right now." I dip my head at the two women. "Thanks for meeting up, man. Sorry I'm not good company."

Jason shrugs on his jacket and follows me out to the parking lot, shoving fries into his mouth.

"Listen, man. I wish I knew what to say. Thing is, as much as you want to, you can't control him."

I stop in the middle of the parking lot, the fresh air bracing enough to make me listen to my friend's words.

"You can't make him act how you think he should act. Even if we're both one hundred percent certain he's in the wrong. It's out of your hands."

I groan. "I know. *I know*. It's just hard to figure out what to do."

Jason blows out a long breath. "Maybe you don't have to do anything. Maybe you just be sad right now."

I nod, unlock my truck with my key fob.

"Does Charlotte know?"

I shake my head. "I'm not exactly eager to tell her."

"You're not asking me to keep this from Laney, are you?"

I roll my eyes. "Wouldn't dream of it." I elbow him. "It's all good, man. Pretty soon all of Bar Harbor will know Paul Garrison is a complete and utter scum bag."

THE NEXT DAY, I'm pulling a toilet from the guest cottage on Charlotte's property when the spunky older woman comes up behind me. "Good morning, dear. I didn't even hear you sneak in." She offers a plate of scones. "Hungry?"

I peer around the toilet I'm currently hugging. "They look great, Charlotte, but I've got my hands full at the moment. Maybe in a minute?"

"Sure thing. I'll wait outside."

I finish moving the toilet and wash my hands in the still-working sink before stepping out of the guest cottage. Spring sunshine sparkles off the Atlantic and there, across the sturdiest footbridge this side of the Mississippi, sits the shining Beacon, white and gleaming, the automated light like a crown atop her head. I've never worked on something that meant more to me than this lighthouse. Gutters . . . gutters are important. As is power washing and bathroom and kitchen remodels. But restoring a centuries-old lighthouse? Now that was worth jumping out of bed for.

"I can't get over how beautiful she is." Charlotte's gray curls frame a weathered face that hasn't quite given up its hint of youthful beauty. "Jack would be so proud of you."

I blink. We are not going there. No doubt, Laney told Charlotte about my parents, and this is her way of trying to make me feel better. Her husband had been like a second father to me.

I hold up the blueberry scone after taking a bite. It's sweet and crumbly, with just a touch of icing drizzled on top. "Thanks for this. It's good."

She clears her throat and places the plate of scones on the small metal table outside the cottage. I hold back a groan. Here we go.

"I spoke to Laney this morning, honey."

I guess we are going there.

"She told me about your parents. I'm so sorry, Zack."

I shrug. Though I had thought to call her when I first received the news, the last thing I had wanted to do was relive that conversation. "I guess this stuff happens. People fall out of love. They let you down."

She stares up at me, her tiny frame sturdy enough to stand against a coastal hurricane. "You don't have to pretend to be brave with me. You may be a grown man, but you're allowed to have feelings, especially when it comes to your parents."

I rake a hand through my hair. Past the Beacon, the white sails of a boat stand taut in a gentle breeze. "I can't control him." I repeat Jason's words from the night before. They sound good. They'll make Charlotte feel better. But deep down, I'm still desperate to make my dad see reason. Either that or disown him forever.

"That's true." She sighs. "I won't press you anymore but know I'm here and that I love you and I'm praying for all of you." She opens her mouth, seeming to want to say something else, but then closes it.

"Thanks, Charlotte. And thanks for the scone. It hit the spot."

She gestures to the cottage. "How's it looking in there?"

"The leak was pretty bad, but considering the entire place could use some work, maybe it's not such a big loss."

"Make sure you charge me what you're worth, young man. Understood?"

I nod.

"I mean it, Zackery Garrison. I spoke to Mrs. Darling at the Garden Club last night and she told me you're coming by to clean her gutters. Didn't you just do that a few weeks ago?"

"I consider it a win that she remembered she spoke to me." I crack a smile.

"She also remembered that you gave her a great deal on repainting her garage. Honey, I love your sweet heart, but you have a business to run. Everyone in this town knows you and loves you. It doesn't mean you have to give them a deal. You have talent—look how much talent you have!" She flings a hand toward the lighthouse. "Make sure you're paid what you're worth."

I wink at her, uncomfortable with how far this conversation has gone. "Yes, ma'am. Hear you loud and clear. I will double your bill."

She slaps me on the shoulder. "Oh, kiddo. You do remind me of Jack so much sometimes."

I sober. "He taught me everything I know about fixing things."

She smiles, her eyes watery. "I'm glad you didn't move to New York."

I straighten. "I need the coast. I thought I needed my family." Thought they needed me.

She squeezes my arm. "Your dad loves you, Zack. You've always had a high view of him."

My mouth tightens. She's right.

"Honey, every person in your life has the potential to disappoint you, if they haven't already. There's only One who won't disappoint."

I push out a noncommittal sound. I know she's right—I

believe she's right. I just don't feel like hearing it right now. "Thanks for the scone, Charlotte. I better get back to work."

51

Chapter Nine

There's an old saying, maybe even from the Bible, that says beware of wolves in sheep's clothing. I say beware of wolves in Gucci business suits.

~ SCOUT SWIFT'S JOURNAL

It would have been easy to blame Mom's death on my leaving home. But for some reason all that comes to the forefront of my mind when I think of the past, of the reason I left Maine, is the man who broke my heart.

Gregory Showalter was a ball of fire and success wrapped tight in the most attractive set of XY chromosomes I'd ever seen.

Okay, those are not my words—they were Lexie's. Unlike my best friend, I wasn't one to get all steamy about the opposite sex. But Gregory shook me up. He was like none of the other boys I knew. Not my elementary childhood crush, not my first boyfriend who asked me out in the fifth grade via a series of Chinese folded notes. Not even the boy I spent most of late middle school and high school mooning over, Zack Garrison. Zack used to mow Jack and Charlotte's lawn and had given me my first taste of unrequited love with how little he acknowledged my existence.

Gregory was older, sophisticated, and drove a BMW. He had a lucrative job in a marketing firm and was vacationing in our small, tourist-filled town when I first met him the summer after high school. I was waitressing at The Terrace Grille at the Bar Harbor Inn. Mom's death four months earlier still had its sharp talons in me, and I'd decided to put off college for a year.

Rugged and dark, in clothes fit for Wall Street, Gregory showed up at one of my tables and didn't take his eyes off me. Far from repulsive, but nothing to write home about, I wasn't used to my plain looks garnering such attention. I was grasping, but for what, I didn't know. Something beyond my world, beyond my grief, beyond the heavy cloak of sadness that was now my father's and my home. When Gregory asked if I wanted to take a walk after my shift, I surprised myself by saying yes.

He told me about his new job near Myrtle Beach. Actually told me about the hefty six-figure income it would bring in. He confessed he wasn't sure he was doing what he loved, confessed he wanted to go back to school for a teaching degree someday but wanted to make enough money to pay cash for it first. I was too young, too enraptured, to see through his lies.

The vicious argument I had with my father that week only served to push me farther into Gregory's arms. We spent every moment we could together, me baring my secrets and soul and body to this man I was certain was *the one*, him spinning his lies in a thick web around me, saying what I longed to hear, filling the fast-draining spaces in my heart since Mom died.

I told him I longed to break free of my small town, my insignificant life. That I wanted to *matter*. That the thought of more school terrified me and that I didn't know if I could stand to be under my father's roof another night. I told him I longed to pursue my painting but was discouraged over the prospect of making a career out of it. I told him about the sizable sum of money I had in the bank, my portion of Mom's life insurance money.

I was stupid. There's really no other excuse for what I did. He convinced me too easily to leave town with him, to withdraw my entire savings, to say goodbye to my father and my friends, and begin a new adventure in North Carolina. He said he would buy us a house on the water, complete with an art room overlooking the waves, that we would marry the next year, and he would fly my family and friends down to celebrate with us.

Lexie tried to stop me, going so far as to threaten to chain herself to the top of Bass Head Light if I left town with Gucci, as she chose to refer to him. Dad's resistance was more subtle—an attempt to cook supper for me, to ignore the nasty tension hanging between us that I had no intention of ignoring. Even Charlotte tried to talk some sense into me. But I was a goner. A goner for a make-believe perfect life. A goner for the promise of something better than waitressing tables and swimming in grief.

The weird thing is, part of me doubted Gregory's sincerity from the beginning. Part of me saw the truth. And still, I closed my eyes and shut my ears against it.

It didn't take much for me to transfer my money into one of his accounts, as he'd convinced me he knew how to handle money. I packed everything I could fit into Mom's old suitcase, gave my grim-faced father a tense hug, and hopped into Gregory's BMW without looking back.

Six hours later, after a pit stop at a Walmart fifteen minutes east of Providence, I emerged into blinding sunlight to find no BMW waiting for me. No Greg. No wallet. No phone. No hope.

It's pathetic how long I waited on that hard blue bench outside that Walmart, the sun burning my face and my flip-flop clad toes, certain the man I loved would return. He wouldn't just leave me there. I'd given him *all* of me, everything. All he'd left me with was a lousy three dollars and fifty-four cents alongside my driver's license in the pocket of my jean shorts.

When the sun made its descent and I finally realized he wasn't coming back, my breaths came fast. My chest squeezed. Is this how it would all end? On a Walmart bench, the victim of one of the panic attacks that frequented me since Mom died?

I focused on a dried-up wad of bright pink gum at my feet as I forced my breaths to slow, to grow longer and deeper. For the next ten minutes, it was just me and that lumpy, used gum. I emptied my mind of everything around me and slowly, my breaths came easier.

I'd learned the technique from a Google search. It seemed to work—at least, I hadn't died from an attack yet.

As I calmed, I mulled over my options. I couldn't go home, I couldn't face my father, Lexie, or Charlotte. The entire town knew what I'd done. I'd be humiliated forever. What's worse, none of this changed the fact that I needed to escape from my father and his terrible secret—a secret that called me to an action I wasn't brave enough to fulfill.

Why would I go back home? To grief and sadness and secrets?

As the sun descended, I went back inside the store, bought a bottle of water and a protein bar, spending all but twenty-six cents. I wandered around Walmart until closing time dumped me out into the well-lit parking lot. I walked around the building for most of the night until my flip-flops were near-worn through. I thought of my mom, of Greg. Anger roiled inside me until big sobs pushed up my diaphragm.

When they were finally spent, I fell asleep on a bench, grateful that at least the night proved warm. When I woke the next morning, my stomach growled, prompting a deep, desperate hunger that propelled me to action.

I visited the restroom, where I rinsed my mouth and washed my face before visiting the service desk and asking for an application. After I borrowed a pen to fill it out, I returned the papers, requesting to speak to the store manager.

"He's very busy." The heavyset woman behind the counter had

something green in her front teeth. "I'm sure you'll hear soon, though. Walmart's always looking for help."

But I had no phone to be contacted at. I had nothing and no one.

"I don't mind waiting until he's available," I said, determined now. I stood off to the side of the service desk.

I stood there most of the morning, my body weak from lack of food. I saw the two ladies behind the service desk whispering and sending skewed glances my way. Finally, one of them picked up the phone and turned toward the wall, speaking into the mouthpiece so I couldn't read her lips.

A short time later, a thin woman wearing a navy-blue Walmart smock with a name tag that said *Lisa* approached me. She smiled, but it was tight-lipped as she took in my flip-flops and jean shorts —not exactly interview apparel.

"I hear you're looking for employment?"

I straightened. "I am, ma'am."

"Did you fill out an application?"

"Yes, ma'am."

She walked to the service desk where she obtained my application. She held out her hand. "I'm Lisa. And you are . . ." she looked down at the paper in her hand. "Scout?"

I nodded.

She gave me that tight-lipped smile again but gestured for me to follow her. "We'll conduct your interview in the personnel office."

She led me through the store, past Home Goods and Arts and Crafts, into Electronics, then through a set of gray double doors and around a corner to a large windowless room with three sets of rectangular tables pushed together.

"Have a seat."

I did, grateful to hide my bare legs and toes beneath the table.

The room lay quiet as she read over my application. A pile of papers lay to my side, one splayed out from the rest. Following instinct, I picked them up and banged them lightly on the counter to align them before realizing my actions. I put them down.

Lisa didn't seem to notice.

"Says here you live in Bar Harbor, Maine."

I swallowed. "I just moved here."

She took her pen and crossed out the address I'd written.

~~34 Sand Point Road~~

The simple act of crossing out my childhood home, of crossing out all I'd left—happy memories of Mom, long talks on the phone with Lexie late into the night, Christmas mornings filled with pretty wrappings and shimmering trees—served to do two things. First, it made me realize the gravity of what I'd done in leaving the only place I'd ever known. Second, it made me realize there was no going back. This was a new chapter, a new beginning. Nothing else for me to do but to embrace it.

Lisa looked up, pen poised. "What's your new address?"

I pressed my lips together before answering. "I . . . I don't have one yet."

She straightened, but I thought I detected a hint of softening about her. "Do you have a license, honey?"

I perked up at the remembrance of putting my license in the back pocket of my jean shorts. I had shoved it there my last night in Maine when I drove to meet Lexie for a walk to Bar Island. I hadn't wanted to bring my entire wallet to leave in Dad's car, so I'd tucked my license in my shorts for the ten-minute drive.

I had donned the same shorts the next day, when I left home with Greg.

That was not even forty hours ago, and yet it felt an eternity.

She took my license. "Social Security card?"

"Uh, not with me." How had I forgotten to get that out of the family safe? "But I could get it." Surely, I could borrow someone's phone and ask my father to send it to me . . . once I figured out what address he could send it to. Or maybe I could just request it from the government. But would that take too long?

"All right, I'll need that ASAP." She turned and walked into a small office off the large room. The hum of the copy machine sounded, and she came back, handing me my license. She sat down, rubbed one temple, and looked at my application again.

"What sort of customer experience do you have?"

"I've waited tables for a couple years now, so I've dealt with plenty of people, even the mean ones. I know it's important to be nice even when it's challenging. I'm a pretty patient person."

She nodded, continued looking at the paper. Finally, after what seemed an interminable amount of time, she raised sharp green eyes to mine. "I could take you to the bus station if you'd like. I'd even pay for a ticket back to Maine."

I tried not to let it irk me that this near stranger thought she knew what was best for me. My father thought he had, Lexie, and even Charlotte. Now this woman.

I raised my chin. "Thank you, but I'm determined to stay here, in . . ."

"Swansea."

"Yes. Swansea."

She studied me like Mrs. Gardner had done in the third grade after I'd swallowed my gum so she wouldn't be able to prove I'd been chewing it. "Are you sure you shouldn't go back home?"

I inhaled deep. "Miss Lisa—"

"Just Lisa, please."

"Lisa . . . have you ever wanted to be free of something that gripped you? Have you ever wanted to just start over?"

She held my gaze for a moment before her brow scrunched, and she closed her eyes. "Yes, Miss Scout, I suppose I have."

"Please, just Scout."

She smiled, and it was a kind smile. A bit tired and tried around the edges, but kind.

"Ma'am, I *can't* go back home. Please, I'll be your best employee in whatever department you put me in. I'll stock shelves, I'll clean toilets even. I clean toilets really good." Not that I would relish the task, mind you—in fact, now that I thought about it, cleaning up a public bathroom might very well kill me . . . but even that was better than going home.

The corner of her mouth lifted in a smile. "I don't have any positions in Maintenance, but I do need someone in Lawn and Garden. How does that sound?"

"It sounds great. Thank you. Can I start today?"

"No, I'm afraid we have more paperwork. Training starts next Tuesday."

"Oh." How would I survive until then?

"Scout . . . you say you clean toilets well. I know of a part-time housekeeping position in the next town over. Comes with a small signing bonus and room and board. To start immediately. Are you interested?"

"Well, yes. Definitely. But I wouldn't want anything interfering with my Walmart job."

She shook her head. "It's flexible hours."

"Sounds too good to be true."

She smiled. "I get off in an hour. I can take you there if you'd like."

A short time later we pulled into the driveway of a small Cape with a porch. I followed Lisa inside where she dropped her purse and keys on a chair. She held her hands out. "It's not much, but it's home. And as you can see, it needs a good cleaning."

"This is your place?" I sputtered.

"All mine, since the husband left five months ago."

I crossed my arms over my chest. "I'm sorry."

She leaned against the wall. "I'm going to be honest. I've never done anything like this, and I'm not even sure it's a good idea. I'm thinking we give it a one-week probationary period. After that, either of us can bow out if things aren't working, no awkwardness and all that, and absolutely no endangerment to your position at Walmart."

"That sounds reasonable."

She walked past the kitchen where dishes piled high in the sink and then down a corridor. "Let me show you your room."

She led me to a spacious guest bedroom with a window facing north where birds feasted upon abundant seed. Strange how Lisa couldn't keep up with her dishes, but she obviously made it a priority to feed her winged guests.

I tore my gaze from a cardinal to study the rest of the room, walls bare save for a single picture of a little girl sitting on a tree stump, reading a book. It felt . . .empty. As if it, despite the picture, had never known a child's laughter or breathing, heavy with sleep.

We both stared at the picture for a moment. Finally, I spoke. "Why are you doing this?"

"You saw my kitchen. I need some help around here."

But she didn't. Not really. As far as I could see she was a capable woman who I guessed could clean her own toilets and put her own dishes in the dishwasher.

What must have been a pained look crossed my face as I tried to measure up the situation.

Lisa turned toward me. "You want to know the truth, Scout?"

I nodded.

"Someone once told me the best way through hurt is helping someone else. I guess I'm testing out that theory is all." She left me alone in the room, the walls hugging the echo of her words.

I would never forget them.

Chapter Ten

I don't know where else to go, so I will look to the Light.

~ SCOUT SWIFT'S JOURNAL

Reagan and I make our way lazily up the coast of New Hampshire and Maine over the next few days. Portsmouth Harbor Light, Cape Neddick, Cape Elizabeth, and Portland Head Light. As we drive farther and farther north, I begin to feel anxious and worn out. Anxious about going home and seeing my father, worn out with the feeling that there should be more to this lighthouse goal. Maybe I am just going through the motions of checking each lighthouse off without really seeing what Mom would have wanted me to see.

What *did* she want me to see?

This isn't what our trips had been about. Probably why we hadn't gotten farther in making our way down the list in four years. Back then, it had been a relaxed thing. A no pressure time together. More like a leisurely stroll with a friend than a hard-core marathon. And that made it special.

At Marshall Point Light, I ask a passerby to snap a picture of me and Reagan on the bridge in front of the lighthouse. Reagan doesn't bother hiding her surprise but asks if I can text her the picture. I do.

The girl is growing on me, and as we drive closer to home, I wonder what her future holds. How will she find her family? And how can I help?

The next morning as we sit in the hotel lounge eating the continental breakfast, I pull out a small package wrapped in green paper and hold it out to Reagan.

She shakes her head. "What's this? You've given me enough, Scout."

"It's for your baby. I think—I think it's time to head home. I can visit more lighthouses on the way back, but we're both tired. You need to find your family. And I need to face mine."

"Oh." She sounds disappointed, which surprises me. I thought she'd be ready to move on to whatever's next by now. "Is this a goodbye gift, then?"

I smile. "Not at all. I want to help you find where you need to be. But it could take another ten days for me to see all the lighthouses I need to see, plan the ferry trips and overnight stays. This is supposed to be enjoyable, not taxing. And you're not getting any less pregnant. Soon you'll need to see a doctor for more regular checkups. And strangely enough, I think I'm ready to get home."

"I guess I am, too." But her voice is wistful, full of mystery. She flips the package over and carefully unwraps it, gasping at the bound notebook and set of fancy gel pens within.

"I spotted it at that Barnes & Noble in Portsmouth. I thought it'd be perfect for your baby's journal. I'm guessing you're going to run out of room in that memo pad soon enough."

She runs her fingers over the leather-bound journal, tracing the lighthouse on the cover and then, the words above it.

Hope
sees the invisible,
feels the intangible,
and achieves the impossible.
~ Unknown

"It's perfect." Reagan swipes at her eyes before lunging at me with a hug. "Thank you."

I squeeze her tight, realizing for the first time how much I'm going to miss her. She doesn't know it, but I bought myself an identical journal, had tentatively started putting my thoughts on paper in the early morning hours when Reagan still slept. While I couldn't see what good it would do, I did feel myself opening up. Some of it was painful, some of it bittersweet. All of it, I was quite sure, was progress.

When we part, I inhale a deep breath. "You said this is a beginning for your baby. That's what this trip is. But Reagan, you have to tell me more about your family if I'm going to help you find them. Do you have someone you can get in touch with that would know where to find them?"

She rubs her temples. "It's . . . complicated. I want to make my own way, Scout. Not as a charity case, but as a girl who can stand on her own two feet. Maybe you can't understand . . ."

She had no idea how alike we really were, how I could have just as easily gotten pregnant at eighteen with Greg.

"What do you want, then? You want to make a life for yourself up here? How? You could get a job, but what about when the baby comes? How will you work and take care of a child, find somewhere to live?"

She swallows. "I—I don't know."

I breathe around my frustration. When I'd offered to take Reagan to Maine, I'd assumed a week-long commitment. Yes, I'd grown attached to my new friend, but that didn't mean I was ready to take responsibility for her.

I rub my forehead. "When did you say you'd turn eighteen? Two more weeks?"

She bites her bottom lip, stares at the journal I gave her. I can almost see the inner battle waging within. "About that . . . I might have been a little less than truthful."

My thoughts sputter on her words. "*How* less than?"

She scrunches her nose. "Five months . . . give or take a few weeks?"

I close my eyes. "Oh, Reagan." When she has her child, she will still be a minor. Perhaps that would work with supportive parents or grandparents, but on her own?

"I only have a few more months until I age out. I can't go back in the system. They'll take my baby, give her away without even consulting me."

The system. She'd been in foster care? I don't know what I thought—that she'd run away maybe, or was emancipated. But this changed everything. What if the family I was urging Reagan to find wasn't healthy for her to return to? And the girl had already lied to me, more than once. What if this was just one more fabrication to add to the layers she seemed intent on building?

And, I'd brought her out of Massachusetts, which I assumed was where her foster family lived. Unless . . .

"Reagan, I can't help you if you're not completely honest with me."

"I'm not stupid. I know how things work. I've been handed off all my life and this time, with my baby depending on me, I'm taking matters into my own hands. Maybe it's best if we part ways here."

Her words cause chills to race up and down my spine. She's young. So young. How will she survive?

"No. I said I'd help, and I will." I take in a long breath. "What kind of a plan do you have?"

Her eyes shine, clear and genuine. "I'm not exactly sure yet, but I *will* raise this baby."

Tentatively, I reach out my hand and place it on her pale one. "Honey, I know this is hard, but there are lots of nice couples who would give anything to have a baby. You could give your child a good life. You could give him or her their best chance."

She clasps the notebook in her hands so tight her knuckles turn white. She stands, pushing out words through clenched teeth. "I *am* my child's best chance. This is *my* baby. No one will love him or her like I do. And what right do you have to pretend like you know best? I've known you for all of five days."

I glance at the woman at the desk, who shifts in her seat at Reagan's strident tone. I hold back the urge to shush her.

"I appreciate your help, I really do. But this is my child—the only thing I have in this world. And I will do anything—*anything* —to protect him or her. So don't pretend like you even know me or what I'm about, okay?"

She stomps away. I follow her to the elevator. "Reagan, stop. Don't—you can't just run away when things are tough." Huh. Like that isn't the pot calling the kettle black.

She flips her dark hair over her shoulder and jabs at the elevator button. "Can't I?"

"I might be able to understand if you'd open up, tell me more about your family, where you've come from, what you've been through. I'm your friend, aren't I? Isn't that what friends do?"

The elevator opens and she steps inside. "It's a two-way street, Scout. And as far as friends go, I don't know much about them. I've never been good at keeping any."

The elevator door closes. I lean against the opposite wall. This wasn't supposed to be so complicated. I only wanted to help. Reagan should be falling at my feet with gratitude. I could have reported her to the authorities, dropped her off at some shelter, and called my duty done. But I'd tried to do something good. Instead, it backfired.

I rub my eyes. Some vacation. I'm supposed to be focusing on home, on sealing past fissures that have long grown moldy. Instead,

I've saddled myself with the responsibility of an underage pregnant teenager.

I groan long and loud, sucking air deep into the pit of my belly.

"Mom, I miss you," I whisper. "What should I do?"

No voice comes to me, no audible sound. Instead, a distinct impression, more like a feeling.

Take Reagan home.

I almost laugh thinking what Bud Swift would say to have not only his long-lost daughter back, but her pregnant friend as well. But the fact remains that I am out of answers, out of options.

Take Reagan home. My father won't be able to help of course, but maybe someone else can.

I think of Charlotte's warmth, the gift of her hospitality that melts boundaries and soothes nerves. The Beacon Bed and Breakfast is more than an inn, it's a refuge.

I straighten. My mother's best friend will have answers. As long as she doesn't hold a grudge against my years of silence, as long as she still lives at the Beacon, I'm certain she'll help.

I can hope, anyway.

Chapter Eleven

Today I came home, but it was all gone.

~ SCOUT SWIFT'S JOURNAL

My first thought when I pull into the drive of my old home is that my car engine sounds as tired as I am. My second thought is that Dad must have hired help in the past ten years. The landscaping is impeccable—neatly edged and mulched around Mom's hydrangeas. Her black-eyed Susan's are gone though, as are her bleeding hearts. Mom always loved a little bit of wild in her garden and, unfortunately, whoever Dad hired—or maybe even Dad himself—didn't feel the same way.

"Wow, this is nice," Reagan says where she sits beside me.

We haven't spoken since that morning. I feel her pulling away, almost holding her breath over what our next steps will be. Does she see me as a threat to her future with her child?

A pain squeezes my heart.

I open the car door. Maybe I should have gone to Charlotte's first, but I'd purposely missed the turn that would have taken me to The Beacon Bed and Breakfast—not because seeing Dad would be easier, but because finding a solution to Reagan's predicament might prove so much harder.

"This is where I grew up. A regular old log cabin, the woods at my front door, the sea at my back."

She sighs with longing. "Sounds perfect."

"I'll just be a minute, okay? Just want to make sure my old room's open. Can you sit tight?"

Reagan nods, the unspoken question hanging between us. No doubt, my room is still open. Dad and I may have had a horrible disagreement that never settled, but he would be glad to see me. He'd never begrudge me my old room. Where then, did that leave Reagan?

I trot up the stairs to the front door, feigning confidence. He *would* be happy to see me, wouldn't he?

Maybe I should have called. What if he's off on the boat for a few days? What if this entire trip is a horrible idea?

But no. The success of this trip is not dependent on my father. Its success is dependent on me. On my goal to see Mom's lighthouses. On finding closure somewhere in this seaside town.

I knock. Dad had never been a fan of doorbells; said they were too impersonal. A good-ol' loud, neighborly knock did the trick, he'd say.

I look at the shiny Chevy truck in the drive. He liked to keep his vehicle home even when he was away, so its presence didn't mean much.

But then I hear footsteps beyond the door, the slide of a bolt—when had Dad ever locked the door?—and the squeak of hinges.

"Can I help you?"

A woman in her seventies peers through the screen door. I stare at her a moment, still expecting my father to appear from somewhere within. "I'm sorry to bother you. I'm looking for Bud Swift."

The pinched features of her face relax. "Oh, Buddy Swift! Such a nice man that one is. But he hasn't lived here for some time . . . let's see, going on almost four years now."

I step back, reeling from the news. "Oh, I didn't realize . . ."

My childhood home. While I hadn't treated it as precious these last twelve years, it was still . . . home. I could visit if I wanted. Sleep in my old room. Lay on the backyard hammock where I'd devoured countless Nancy Drews and Sweet Valley High books. I'd taken it for granted that it would be mine forever.

"You look a bit peaked, dear. Can I get you a glass of water?"

I shake my head. "Thank you, but I'm fine. I'm sorry to interrupt your afternoon." I turn and nearly stumble down the steps, telling myself that my internal reaction to this news is not warranted. I must pull myself together. And I have ten steps to do it.

At the last minute, I turn. "Do you know where he is?"

"Buddy? He's still in town, although I'm not sure where he lives."

"Thank you."

I walk the few steps to the car and sit in a lump in the driver's seat. "He sold it."

"And he didn't tell you?"

I shake my head, not wanting to explain how I pushed him out of my life a dozen years ago.

"Scout . . . I'm sorry. Are you okay?" Reagan reaches out a hand, then draws it back, as if scared to touch me.

I start the car. "I'm fine. Just a surprise, is all."

I push the gas harder as I turn out of the drive. That house was one of the last tangible things of Mom that still existed. Charlotte had written to tell me that her bookshop had been sold and renamed nine years ago. So, in some ways the house was all that was left of Mom. Why had I not realized how easily that last tangible thread could be cut away?

"Could you call him? Your dad?"

"I could." But I wasn't ready, not yet. How could he sell the house without telling me? I didn't want our conversation to be marred by my fresh anger.

I drive out to Route 3 and turn south, breathing deep into my belly, commanding myself to remain calm. We go through the downtown area, and I glimpse the Bar Harbor Inn and Terrace Grille, where I'd worked so many years ago and where I'd met Greg.

I stare straight ahead, feeling like I'm racing wildly, searching for home around every corner but not finding it, even though it should be here.

All of it right here.

In a half-mile or so, I see the sweet, rustic sign telling me that The Beacon Bed and Breakfast is just down this drive. But instead of calm, sudden panic seizes me. Because what if it has all changed too? What if Charlotte isn't here? What if she, like Mom, is gone forever?

My breaths come fast, and I recognize a panic attack coming on. Maybe this is all just one big fat mistake. Or maybe I am only meant to bring Reagan to Maine to find *her* family, *her* place to belong—maybe that's what all this has been about from the beginning.

I pull over and unsnap my seatbelt.

"Scout?"

I push open the door, gulping for breaths. I place my elbows on the roof of my car. The scent of oil or gas makes me nauseous. Is that white smoke coming from my car or am I hallucinating? Vehicles whiz past, and I feel the air from their movement at my back. From somewhere far away, I hear Reagan get out of the passenger side.

"Scout, are you okay? Should I call someone? An ambulance?"

I shake my head, hard and fast, as I drag deep breaths into my nose, forcing normalcy into my veins.

"Please, Scout, you're scaring me. Tell me what I should do!"

I grab for the first thing to come to mind. "Sing."

"What?"

I attempt to suck in a breath but hit a wall. I shake my head.

Black spots dance before my eyes. My chest constricts. Reagan supports me as she guides me to the side of the road to a thatch of green grass. I collapse onto the ground, my overheated skin welcoming its cool softness. Then, out of nowhere, the sweetest sound surrounds me, singing the most childlike of songs.

"This little light of mine, I'm gonna let it shine. This little light of mine, I'm gonna let it shine."

Reagan begins clapping along with her voice. I'd laugh if I'd had any extra air to do so.

"This little light of mine, I'm gonna let it shine. Let it shine, let it shine, let it shine!"

From somewhere deep within, whatever fear had been gripping me begins to loosen.

I listen to Reagan's sweet alto, singing about not hiding her light under a bushel but letting it shine, shine, shine.

When she's done, I open my eyes and straighten. I glimpse the shimmering sea at the end of the road, the white beacon before it. I breathe in one more satisfying breath.

"Thank you." Another few minutes of steady breaths. "I'm sorry about that."

"Next time you do something like that give me some warning, okay?"

"I guess being home's shaken me up more than I thought." I should have been better prepared. Did I really expect nothing to change in the decade since I'd been gone?

"Well, nice to know you can be shaken."

I tilt my head to one side in question. "You did witness my neurotic cleaning tendencies the past five days, didn't you?"

She shrugs. "It's just nice to be the one helping you for a change."

"That song was beautiful, and you handled my crisis like a champ. So, I take back what I said about giving up your baby. You're going to make an awesome mom."

Her smile lights up her face, and it's enough to push me to my feet, to face whatever it is that's ahead.

Chapter Twelve

I read somewhere that we lose ourselves when we forget to dream. I wonder if it's not just forgetting to dream that causes the loss of ourselves.
Perhaps it's forgetting to love.

~ SCOUT SWIFT'S JOURNAL

Tucked away beyond the pines, The Beacon Bed and Breakfast emerges like a billowing harbinger of hope against the crystalline ocean. The raised garden beds to the right of the footpath are wild in an endearing sort of way—lavender alongside parsley and mint. In another, young tomatoes grow. They will be sliced and grilled, topped with basil and mozzarella and served as a side dish for Charlotte's famous breakfasts.

We pull up to the large home—part Cape, part farmhouse with a huge wraparound porch boasting plentiful seating for guests. Wisteria vines climb the columns and curtains billow behind window screens. In the back of the main building and what had once served as the lightkeeper's cottage, sits a generous guest cottage and a small building, the Oil House, which was once used to store oil that originally fueled the lighthouse. While the guest cottage is its own generous suite, the Oil House claims no more than two hundred square feet. Guests adventurous enough could stay there and use the outhouse, which, in my opinion, is the most adorable and pleasant outhouse one would ever have a chance to use.

And beyond all that, ruling the granite ledges and offshore islands and shimmering sea, is what, in the end, makes The Beacon Bed and Breakfast so endearing—the Beacon. The white light-house stands atop stone. A white-painted footbridge leads to its home on the rocky outcropping, nearly jutting into the ocean. A small door beckons visitors up to the light, where a majestic view of Maine's wonders awaits. Its whitewashed brightness in the late afternoon sunlight catches me off-guard. It looks nearly new, not exactly how I remembered it. More beautiful, if possible.

"Um . . . wow," Reagan breathes. "I've never seen anything like it. I mean, this place is perfect. It feels like . . ."

"Home," I murmur before I can censor myself.

"You think your dad is here?"

I shake my head. "No. Charlotte. She was my mother's best friend. Sort of like an aunt or a grandmother, but I haven't spoken to her in a while. I'm not even sure she's still here. But this is the only place—"

The only place I can think of going to after all these years.

Yes, I have my father's cell number. But Charlotte can probably tell me where Dad is and why he sold the log cabin. Hopefully she will know how I can help Reagan, too.

"Ready?"

Reagan grins. "Are you?"

"We'll see." I push open my door and grab my phone, shoving it into my back pocket.

We take the cobbled path up to the main house. A heavy metal wind chime sounds gently from the side of the porch, as if dancing along to the familiar singing I hear coming from the backyard. I smile.

Charlotte is still here.

I follow the porch, and the slightly off-key melody, toward the back of the house. Some things never change, I suppose—like Charlotte's love for Elvis.

We round the corner, and I glimpse Charlotte in a broad-brimmed sunhat, hose in hand, spraying a thin sheen of pollen off the deck boards. She's petite in every sense of the word. In fact, she doesn't seem to have aged at all. I can only wish I'll look that good when I hit seventy.

She doesn't see us, but continues to spray the deck, putting a little twist in her hips as she sings about not stepping on her blue suede shoes. All the tension inside me melts.

"Don't the guests ever complain about all that racket?" I speak loudly, unable to stop the corners of my mouth from inching upwards.

She jumps and looks at me. For a moment, I fear I've made a mistake in my joke, in pretending things are as they once had been.

She drops the hose, water still spewing out of the end. She places a hand on her chest. "Lillian . . .?" She shakes her head. "Saints alive, of course not. Scout! Oh, my stars, it's really you." She rushes over to me but stops short of pulling me into an embrace, instead holding me at arm's length. "Well, you have her eyes, of course. Pure beauty. Oh, Scout . . . thank the Lord, you've come home."

Home.

She squeezes me in her soft arms. Arms that petite have no right to make someone feel as if they are wrapped in a large, warm blanket, but they do.

I swallow down the lump in my throat. Charlotte isn't mad. She hasn't held a grudge. I deserve none of this warm welcome.

When we finally part, she wipes her eyes. "Well, how about some tea? I made hummingbird cake this morning. I hope it's still your favorite. Oh, the hose!" She rushes over to shut off the nozzle but stops short at the sight of Reagan. To her credit, she doesn't waver. "Oh, I'm sorry, I didn't see you." She holds out her hand. "I'm Charlotte."

"This is Reagan. She has some family in Maine we're trying to find."

Charlotte pumps Reagan's hand. The girl grins wider than a Cheshire cat, seeming absolutely enamored with the older woman. "So nice to meet you. This place is beautiful. I feel like I've entered a fairy tale."

Charlotte peers out at the lighthouse, where an older couple crosses the footbridge for a visit. "It never gets old, either. The work does sometimes, but the view . . . never." She smiles at me again, seems to have trouble tearing her gaze from me. "Come on in then, girls. I need some libations myself after such a surprise."

"I probably should have called first." I follow Charlotte inside, using the back door that leads straight to the kitchen.

She swats my arm. "Oh, come now, you know I don't stand on ceremony. I'm just glad you're here, honey."

I breathe in the scents of basil and rosemary mixed with the faint smells of sausage, likely from breakfast. The spacious kitchen boasts a butcher-block island and antiqued cream-colored cabinets that bring out the rose gold of the granite countertops. Charlotte heats a pot over the commercial gas stove and sets three mugs on the island. A sideboard table along the wall is designated for the guests. It holds a pitcher of ice water, sliced lemons swirling at the top, and a platter of what I recognize as Charlotte's famous hummingbird cake.

"The place hasn't changed. It's still as perfect as ever."

"Well, I don't have the bookshelves any longer, I'm afraid. And the Beacon got a makeover this past year. But other than that, yes, we don't try to make too much progress around here all at once." She winks and scurries around the kitchen until she holds a tray of three teas alongside three slices of cake. "Outside, shall we?"

I take the tray from her and follow her back toward the sea. Three Adirondack chairs sit beneath a towering cedar, a stone fire pit nearby. I place the tray on the side of the pit and pass out the mugs and cakes. Reagan doesn't sit. She seems suddenly very young and unsure of herself—nothing like the snappy, self-assured young woman who'd put me in my place this morning in the hotel lobby.

Charlotte sits back and sips her tea. "Now tell me, Scout. What have you been up to these last live-long years?"

"I'm sorry I haven't been great at keeping in touch. Okay, that's the understatement of the year. Charlotte, I have no excuses. I'm sorry." Though I wanted to say those things when I was alone with Charlotte, the press of their weight crushes me now that I am in her presence. Better to say them sooner rather than later. For how could I sit here and drink her tea and eat her cake and share her conversation and pretend like I haven't committed a grievous wrong against this woman—this woman who, in many ways, was more family to me than my own father?

"Honey, there isn't anything good that can come from getting stuck on all of that. What matters is you're here now. I'm thinking we have some good talking to do at some point, but today is a day for celebration."

I close my eyes, her grace brushing the shadowed corners of my heart. It had been a mistake to push her away, to fool myself into thinking I could avoid everything and everyone here in order to escape my pain. "Thank you, Charlotte."

She squeezes my hand. "I've missed you, honey. Losing your Mom, and then you . . ." She shakes her head, breathes deep, and forces a smile. "But we just decided we're not doing all that now, didn't we?" Her eyes brighten. "Oh! And I can't wait for you to meet my granddaughter!"

"Your granddaughter?" A hazy recollection that Charlotte had an estranged daughter comes to me.

"Laney. You're going to love her as much as I do. She's been helping me run this place. I'll probably hand her the reins in a few years. Despite what it looks like, I'm not as young as I used to be." She winks and we share a laugh.

"I'm so happy for you." And I am. I always thought she deserved more than a dead husband and a daughter who ran out on her. Then again, somebody could say similar things about Dad.

Charlotte turns to Reagan. "Where's your family out of, Reagan? You'd be surprised by how small Maine can seem. Maybe I know them."

Reagan's frantic gaze flies to mine. I cock my head at seeing her retreat into herself. But can I blame her? She doesn't know what's in store for her these next few months, probably doesn't know who she can trust.

I don't want to explain to Charlotte even the small part I played in all of this. But I need to. And I would. Later, perhaps, without Reagan around to shrivel into herself even more.

I recall her singing "This Little Light of Mine" on the side of the road as I faced my panic attack. Or not blinking an eye over the number of times I stripped perfectly good hotel sheets from a bed to replace them with my own. The girl had been a support every step of the way, never judging or asking too many questions. Now, maybe that's what she needed—less judgment, less questions. Not answers or solutions that seem easy on the surface, but simply to know she has a friend.

"We're still trying to locate them," I say when it's apparent Reagan has frozen. "It might take a bit." I push my fork into the pointed end of the slice of hummingbird cake and lift it to my mouth. Moist pineapple, nuts, and a hint of banana combine with the cream cheese frosting to burst on my tongue. I release a groan of pleasure. "This is better than I remember."

"I made a small adjustment on the recipe to cut some sugar. It suits, I think."

"I'll say." I put the plate in my lap, wash the bite down with some tea. The call of gulls overhead soothes, even as I think of my next task. "We stopped by the log cabin. I didn't know Dad sold it."

"Yes, several years ago. After he and Brenda got married, he thought it was time for a change. But he's still . . ."

Brenda. *Married?* My mind stalls on the two words, unable to hear the rest of her sentence.

But he hadn't said anything. Not in his handful of texts, not even in that one phone call last Christmas.

Dad, remarried.

"You didn't know." Charlotte sits solemnly with her cake in her lap.

I shake my head. It shouldn't be a surprise. My father's a decent guy, I suppose. Hard-working, honest, and handsome. It had been almost thirteen years since Mom died. Did I think he'd remain alone forever?

But Dad and Mom . . . Mom and Dad . . . that had been a constant. Like a guiding star in a black night surrounded by a deep sea, they had been the one sure thing in my life. Until the sickness. Until everything crashed down around me.

"I'm sorry, honey."

"We haven't been close, but maybe an invitation to the wedding would have been appropriate?"

Reagan kicks the ground. "I, um, need to use the bathroom."

Charlotte twists in her chair. "Help yourself, honey. Back inside, down the hall. Second door on the right."

"Thank you." Reagan takes her empty cake plate and mug with her. I appreciate her disappearance. This conversation is hard enough without an audience.

Charlotte studies me. I can't hold her gaze.

"It was a small wedding, Scout. Just a couple friends who served as witnesses. And I only know this second-hand."

"But I'm his daughter."

She reaches a warm hand out to lay on my arm. "I think Bud thought it would be just too painful for you. And honey, it's not as if you two have been close these past years. You've lived your own lives, isn't that right?"

I nod. The lack of an invitation *is* my fault. I'd pushed away every instance when he'd offered a piece of himself. And if I received an invitation, I would have crumpled it up and thrown it away without a by-your-leave. But it didn't change the suspicion that my father simply hadn't wanted me there. Surely, my presence would have reminded him of Mom.

I pull my arm from Charlotte's fingers, lay my head back in the Adirondack chair, and listen to the lull of the not-so-distant waves beating at the rocks below. "You're right. Any cracks in my relationships here are my fault. I haven't made an effort. But . . . he's my father. The only family I have left."

Shouldn't he have made more of an effort? Chased after me?

"He's still your family. And for what it's worth, so am I."

I turn my head to look at her. "Thank you. I hadn't realized how much I missed you until I heard your singing."

She guffaws. "Oh, that would bring back memories, wouldn't it?" We quiet for a moment before she gestures to the lighthouse. "We had quite a time getting the Beacon restored. Laney and her fiancé Jason had a big hand in that. And of course, Zack. You remember Zack, don't you?"

"Yes." I hope she doesn't see the blush that rises to my face. Zack Garrison. Hard to believe he is still around. How many of my girlhood summers had been spent watching him from afar as he helped Charlotte's husband with some maintenance project or mowing the lawn? Five years my senior, he paid no attention to the rail-thin preteen who sometimes brought him lemonade at Charlotte's request. By the time my teenage years came around, I spent less and less time at Charlotte's. Then, Mom got sick. By the time I met Gregory Showalter, Zack Garrison was nothing but a childhood memory.

Charlotte shifts in the Adirondack chair. "Anyway, it took forever to put that plan in place. The votes, the funding. We restored the stairs and the catwalk, the wainscoting in the lantern room, the leaks in the cupola. Zack removed the rust and lead paint, repaired the masonry and the footbridge, and finally, we automated the light." She breathes deep. "My point, Scout, is that repairing what's broken takes a lot of work. But every day when my guests see that light shining over dark seas, I know it was all worth it." She smiles. "Maybe your being here is your first step in restoration."

Isn't that why I'm home? Yes, I want to finish what Mom and I started all those years ago, but deep down, haven't I come to mend the cracks and restore my past to something that resembles healing and hope?

"Maybe," I whisper. "Thanks, Charlotte."

"Anytime, honey." She sighs. "I was just listening to a CD your mom gave me the other day. I sure do miss her."

"Me, too."

"She filled a room with light. And those flowers she made up for the guest rooms added just the right touch."

"She did love her flowers. But she loved her books more, I think."

"I've let the bookshelves go. They started getting rickety. I pulled some from upstairs to try to resurrect the shelves, but it's hard to keep up with it. Your mom always had the best suggestions on local history or classic literature."

I remembered the two shelves in Charlotte's living room that Mom had curated with beautiful books for guests to browse or purchase. It didn't make a ton of money, but Mom loved it, and so had the guests.

"How are things with you? You never remarried without telling me, did you?"

She laughs as if getting married again is the most preposterous idea in the world. "Oh, no. I think the right man only came along once for me." She slaps a hand on her thigh and heaves herself up. "You're staying for a bit, aren't you, dear? I'm afraid the main house is booked, but if—"

"I wouldn't dream of imposing on you and your guests, Charlotte. I admit I thought there'd be room for me at the log cabin, but Reagan and I will find a place in town. I have a couple of weeks, and I want to settle in . . . maybe try my hand at some of that restoring you're talking about." I wink at her.

The corners of her mouth turn downward. "It's peak season. You'll be lucky to find anything, and if you do, it'll cost you an arm and a leg. But I might have a solution."

"That's kind of you, but I can figure out—"

"Scout Swift, will you let me talk for one minute and accept a little help when it's offered?"

Reagan approaches us, seeming hesitant to interrupt, but Charlotte waves her over. "Come on over, honey, I was just talking to Scout about your accommodations."

The girl looks at me. "Accommodations?"

I shake my head, but Charlotte rushes ahead. "The guest house kitchen and bathroom are being renovated. Both suffered a nasty leak this past winter. I've closed it to guests for the next month. You'd have to use the main house bathroom but it's more than enough to fit the two of you with the sleeping loft. If you don't mind using a flashlight for any nightly bathroom trips and being woken a bit early to some hammering and all that, it might be a perfect solution for the two of you."

"That's very generous of you Charlotte, but I don't know if we can accept—"

"Why the Sam Hill not? It's a perfect opportunity for you to do some of that restoring, isn't it? And don't tell me you're going to turn down my famous breakfasts?"

I groan. "You're pulling at my weak spot here."

"Then it's settled." She stands.

"I insist on paying you something. At least for the cost of electricity and food."

"And I insist on not accepting. Let me do this for you, Scout." She looks at Reagan. "For both of you."

"I could help around here," Reagan pipes up. "Whatever you need. Housework, weeding. I can cook a little. I—I saw a pile of old books at the base of the stairs. I could . . . organize them."

"Another book lover! Magnificent. You'll fit right in. And you help yourself to any of those books, you hear?" Charlotte taps her chin. "Come to think of it, I wonder if you two might be up to bringing back Lillian's bookshelves? I have books galore throughout this house that I've been meaning to go through. If you have any suggestions, maybe we could order some newer ones. Would that suit you?"

"I'm not sure I could come up with anything half as perfect as Mom did, but I suppose we could wing it."

Reagan's eyes shine. She nods enthusiastically. "I'd love that. Or to help with whatever else you need. I can't believe I get to stay at this place."

No question my young friend is loosening up. I look at Charlotte and shrug. "The minute we become a nuisance, we'll pack our bags, agreed?"

She rolls her eyes. "Yes, dear. As long as you don't disappear for another ten years, we're in agreement."

The comment snags, but I don't deserve any less. I look at the two women, then at the Beacon, standing tall and proud as it faces the glimmering sea. Everything seems to be falling into place. Could it be too much to hope that the rest of my trip will be just as smooth?

Chapter Thirteen

I met a man who hates me today.

~ SCOUT SWIFT'S JOURNAL

I wake with a start, the sound of a compressor jolting me from a dreamless sleep.

I grope for my phone and squint at the time. Seven-fifteen. I'd meant to set my alarm earlier, to be dressed and out of the way for the construction crew Charlotte told me would be arriving early.

I roll out of bed and pull on jeans and a large sweatshirt. Outside the window, the sky is a cerulean blue, the water twinkling like a thousand diamonds beneath it. After breakfast, I'll take a trip to the light. A few morning moments at the top of the Beacon is good for anyone's soul.

I grab my hairbrush, toothbrush, and makeup bag to take over to the main house bathroom. I wonder how Reagan made out last night navigating in the dark for her frequent bathroom trips. She'd taken the loft by the living area, insisting it would be easier for her to be closer to the door so she wouldn't have to disturb me during the night.

I guess it worked. It had been months since I'd slept so soundly.

Rubbing sleep from my eyes, I step out of the bedroom. A man with dark blond hair works a drill from beneath one of the upper kitchen cabinets. I glimpse his arm muscles and the farmer's tan starting at the ends of his T-shirt. The cabinet comes loose from the wall, and he places it on the floor before noticing me.

"Oh, hi." His green eyes meet mine, and I desperately wish I'd made more of an effort to wake earlier and run a brush through my hair.

Zack Garrison. Only he's not a teenage boy anymore. His long body has to be over six feet. Strong features and facial hair have replaced pimples and a smattering of youthful whiskers. My heart thumps. Hard.

"Hey, sorry to be in your way." I point toward the door. "Just heading out."

"Scout, right?"

"Um, yeah. You're Zack, right?" I echo, wanting to stuff my foot as far as I can into my mouth.

He holds out a hand, but something hard—or maybe challenging?—carves his pleasant face. "That's me. Charlotte told me you were here. I tried knocking, but you must have been dead to the world."

I shake his hand, try not to allow his grip to intimidate me. Any residual and initial attraction I'd felt for him simmers. Unless I'm reading him wrong, he doesn't like me. But why not? Because I slept too late?

I wrench my hand from his, grasp my makeup bag tighter, and look around for more people. "You're the construction crew?"

"I am."

"Well . . . we'll try to stay out of your way."

"Sounds like a plan."

Was that a word of warning? Stay out of his way or . . . or what?

My eyes meet his. Oh, yeah. That was a warning.

I walk out the door and up the flat stone steps toward the main house. What is with him? I will definitely make it a point to stay away from the guest house while he works.

The scents of coffee, bacon, and something sweet baking in the oven greet me when I enter the kitchen.

"Morning!" Charlotte calls from the island where she cuts up kiwi and strawberries. "Coffee's right there." She points to a Keurig on the side table where the hummingbird cake sat the day before.

"Oh, you're my morning savior." I look over the coffee carousel and pick out a French Vanilla pod, popping it into the machine. "Have you seen Reagan?"

"Have I! That girl was up at dawn's first light offering to help with breakfast. She made the batter for the pancakes and then insisted on starting on the books right away. She's a hard worker, I can tell already."

"Oh, wow. That's great. I should have been up already, too, but I slept like a rock last night. Must be the magic of the Beacon."

Charlotte stops peeling a kiwi with her paring knife and casts me a meaningful look. "The magic of home."

I resist a roll of my eyes and lift my makeup bag. "I'll be right out to help you. Just need to freshen up. I don't want to offend you with my dragon breath." Maybe that's what offended Zack.

The beautiful, merry sound of her laughter warms me straight to the bones.

After I finish brushing my teeth and applying a small amount of makeup, I find an empty spot in the bathroom cabinet to store my things. When I emerge, Charlotte spoons pancake batter on the griddle with a measuring cup.

"Did you see Zack?"

"Uh-huh."

She raises an eyebrow. "He's a looker, isn't he?" She elbows me. "And sweet as cream."

I snort. "I don't think you have to worry about playing matchmaker, Charlotte. Your handyman isn't too happy I slept past his starting time."

Charlotte's brow bunches. "Now, that doesn't sound like Zack at all."

I shrug as I stir cream into my coffee. "Whatever. He's right. I should have been out of his way."

"Well, I'll have to have a talk with him about that. You're my guest and—"

"No!" I wince. "Please, forget I said anything."

She presses her lips together. "Zack's had a tough week, honey. He's a good kid. Give him some grace for me?"

"Of course." I remember his brisk handshake, his hard look. Must have been some week. "And I think it's pretty funny you still call him a kid." That mass of muscle was clearly one hundred percent man.

At the thought, my skin heats. I open the cabinet to retrieve plates so Charlotte won't catch my embarrassment over my inner thoughts. I am not attracted to Zack Garrison. The guy is plain rude, and no amount of manly muscle can make up for that.

"When you're as old as I am, honey, everyone is a kid."

I laugh, reaching into the silverware drawer.

Charlotte waits for the pancakes to bubble on top before flipping them with the same spatula I remember from childhood.

"So, when do I get to meet Laney?"

Charlotte leans back to glance at the clock. "She should be down any minute."

"Oh, she stays here too?"

"Just until the wedding in four months. Jason's bought a house right down the street."

If Charlotte's not charging me, she's definitely not charging her granddaughter who's going to take over the inn someday.

"Would you go fetch Reagan, honey? These are just about ready."

I walk into the sitting room and around the corner to the stairs, where Reagan sits cross-legged on the floor, thumbing through an old book that sits on her massive stomach. "Finding anything good?"

She flips the book over to reveal the cover. "This is a beautiful copy of *Little Women*. The gold edges are still crisp. Maybe not to sell, but it would be nice to display it."

I swallow down a lump in my throat, memories of Mom reading the story aloud to me brimming to the surface. "Sounds like a good choice." I gesture to the two piles she's accrued. "Pancakes are ready. I'll help you move these out of the way." We work to keep the piles separate from one another. *Flowers in the Attic* catches my eye. "Which pile is this?"

"Donate. I think we need to be selective about what books to pick. Too many choices with only the spines showing intimidates people. Less options with the covers facing outward will draw them over and invite them in."

One side of my mouth hitches up in a smile. This girl is a rarity. How in the world did she find herself in such a predicament?

But I know. Love can make us do stupid things. Besides, maybe I should give her more credit. She left Jaden—something that took both smarts and courage.

"You're pretty good at this, aren't you?"

She gives a half-shrug. "I like bookstores. And books."

"We'll have to make sure Charlotte takes a look at the donate pile before we get rid of them."

"Of course."

I hold out my hand. "Need help up?"

"If you think you're strong enough." She giggles, accepting my help. When she stands, she rubs her back. "I am not sure how this baby can get any bigger . . . or how he or she is going to make its way out."

I bite my lip, study Reagan's small frame. I suppose I'd be worried about those logistics too if I were in her shoes. "Mamas have been managing since the beginning of time. You will, too."

But something—maybe fear—clings to her expression. A fierce, almost motherly sense rises within me. I place a hand on her arm until she meets my gaze. "Reagan, I know there's *a lot* still up in the air for you. But no matter what, I promise when you go into labor, you will not be alone. Okay?"

Her eyes water and without warning, she flings her arms around me. "Thanks, Scout."

I sniff, forcing my own emotions aside. "Okay, let's go feed that baby some pancakes."

Chapter Fourteen

ZACK

I've just finished taking all the old, rotting cabinets out of the cottage kitchen when Charlotte waves to me from the back porch door of the main house. "Breakfast!" she calls.

And she expects me to charge her full price. Not on her life. Not when she feeds me three-course breakfasts fit for a king.

I place the cabinet in my arms outside the cottage and trudge up the hill. I think on my meeting with Scout. Maybe I'd been a little rude. Seeing the gorgeous, doe-eyed woman emerge from the bedroom, her dark hair tussled, her oversized sweatshirt nearly covering the bottoms of her shorts, stirred a reflexive reaction within me.

I knew all about beautiful women. And I knew all I needed to know about Scout Swift from the acute memory I held twelve years ago. I'd come to the bed and breakfast to mow the lawn one Saturday morning when I found Charlotte crying on the back porch.

"Charlotte, what's the matter?" My first thought was that she received bad news about her daughter. Though I'd never met

Miriam, I knew she left her parents a long time ago, when she was still a teenager. I couldn't imagine how she could leave Jack and Charlotte, two people who had become like grandparents to me.

The Jacobs led the youth group at our church, and I'd gravitated to them like a hammer to a nail. When I started a lawn mowing business, they hired me and spread the word. Jack taught me everything I know about cars and small engines.

Charlotte swiped at her tears. "Oh, you never mind me, Zackary. I didn't hear you drive in. I'm okay. Just received some unpleasant news is all."

"About Miriam?"

Charlotte stood and straightened, wiping just below her eyes with the back of her pointer finger. "No. Bud called to tell me Scout left home."

Scout. I remembered the skinny girl who used to bring me lemonade. I hadn't seen her around much lately.

"She didn't stop in to say goodbye?"

Charlotte shook her head, fresh tears welling. "No. I'm sure she has a lot on her mind. She's grieving her mom."

I wrapped Charlotte in a rare hug. "But so are you."

I've held a grudge against Scout Swift ever since. And now that she's no longer the bean pole I remembered, but a beautiful grown woman, I'd nurse that grudge for all it was worth. If for no other reason than she reminded me of Priscilla—in more ways than one.

I bang my boots on the back steps and open the porch door of the kitchen at the same time I doff my baseball hat. The smell of bacon and pancakes and maple syrup teases my nostrils. Laney turns from pouring five glasses of orange juice. When she sees me, she comes over and gives me a quick hug.

"Hey, how's it going?"

I pull away from her. She is tan and glowing; she's going to be a beautiful bride. She flips her long ponytail over one shoulder. "I'm sorry about your parents, Zack. That really stinks."

"Thanks. And thanks for letting me borrow Jason's ear the other night."

"You kidding? That guy would kill for you. You're like a big brother to him."

I clear my throat. "Well, the other night I was a whiny big brother."

She smiles, but it doesn't quite hide her look of pity. We walk into the dining room where Charlotte is bringing a fresh stick of butter and a small pitcher of syrup. She and Laney eat before the guests come down for breakfast at eight. Sometimes, I join them. From the multiple place settings at the table, it looks like Scout will be here as well.

A moment later, she walks into the room, a very young, very pregnant girl beside her. I try to hide my surprise.

Charlotte claps her hands. "Scout, this is my granddaughter Laney. Laney, this is Scout and her friend Reagan. I think you both already met Zack?"

Laney smiles. "It's great to finally meet you. I've heard so much about you and your mom." She holds out her hand, which Scout seems hesitant to take.

Why was she being rude?

With much hesitation, Scout finally puts the edge of her fingertips in Laney's. "It's wonderful to meet you as well. When Charlotte told me she found her granddaughter, I was so happy for her."

Laney shakes Reagan's hand while Scout disappears from the room.

"Well, let's sit and eat before these pancakes get cold." Charlotte gestures to the table beside a window that looks out on the Beacon, the background of a glowing sun climbing over the Atlantic a sight that never gets old.

Scout slides into her seat and Charlotte bows her head, thanking God for the food before we dig in.

"How long was the drive up?" Laney asks when the silence around the table becomes stilted.

"We took our time and saw some lighthouses along the way. About five days?" Scout looks at Reagan for confirmation and she nods.

"Where'd you travel from?" I ask.

"Massachusetts." Scout spreads a healthy pad of butter on her pancakes. For some reason, the act surprises me. With a figure like hers, one would think she'd stay far away from pancakes and butter. I watch as she drizzles maple syrup on top.

What is wrong with me? I'm making assumptions I have no right to make. Just because Priscilla didn't let anything that wasn't green past her lips didn't mean that all pretty women starve themselves.

"Laney's from California." Charlotte beams at her grand-daughter and for the millionth time, I thank God that they found one another, that Charlotte has family again and doesn't have to run this place by herself.

Reagan's eyes widen. "Wow, have you ever been to Hollywood?"

Laney laughs. "I have. But I'd take this light"—she gestures out the window—"to the Hollywood stars any day of the week." She reaches for an extra napkin. I catch Scout staring at Laney's arms, surprise—or more likely, judgment—plastered on her face. The pale pink horizontal scars tell a story all by themselves, one I only know through Jason. When Laney first arrived in Maine, she kept her arms covered, wearing only long-sleeve shirts. But thanks to Charlotte, Jason, and her friend Kiran, she'd done a lot of healing in the last year. She no longer shied away from wearing T-shirts when it was hot like today.

"So, Scout . . . I've never heard of anyone with that name—except for the little girl from *To Kill a Mockingbird*, of course," Laney says.

Scout smiles and it's astounding. It transforms her entire face into a beam of light I can't take my eyes from. "Mom loved that book. I tried to convince her to change my name to Jean Louise once, but she wouldn't have it."

Charlotte laughs. "I remember that! Lillian was mortified."

Reagan wrinkles her nose. "Scout is a much better name than Jean Louise."

"Your mom must have really liked books to name you after one of her favorite characters," Laney notes.

I shovel in a bite of pancakes, sweet moist maple and butter-milk goodness.

"Laney is a writer," Charlotte says proudly.

Laney rolls her eyes. "Nana . . ." She turns to Scout. "The way she talks, you might think I've actually published a novel—or even completed one."

"What do you write?" Reagan asks.

"I'm still trying to figure that out. But I'm thinking of focusing on beach-read fiction."

"Reagan likes to write." Scout takes a sip of orange juice.

Laney's eyes light up. "No way! You should come to our writing group on Monday night. We'd love to have you."

A look of panic crosses Reagan's face. "Oh, I'm only writing in a journal for my baby. Scout writes too, though."

Scout's head snaps up.

Reagan raises her eyebrows as if to say, *If I'm going down, I'm taking you with me.*

"I just journal. I don't think that's reason to go to a writing group."

"That's how I started. No pressure, though. If you guys are around Monday and want to join, it's right down the street. And you'll love Kiran." Laney wipes her mouth with a napkin. "Oh! There's a box of Scout's mom's things upstairs, remember, Nana?"

Charlotte taps her chin. "That's right." She turns to Scout. "Your father gave it to me several years ago. I saved it for you."

Scout lowers her fork. Her bottom lip trembles. I momentarily forget my grudge. All I see is a woman who is scared, maybe even still grieving. She swallows. "I'd like to take a look, thank you."

Laney places her fork and knife on her plate. "I'll bring it down after breakfast."

"No." Scout clears her throat. "I mean, I'm going to take a drive to see a couple lighthouses today. I don't think I'll have time to go through it today."

"Okay . . . no problem. Just let me know when you want it. I don't want Nana carrying the box downstairs."

"You worry too much, my girl." Charlotte stands and begins gathering empty plates. Scout follows suit.

"When are you getting married?" Reagan asks Laney as she shovels in the last of her pancakes.

"August sixteenth. Nana's friend Hannah has a bed and break-fast two hours from here in Camden. They have a gorgeous barn they offered to us for the reception. I can't wait."

"That sounds amazing." Reagan places her hands on her swollen abdomen.

Laney gestures to Reagan's middle. "When are you due?"

"August twenty-second." They share a smile.

"You know what it is?"

She shakes her head. "I want to be surprised." She stands and begins clearing off the butter and syrup.

I slide my fork along the bottom of my plate to scoop up the last bits of pancake soaking in syrup before wiping my mouth and taking my plate and glass to the kitchen. "Thanks Charlotte. Delicious as always."

"Zack, I was wondering if you might find time to take Scout and Reagan on Park Loop Road? Reagan's never been, and I'm sure she'd like to see the sights."

Scout looks horrified, her mouth hanging open as she stares at Charlotte.

I rub the back of my neck. "Um, I'm kind of busy this week with work and all." Not to mention the golf fundraising tournament on Saturday, mowing the town pavilion Friday night, and in between, somehow accepting the divorce of the parents I thought would live happily ever after.

"Charlotte, that's not necessary. I have a car. I can show Reagan the sights—I remember them well enough," Scout says.

"Well, I just thought you two might want to catch up."

Scout scrunches her brow. I'm with her on this one. Catch up from when? From when she last brought sixteen-year-old-me lemonade?

I kiss Charlotte's cheek. "I think breakfast was the perfect time for us to catch up, Charlotte. Thanks for that." I wave to Scout and Reagan. "See you around."

She waves back. "See ya."

I can't get out of the house fast enough. I love Charlotte, but sometimes she's too well-intentioned for her own good. I know she wants to see me happy, but who's to say I need a woman for that? Especially when any attachment to Scout would likely blow up in my face eventually. Those who have no loyalty for family, surely have no loyalty to anyone other than themselves.

Chapter Fifteen

I came back home for closure. Why then, am I so scared to see what's in that box?

~ SCOUT SWIFT'S JOURNAL

As soon as Zack's tall form reaches the sidewalk, taking languid steps back toward the cottage, I whirl on Charlotte. "What was that?"

She pulls on dish gloves and squirts soap into the sink of running water. "I'm sure I have no idea what you're referring to, young lady."

"I told you not to play matchmaker—"

She pauses her scrubbing, gazes up at the ceiling. "I seem to remember you saying I don't have to *worry* about playing matchmaker. And I'm not worried at all. In fact, I quite enjoy the role."

"If I didn't love you so much, I'd be furious with you." I adjust my voice to pretend a Charlotte imitation. "Do you think you could take little ol' Scout on Park Loop Road, Zackary?" I flutter my eyelashes, eliciting a smile to tickle the corners of Charlotte's mouth. "As if I'm some helpless damsel from the thirteenth century."

"Dear, don't you think you're overreacting? If you didn't like him—and I know how much you used to like him—you wouldn't be so upset with me."

I open my mouth to argue, but words fall from my lips. "You—you knew?"

"Of course, I knew, honey. But he was too old for you back then. Now . . . well, now is a different story."

I prop a hip against the counter and cross my arms. "Is it? Because now he seems to dislike me."

"I told you, he's just having an off-week."

I snatch up a dish cloth and begin wiping down the counters. "Seems I might be, too."

She elbows me until I look up. Her endearing smile causes me to give in to one of my own.

"I love you, honey. I'm sorry. Please don't be angry with me. I don't want us to fight, not after finally getting you back."

My shoulders slump. "I wasn't angry with *you*, Charlotte. Not really."

"You going to call your dad?"

"Are you butting in, again?"

She tilts her head. "Seems to be it's what I do best."

AN HOUR LATER, I'm sitting in my Corolla, pleading with it to start. I turn the key in the ignition. "Come on, Chip. You've always been good to me. You got us all the way here. Don't let me down now."

I take the key from the ignition, reinsert it, and try again. Nothing. I remember the sound of the tired engine when I pulled into my old home, as well as the scent of oil and smoke while having my panic attack.

I get out of the car and shut the door. What I really want is some privacy to think this out, but I can't retreat to the guest cottage because Zack's there. I walk to the Adirondack chairs we sat in the day before and sink into one, resting my head back and looking at the tufts of white clouds floating lazily across the sky.

For the first time since I left Swansea, I miss my birds. Have they run out of seed by now?

"I thought you were leaving, honey."

I turn to see Charlotte has resumed her hose-spraying from the day before.

"My car's dead."

"Oh no. You need a jump?"

I shrug. "Maybe? I don't know much about cars."

"I know someone who does." Her tone is sing-song.

"If his name starts with a Z and ends with a K, I think I'll explore another option."

"The other option is to have it towed to a shop, but that will run up quite a bill."

I'm not sure which is worse: calling my father or asking Zack for help.

Another idea hits me. I sit up quick and enter the front door of the bed and breakfast, where two couples file down the stairs, talking and laughing about how frightened they'd been on a steep hike the day before. I return their smiles and thank one of the men for holding the door open for me.

I find Laney coming down the stairs with a basket of laundry. "Hey!" she says brightly. She really is sweet. I do hope to get to know her better while I'm here.

"Hey. I'm wondering if you might be able to give me a jump? My car died, but I have cables in the trunk."

"Absolutely. Give me a sec and I'll grab my keys."

"Thanks. I owe you."

I open the web browser on my phone. I've jumped a car before, but I always second-guess which cable goes on what part of the battery. There. Red, positive, black, negative.

I head to the small parking lot and dig out the cables. Laney pops the hood of her car and starts it. I hook up her car and then run the wires to mine.

Moment of truth. I slide into the driver's seat. Turn the key. Nothing.

I try again. Still, nothing. I groan.

"Not doing it?" Laney asks.

I shake my head.

"Want me to run and get Zack? He's a pro at working on cars." Of course, he is.

"I hate to bother him."

"Are you kidding? He loves this stuff. Practically lives for it." What other option do I have?

"Well, I guess if he practically lives for it . . ."

"Be right back." Laney jogs to the back of the house and a few moments later, she and Zack are walking past the raised garden beds.

"Won't start?" He peers over the hood.

"No." Was there an alternative reason for my car being hooked up to these cables?

"Well, you hooked these up right."

I roll my eyes, as if I didn't have to look up the right way to do it on the internet. "I know how to jump a car."

Laney shifts from one foot to the other. "Um, you guys done with me? It's check-out time and Charlotte thinks I'm in the house."

"Thanks, Laney."

"Good luck!" she calls, skipping back to the house. She seems so . . . joyful. Is it that she's found the love of her life, that she's so young, that she has her grandmother and this beautiful place—or is it something more?

Zack leans over the hood and begins tinkering with a few metal parts. "You notice anything funny on the way here? Smell? Was it driving okay?"

I shrug. "Chippy's never let me down. He seemed a little tired when we got on the island . . . and I did notice some fumes—"

He holds up his hand. "Whoa, whoa, whoa. Chippy?"

I scrunch my face. Did I say that out loud? "That's . . . his name."

His mouth gives a little tick, making him look ten times more appealing. "Cars are girls."

I cross my arms in front of my chest. "Tell that to Lightning McQueen."

The tick turns into a full-on laugh that makes his striking green eyes twinkle. "Chippy the Corolla, huh?"

I thought it was cute. "Can you help me or not?"

He bends over the hood, unscrews something, and looks beneath it. He groans.

I step closer to see. "What is it?"

"Well, I'll tell you what it isn't—good news. You said the engine was struggling and smoking?"

I nod.

He points to the cap he holds in his hands. "This is your oil filter cap. See that milky buildup? Ninety-nine percent of the time that means a blown head gasket."

"Can it be fixed?"

"It can. Question is, is it worth it? How many miles does ol' Chippy have on him?"

I roll my eyes. "Around one hundred thousand."

"Worth replacing, but it's not an inexpensive job. I could do it for you, save you some money, but it'll probably take a few days for the part to come in."

"I—that's nice of you."

"Any friend of Charlotte's is a friend of mine." He stares at me intensely as he says the words and I shift my weight from one foot to the other. "You are her friend, aren't you, Scout? You're not going to break her heart by leaving again, are you?"

I grab the cables from Chippy's battery. "Not that it's any of your business, but it was nothing against her the first time I left."

"Then why didn't you say goodbye?"

"I don't see what right you have to ask that question." Though it unnerves me that he knows I didn't say goodbye. In order for him to know, Charlotte must have told him. In order for her to confide in him, it must have bothered her.

"She already lost her daughter and granddaughter. Then she lost her best friend. You were just the icing on the cake." He flings a hand in the air, his tone pointed and accusatory.

I grit my teeth. "You know what? I don't need your help, okay? And for the record, you have no right to judge my decisions. I'd just lost my mom, and I did what I had to do." I throw the cables in the trunk, not even caring that they're not wrapped in a neat circle. I take my keys from the driver's seat and slam the door. "Thanks for your help." I stomp off toward the bed and breakfast, fuming that I'd allowed myself to ever be attracted to this guy, fuming that I wasted so many daydreams on him as a girl, and fuming that I'd been obvious enough that Charlotte knew.

Zack probably knew, too.

Most of all, though, I'm angry at myself for hurting Charlotte.

I release a frustrated breath.

"Scout, wait."

I ignore him.

"Scout, I said wait. I'm sorry."

I stop just as I reach the steps.

"I'm a little messed up right now, and the thought of Charlotte getting hurt again just about drives me batty. But I shouldn't have accused you. You're right—I don't know your story, and I'm sorry."

I turn, my anger melting at his words. We both love Charlotte. Can I blame him if he wants to protect her?

And now I understand the cold shoulder he gave me this morning. It wasn't because I slept late and got in his way, it was because I hurt someone he cared about.

I deserved his cold shoulder, and so much more.

"Thank you," I say, my voice softer. "I guess I understand why you don't trust me."

He looks as if he will say something else but instead turns back to my car. "So, what's the verdict? You going to let me handle the Chipster?"

I scrunch up my face. "Chippy. And I would appreciate your help. But I insist on paying you for your time."

"Whatever makes you happy. I'll order the part this morning. Hopefully, it will come in by Monday. It's kind of a big project but I'll see if I can get it done in an afternoon for you."

"Thank you. Really."

He screws the oil cap back on and closes the trunk. My eyes are drifting to his chest and when I realize what I'm doing, I force my gaze away. It lands on his face where he's watching me, an amused look on his face.

Shoot. Shoot, shoot, shoot. My skin heats. "Guess I'll have to cancel my lighthouse trip, but if I have to be anywhere, I'd say this is the place to be."

"I'll let you know when the part comes in."

"Wait. I need to pay you for the part."

"No worries. We'll square up after it's fixed."

I thank him again and head back into the house, fanning myself furiously with my hand when I enter.

Reagan looks up from her pile of books. "What's got you so hot?"

"It's warm out there."

"Nothing to do with the contractor guy checking out Chippy, I suppose?"

I swat her on the shoulder. "Keep to your books if you know what's best for you, girl."

Chapter Sixteen

I told myself I either had to text Dad or go through Mom's box.
What I decided surprised even me.

~ SCOUT SWIFT'S JOURNAL

SCOUT: Hey, Dad. I'm at Charlotte's for a little, but I don't have a car. Just wanted to let you know I'm around.

BUD (One Minute Later): Scout, so good to hear from you. You have dinner plans tonight?

SCOUT (Panicking): I actually think I do. Maybe tomorrow?

BUD: That works. Pick you up at five?

SCOUT: Okay.

BUD: You need to borrow a car?

I tap my pointer finger on my chin and gaze at a barge drifting off the coast. The scent of salt and wild roses weaves its way around me, reminding me of my childhood summers.

If I borrow a car from Dad, I could get my lighthouses in. Then again, what if he gives me Brenda's car?

SCOUT: I'm good, but thanks.

I PLACE the phone down and try to come up with dinner plans tonight so that I don't prove myself a complete liar. A small problem considering I don't want to expect Charlotte to feed me, and I don't have a car. And what about Reagan?

I scroll through my contacts until I find the name I'm looking for. If I text, Lexie might ignore me. Without overthinking it too much, I push the call button, praying this is still her number, praying she won't ignore an unfamiliar caller.

Four rings in, she answers. "Hello?" She sounds unsure, uncertain.

"Lexie?"

"Yes . . ."

"Hey, it's Scout."

Silence.

"You there?" My entire body tenses and a kink starts in the back of my neck.

"Scout?"

I clear my throat. "Yes. I . . . I know it's been a while but I'm in town and . . ." I let my voice trail off, waiting for something. An *I can't believe you're in town!* Or a *You have some nerve to call me after all these years!*

When she speaks, it's like a kick to the gut. "Scout—Scout

who?" She's chewing gum, and I can hear it smacking in the background. My heart aches with how familiar it all is.

I blow out a breath. "Come on, Lexie. Scout Swift, your former best friend."

"Ahhh, I think the key word in that sentence is *former*."

So, she is mad at me. Well, take a number and get in line.

I chastise myself. These people—Zack, Lexie, even Charlotte—all of them have a right to be mad at me. I just didn't realize how far-reaching my actions of twelve years ago had been. How much pain I'd caused.

I had been selfish, thinking only of my own hurt and trying to escape it. Now, it was wrong of me to presume on forgiveness after so many years of silence.

"I'm sorry, Lexie. I have no excuses and if you want to hang up on me and never speak to me again, I won't hold it against you."

"No, Swift, I'm not going to do that. You know why? Because that's not what best friends, or even *former* best friends do."

"You're right." This was hard. Maybe harder than facing my dad or going through Mom's things.

"And how do I even know it's you? What if you're an imposter? After all, I thought you died. Because what other reason does a best friend—ahem, *former* best friend—have for acting like she's fallen off the face of the earth?"

"I was a wreck, Lexie. I missed my mom. I was mad at my dad." Same old story. I sounded like a whiny woman on a soap opera.

"And that is exactly why you need a best friend, Scout. You don't ditch her for Gucci suits and a painting studio."

Painting. It had been way too long since I'd picked up a brush. Would I even remember how to swipe color onto canvas?

"I know," I whisper.

A moment of silence before she speaks again. "Well, did you get your dream life? Gucci all he was cracked up to be? Do you have a house on the water and two and a half perfect children and pieces in European art galleries?"

Each word jabs at me, poking and prodding like tiny pricks of a sharp knife along my spine. It hurts. But at the same time, my anger rises. I'm trying to make things right by calling. I could have ignored her forever, but I'm making an effort at least. Doesn't that count for something?

"No." My voice is small and tinny.

"What? I didn't hear you?"

I'm certain she heard me well enough.

"No. He dropped me off at a Walmart six hours from here and left me. He stole all Mom's life insurance money. I was too ashamed to call Dad or Charlotte . . . or you."

She's quiet again. "For real?"

"For real."

She sighs long and deep over the line.

I tap my foot on the packed earth at my feet.

"So, you want to have dinner tonight?"

I blink. "What?"

"Oh, now who's the deaf one? You want to have dinner?"

"Um, yeah. That'd be great. But my car's currently out of commission."

"I can pick you up, but we have to go somewhere that allows Gumdrop to come."

I wrack my brains. I haven't been on social media, so I have no idea what Lexie's life looks like. Is Gumdrop a nickname for a child?

"Gumdrop?"

"Gumdrop! My dog. I never go anywhere without him—he has full-blown panic attacks if I do."

I can't help but wonder how she realized this.

"Okay. I can't wait to meet him."

"He's going to love you. Even though he's spent hours hearing me complain about you, he might forgive you."

I can only hope she will, too.

AFTER MY PHONE call with Lexie, I check in with Reagan, who's surrounded by books. I know I need to worry about her, figure out how to help her, but we did just get here, Chippy's broken, and I need some time to pick Charlotte's brain. I help Reagan for a couple hours before deciding to search out the older woman, see if she needs help with any other tasks on her list.

But Charlotte is nowhere to be seen. Neither is Laney. I head to the lighthouse.

I pass the cottage, where the sound of banging echoes through open windows. I continue toward the footbridge. The new, white-painted wood is sturdy beneath my feet. When I stand before the white-washed lighthouse, I reach out to greet it like an old friend. It's cool beneath my palm, and I remember the many times I came here with Mom.

She loved this place.

Without thinking, I lean my forehead against its sturdiness, keeping my hand flat against it. I close my eyes, try to imagine Mom's voice.

God speaks to us when we're still, Scout. I think that's why I like it out here. No matter what storm and chaos surrounds this light, it's sturdy and still.

I push back from the structure and walk through the propped-open door of the light. The inside is just as immaculate as the outside. I remember a web of cracks along the interior, a broken step at the bottom. But it all looks as if it was rebuilt. I begin to climb the winding stairs, grateful there are no other visitors. Halfway up, a window allows a glimpse of the endless ocean. I continue until I reach the lamp room, dominated by a giant automated light. I move onto the catwalk.

I grip the black metal rail and stand straight against the wind. Up here, I feel like anything is possible. Slowly, I put my arms out to my sides and lean into the railing. I breathe deep.

God, I know it's been a while but help me. Show me what my mom wants me to see. Heal the parts inside me I can't heal myself.

It was the most honest prayer I'd said in a long time. Was it this place that brought it out, or was it simply time to search for a way forward? A way that was beyond myself?

Here, leaning into the wind, I can almost feel Mom's presence. It's as if her very being is soaked into this place, the essence of her in every scent and stone and patch of earth. It's why I'd run away, why I couldn't stand the aching reminders all those years ago.

But now, instead of sadness, a sense of hope calls me forward, making me brave. Is it God? Or is it simply memories I'm finally ready to face instead of run from?

I think of Charlotte and her steady grace. I think of my dad, of the lighthouses still on my list.

There's a lot to do, but for the first time in twelve years, I feel up to the task.

Chapter Seventeen

ZACK

I can't breathe. The sight of her standing at the top of the lighthouse I worked so long to restore, her arms out, that long dark hair flying in the breeze, pulls me in.

The drill I'm holding slips from my hand, but I catch it by its cord before it hits the ground. I shake my head to rid myself of her pull. Doesn't work.

I think of her leaning into the base of the Beacon, as if seeking comfort. Her head and hand pressed against its whitewashed chest.

My throat grows dry, and before I know it, I'm walking toward the light. She's having a private moment, sure, but I'm due for a break, and I have a legitimate reason to seek her out.

I cross the footbridge, a sense of pride swelling in me as I think of all the work I poured into this place last year. I enter the Beacon and take the narrow stairs two at a time until I'm in the lamp room, just behind her.

I clear my throat, and she jumps, wrenching her arms to her sides and whirling, one hand at her chest.

"What the blazes are you doing, sneaking up on a girl like that?"

I shake my head. "I'm sorry. I wasn't sneaking."

She blows a breath upward and it fans the fringe of hair at the side of her face. Her shoulders relax. "I suppose I was lost in my own world." She turns back toward the ocean. "But isn't that where you're supposed to be up here?"

Every drop of resentment I felt upon learning of her arrival drains out to leave a puddle of bitterness on the lamp room floor. These are not the words or actions of a woman who intends Charlotte harm. The way she is around this light . . . it's obvious it means a lot to her, obvious she's missed it.

I slip onto the catwalk beside her, lean my arms on the railing. "I think that's exactly where you're supposed to be up here."

"You did a great job with it. Charlotte told me how much work you did. It shows. It's new, but somehow the historical significance comes alive."

Yes, that's exactly what I wanted for this place. "It's the work I'm most proud of doing."

"And now you're renovating a cottage bathroom. Is that disappointing?"

I laugh. "I do what needs to be done, though I wouldn't turn down another lighthouse restoration." I hold the rails and lean back on them. "So, I came up here to tell you I ordered the part." That was the logical reason behind my trip up, anyway.

"I appreciate it."

"Only, it's going to take longer than I expected to come in."

Her face puckers, as if she's tasted a sour lemon. "How long?"

"Estimated to come in next Thursday."

She groans. "Okay. Well, there's nothing I can do about that, I suppose. Thanks."

"Charlotte tell you she doesn't drive anymore?"

"What? No, I didn't realize that."

"She stopped last fall. She was having trouble seeing at night. She got in a fender bender and decided to sell her station wagon."

She shifts from one foot to the other. "That's ridiculous. She's not *old*. And she runs an entire bed and breakfast. There's no reason she should give up driving."

"She does well for herself. But I wouldn't exactly call her a spring chicken. She's needed more help around here than she used to. That's why I'm glad Laney came when she did. She's as invested in this place as Charlotte."

Scout swallows. "I'm glad, too. And while I'm here, I intend to help however I can."

I hold her gaze, studying the hazel flecks in her chocolate eyes.

She bites her lip, looks out at the deep sapphire of the ocean, the waves hitting the rocks far below. "I won't hurt her. I promise."

I nod once, hard, as if I'm putting that notion behind me once and for all. "Anyway, my point was that Charlotte doesn't have a car for you to borrow. You said something about seeing a lighthouse close by? If you want, I could take you Sunday afternoon."

As soon as the words are out of my mouth, I'm regretting them. What am I thinking? How did I go from bound and determined to hold a grudge against this woman to offering to take her to a lighthouse?

But the words are out, and I don't see how I can take them back.

"Oh, um, that's real nice of you, but I'll probably see about a car rental for the week. I don't want to inconvenience you."

She's given me an out and since I'm doubting my offer to begin with, I decide to take it. "Kind of expensive but suit yourself. Let me know if you need a ride to the airport. It's about twenty minutes away, closest place to rent a car."

"Thanks."

"Enjoy the Beacon." I turn to head back into the lamp room and down the stairs.

I'm not sure if I'm disappointed she turned down my offer, or relieved.

Relieved, I decide as I jog down the cement stairs of the Beacon. Definitely relieved.

No use getting attached to another woman who has a history of running. Even one that looks like an angel of light at the top of my lighthouse.

I'M PACKING up my tools when my cell rings. I glance at the screen and my stomach curdles.

Dad.

I let it go to voicemail. I finish hauling trash to the dumpster then return to pack up my tools before seeking out Charlotte to say goodbye. I heave my table saw into the back of my work van and climb into the driver's seat.

My phone rings out a tune, signaling a voicemail. I consider deleting it without listening but feel childish even considering the notion. Instead, I head to Mrs. Darling's.

He likely left a message to tell me he doesn't want to hurt me or Mom, that he didn't intend for this to happen. He'll say all the same things he said the other night, and none of it will make the situation better.

I dial Mom.

"Just wanted to check in," I say. Maybe this would become a daily thing. I'd never much worried about my mother. She had Dad. But now . . . now, she only has me.

"You don't have to do that, honey."

"What? Call my mom?"

"Look after me, Zack. But you're sweet to call. I'm okay. The question is, how are you?"

"Just leaving Charlotte's." I purposefully ignore her actual question.

"How is she?"

But I can't take the small talk. "She's fine, Mom. Listen, I just want you to know I'm here for you, okay? Whatever you need, day or night. Don't hesitate to call. And maybe you can come over for dinner once in a while, huh?"

"Did you acquire some cooking skills you've been keeping secret?" She laughs, but it's tight with unchecked emotion.

"Well, I'll grill some burgers or something, anyway."

She sighs, long and deep. "Honey, I'd love that. But you don't have to worry about me. I'm okay. Really. I *will* be okay." She seems to be saying it for her own sake as much as mine.

I want to say more. Tell her I'm so angry with Dad I could pummel him. Tell her I wish I could make this all better, somehow, some way.

But I don't say anything.

"Zack, I know it's hard and I know you're going to need some time, but don't push your dad away, okay?"

"How can you stick up for him?"

"I'm not sticking up for him, I'm sticking up for you. You deserve your dad, honey. Even now."

"Neither of us deserve the man that sat in your living room and said what he did."

She grows quiet. "Maybe not, but that's the only one you have, and no matter how our story's going to end, I wouldn't change any of it because it gave us you—and that is the best gift either of us could have gotten."

My throat thickens. "I love you, Mom. Call if you need anything, okay?"

"I love you too, honey. Take care of yourself."

As I pull into Mrs. Darling's drive, I try to push thoughts of my parents aside. An hour and a cold iced tea later, I've assured Mrs. Darling her gutters are clean. I bid the sweet old lady goodbye and walk out to my van, her daughter Laura at my side.

"Thanks for coming by, Zack. How much do we owe you?"

"To stop by and have a glass of tea?"

She studies me. "Your time is worth money."

"Don't worry about it. I'll add it onto the fall gutter cleanup." I glance toward the house, don't see any sign of Mrs. Darling. "I can't help but notice she's getting worse."

"She's old, Zack." Mrs. Darling's daughter pushes her sunglasses atop her graying head. Red marks spot either side of her freckled nose, where her glasses were.

"She doesn't remember I was here three weeks ago . . . I just, I worry it might not be good for her to be alone."

Laura releases a huff. "You try telling that to a woman as stubborn as my mother."

I rub the back of my neck. "I know you're busy. I just wanted to make sure you realized what danger she might be in."

"I care about my mother, Zack."

"I know you do."

"I have a lot on my plate. Do you know my teenage daughter was just diagnosed with cancer last week?"

I feel like a complete idiot. "No—no, I didn't. I'm so sorry."

"You'll have to excuse me if I think my mother is just fine on her own. Everyone needs me, you know. Sometimes things in life just aren't perfect."

"I understand. If there's anything I can do to help—"

"Zack, I know you mean well, but if you would just stick to what you know, that will be help enough." Her gaze flicks to the roofline. To the gutters. To what I know.

"Goodnight, Zack."

My stomach curls and tightens as if I've been punched by a heavyweight boxer instead of a middle-aged woman's words. "Goodnight."

I watch her retreating back. Had that really just happened?

I shake my head and open the door of my van, slamming it shut. Seems I couldn't win, today. Or this week.

I drive toward home, replaying Mrs. Darling's daughter's

words in my head. Stick to what I know. But I was only trying to look after the old woman. Just like I was trying to look after Charlotte, look after my mom.

I think of her daughter's diagnosis. I say a prayer for the girl and for the entire family. Maybe Laura's right. I should have never intruded on family matters.

I back into the drive of the small Cape I bought two years ago, grab my lunch cooler, and unlock the side door of the house. I throw my keys on the oak table and place my cooler down, bracing myself as Atticus comes barreling around the corner to greet me.

The sixty-pound black-and-white mutt comes hurtling toward me where he slides on the square tiles at my feet, then backs up a few steps to sit on his haunches.

I can't help but smile. "Good boy." I lean down and scratch behind his ears as he pops to his feet, his entire body trembling with excitement, his tail slapping the wall, my legs, my cooler.

"We're going to go out tonight, boy. Find a place to run around." I finish his scratching routine—his ears, his belly, his back, his nose. After a couple minutes, he's had enough, and I wash my hands and empty my cooler. Maybe I'll bring Atticus to Charlotte's tomorrow. He can run around, chase rabbits, get out of the house.

I open the back slider and step onto the porch. Atticus darts out to sniff around and do his business. I dig my phone out of my pocket and tap on the voicemail that dad left.

"Zack, hi. It's Dad. I just had a project come through the office that I think you'd be great for. An old Victorian in the West Street Historic District downtown. Well, anyway, it's a buddy of mine I play golf with, and he asked me for a contractor recommendation. The plans are intense, but I told him what you did with the Beacon, and I gave him your number. Hope that's okay . . . . Listen, son. I know you need time to process and cool off, but I'd really like us to talk. Call me sometime."

I toss the phone on a patio chair and lean over the porch railing. My yard is neat and trim with a blooming lilac bush and a handful of other perennials I can't even pretend to identify, all here when I bought the place. At the back property line lies a thick hedge of woods. I close my eyes.

While I'd like to think the timing of this opportunity is pure coincidence, I can't ignore the feeling that this is Dad's way of offering an olive branch. And it feels slimy and wrong.

He's never referred me for a job from one of his clients before. Although, to be fair, most clients that come to him aren't home-owners, they're the big-name contractors around town, firmly established for decades. I'd give my left arm to work on one of the homes in the historic district, but I'm not sure I'd give over my pride.

But what if I did the job and it turned out just as great as the lighthouse? Could this be the beginning of getting my name out there, working on projects that inspire me?

If you would just stick to what you know, that will be help enough.

If I'm lucky enough for this guy to call me, I'll do everything in my power to give him a reasonable estimate. I'll do everything in my power to do a kick-butt job on his home.

And maybe, just maybe, I'll satisfy something deep inside I'm trying to prove to myself.

Chapter Eighteen

A lot has changed in the twelve years since I've been gone, but Lexie's changed the most.

~ SCOUT SWIFT'S JOURNAL

The woman who gets out of the sleek Nissan Ultima possesses hair blonder than Taylor Swift's. Large, Hollywood-style sunglasses sit atop her head. She's skinny in turquoise capris and a white blouse showing off a chest that makes me think all that praying we did in middle school helped at least one of us. And, in the crook of her arms, is a small lap dog wearing a sweater that, yes, matches the woman's pants.

I step off the front porch and readjust my bag over my shoulder. "Lexie?"

"Scout!" She trots over, though how she does so in her tall platform shoes is beyond me. When she reaches me, she throws the arm not holding her dog around me. She smells of the same Victoria's Secret perfume she wore back in high school and that, at least, is comforting.

She pulls back. "Look at you! You're so—so . . . " Clearly, she started her sentence before the thought fully formed in her head.

"So old?" I offer.

She waves a hand through the air. "You look fantastic, girl. Healthy. That's what you look like, healthy."

I wonder if *healthy* is code for fat.

"Well, you look great, too."

She straightens, thrusting out her chest as she smacks her gum. "Largely thanks to the girls, wouldn't you say? I got them done when I turned twenty-five. Birthday present to myself."

I raise my eyebrows and scratch the side of my cheek to keep from laughing. "And here I thought all those prayers we said as teenagers panned out for you and not me."

Lexie elbows me. "Sometimes, you have to take matters into your own hands, is what I say."

Though I don't argue with her, I know I'd never take this particular matter into my own hands.

"Oh!" She thrusts out her dog. "Meet Gumdrop! Isn't he adorable?"

The brown and black pup hangs limp as a wet rag hung out to dry in her hands. I raise a hand to pet his head, but I swear his lip curls. I withdraw my hand. "He's super cute. Is he a yorkie?"

"No, silly. He's a toy poodle. Bought him when I turned twenty-seven. Birthday present to myself."

"Oh . . . he's adorable. Um, I'd invite you in, but I think Charlotte just went upstairs to lie down." I don't mention Reagan to her—I'd rather not have to explain our complicated friendship just yet.

We walk to her car, and I try to dig out the mental picture I have of teenage Lexie. Slightly on the heavier side, dark long hair, flat chest, thrift store clothes, no dog. What have her last twelve years been like to change her so drastically?

"Nice car." I slide in and school my expression so as not to cringe at the abundant brown fast-food bags on the floor of the passenger's seat.

"Thanks. I got it when I was twenty-nine."

I raise an eyebrow. "Let me guess? Birthday present to yourself?"

She grins. "You got it." She waves at the trash on the floor. "Just throw that in the backseat if it's bothering you."

It is, but although I want to ignore it and say it's not, I lean over and begin crinkling the bags, stuffing them all into a single one before tucking it into the back seat.

"Purell's in my purse, but I'm guessing you have your own?"

I let out a snort. Guess at least one of us hasn't changed that much. "I have some." I zip open my bag and dig out my bottle.

"Of course." She laughs. "I used to think you secretly took a bath in that stuff every night."

"I'm not that bad. I just like things . . . neat." That desire for neatness hadn't morphed into something more until I'd moved to Massachusetts.

"I'm not a slob, you know. Just haven't gotten to cleaning out my car this week. Plus, I wanted to see how you'd react. See how much *you've* changed."

I try not to be offended over the bait I just took. "Guess I've not changed that much."

"Just enough to come back home?" She casts me a sidelong glance as we take a right out of the driveway of the bed and break-fast. Gumdrop's front legs perch on the car door window, his back legs on Lexie's lap.

I shrug. "I guess so." I think to tell her about my dreams of Mom but stop myself. We are not the same people. I needn't open myself up to her just because we used to be best friends.

"Saw the Garrison Construction van in the drive. You enjoying that view?"

I shake my head. "Lexie . . ."

We're not in high school anymore.

What happened to you?

"What have you been up to?"

She heads downtown, shrugs. "Not much. Taking care of Gumdrop. I tried a few things, but nothing panned out."

"Well, what do you do?"

"Do?"

"Like, for work?"

"Oh! I don't."

I lick my lips. "Oh. You still live at home, then?"

She waves a hand through the air. "No way. I've been out since I was twenty."

She's apparently going to make me ask. "Did you have a rich relative who left you a bunch of money or something?"

"Nope. Rich husband."

I blink as she pulls down a side street and parks, taking out her phone to use the parking app. "You got married?"

"Yup."

Two weddings I wasn't invited to?

"I would have invited you, but you didn't leave an address or a number or even tell me what *state* you were in, so you know, couldn't send an invitation. Sorry."

I have a feeling she is very much *not* sorry. This new, passive aggressive Lexie is really something else.

"Well . . . what's his name?"

She taps away on her phone. "Whose name?"

"Your husband's name."

She swipes on her phone and tucks it in her purse before grabbing up Gumdrop's leash and her purse. She pushes open her door. "Ex-husband."

I slide out of her car and shut the door, meeting up with her on the sidewalk.

"I'm sorry, Lex."

"Lexie," she corrects. "And don't be. We weren't good for each other, and he left me with a boatload of money."

"So, you're happy now?"

She throws back her head and laughs. "Happiness, dear Scout, is relative."

"Is it?"

She stops walking. Alongside us sits a historic home with a half-circle driveway behind an impeccable stonewall. "Are *you* happy?"

I hold her gaze a moment. Am I happy? I think of my safe, predictable world back in Swansea. I think of Walmart and Elise and Sherry. I think of my predictable life—working, picking up extra hours to make yet more money, sitting in front of the Hallmark channel at night, going out on dates that never make it to a second, going out with friends, but coming back home to a strange emptiness.

I remember standing at the top of the Beacon, the wind in my hair, a strange sense of peace stirring my spirit. Sitting in that Adirondack chair alongside Charlotte, sweet hummingbird cake filling my mouth.

"I'm trying to be."

"Hmmm."

We continue walking farther into downtown. We end up at The Lobster Bar, which allows dogs on their back deck. I glance over the menu, but there's an awkward tension between me and Lexie.

Gumdrop sits on her lap.

"Lexie, I'm sorry I wasn't there for you. It sounds like you went through a lot, and I was stupid selfish. I assumed you had your parents, that you went off to college and never looked back. Naïve, I guess."

"You're right, Scout. You were stupid and selfish. You left me. I never made friends easily and that was okay because I had you."

I don't know what to say. "I came home one Christmas and

knocked on your door. You weren't home." The excuse sounds piddly even to me.

She bites her bottom lip, gazes out at the water, choppy and white-frothed beneath a setting sun. "I can't believe you actually left, that you cut me out of your life so easily." She blinks so fast, it's a wonder her fake eyelashes don't fall off. A tear leaks out of one eye, and she curses quietly, digging in her purse for a tissue.

I realize then that this journey home is about so much more than making peace with Mom's death or touching base with my father. I left real wounds here. Wounds with Charlotte, wounds with Lexie. Am I the reason Lexie is so far from the fun-loving girl of our teenage years, or am I over inflating my worth to her?

I look at her now, swiping at her lower lids, and see for the first time a glimpse of the girl she used to be. Way down under the professional makeup and dyed hair and fake boobs and nice clothes . . . somewhere is the Lexie I used to know. And somehow, I need to prove to her how sorry I am, earn her forgiveness if I can, and maybe, just maybe, find the woman who used to be my best friend.

Chapter Nineteen

My faults are as obvious as these shining Maine stars.

~ SCOUT SWIFT'S JOURNAL

The next morning is a repeat of yesterday, with the exception that two people at the breakfast table seem much more relaxed. Zack jokes that restoring the Beacon might be easier than finding out how all the water got into the guest cottage over the winter, and Reagan is bubbling with excitement over a rare Virginia Woolf find that will make a great addition for the display. Laney's excited to send out wedding invitations, and Charlotte sits beaming at each of us, seeming absolutely tickled that there's so much laughter and conversation at her breakfast table.

"Okay, Charlotte. I'm all yours today. What do you need me to do?" I spray down the breakfast table after everyone disperses. The scent of coffee cake still permeates the kitchen and dining room.

"Oh, honey, I'm pretty caught up. I plan on making cookies for this afternoon's snack. Care to join me then?"

"Just like old times? I'd love to."

She smiles and slips her dishwashing gloves off her fingers. "In the meantime, there's only one task I can think of."

"Anything."

She gestures for me to follow her, and I do—up the narrow, creaking stairs, around the corner, and down the hall. I peer into the open doors of empty guest rooms. Lavender Room, Wisteria Room. All as I remember them.

At the end of the hall, she pulls down the stairs that lead to the attic.

When we reach the top, she opens another door. "I'm not sure if you've ever seen Miriam's room. Laney cleaned it out last year."

I look out the window of the stuffy room to see the Beacon. "What a view."

Charlotte opens the window and an invigorating sweep of cool air rushes in. She reaches for a box near the foot of the bed. On the top, in black marker, it simply says, *Lillian*. My stomach drops.

"I don't think waiting will do you any good at this point."

I fold my arms in front of my chest, curling into myself. "You're probably right."

"What are you scared of, honey?"

I suck in a breath that goes all the way down to my belly. "Maybe . . . not finding what I'm looking for?"

Charlotte lowers herself to Miriam's old bed and pats the spot beside her. I sit.

"Healing?" she asks.

"Yes."

"Dear, you're a grown woman and you certainly know your own mind. But even if you don't find what you're looking for in this box, will avoiding it make anything better?"

I bite my cheek. "I suppose not."

She sighs. "I've been praying for you all these years, Scout. I'm so glad you returned home, and I'm going to continue praying for you—that you find that healing."

The thought that she's been talking to God about me touches me. I haven't had much will to pray myself after Mom died. I'd prayed a lot while she was sick, and that hadn't done any good.

I hadn't wanted to ask for help. Not from Dad, not from Charlotte or Lexie, and not from God. I hadn't wanted to admit I'd been in the wrong. And so, here we were.

"Charlotte?"

She places her cool hand on mine and squeezes. "What is it, dear?"

My lungs tighten. "I was wrong to leave without saying goodbye."

She pats my hand. "Honey, I want to sit here and tell you not to worry about it because you're forgiven. And you are. But I also want to be honest with you. I grieved you. Losing you was a twist of the knife. The last in a line of hurts. You would have thought my heart would have grown numb to it, but I don't think that's possible."

Tears prick the back of my eyelids. "I know. And I hope you can forgive me one day."

She wraps an arm around my shoulder. "Thank you, dear. Today is the day. And now, let's not speak of it again, okay? Just promise me one thing?"

I lift watery eyes to her.

"Next time you leave, promise me we'll still stay in touch?"

I force a smile and nod.

She squeezes me one more time. "Okay, then. I'll leave you to it."

My pulse skitters. "Here?"

"Does this suit you? It's out of the way. You can spread out whatever's in that old box. The room's not too stuffy, is it? There's a good sea breeze today."

I stare down at the brown box, folded in fours at the top. It's not terribly large—probably won't take me but an hour or two to go through. "Okay. Thanks, Charlotte."

"Let me know if you need anything, and after lunch, let's make those cookies. I'm thinking banana peanut butter."

My mouth waters. "Can't wait."

And then she's gone, leaving me with the box that shouts my mother's name at the top. I close my eyes, breathe a wordless, nonsensical prayer for inner strength and take a large breath—as if I'm ready to dive underwater to swim the length of a pool—before popping open the four corners of the box.

On the top is a green blanket. I reach for it, its parachute material familiar. It was my dad's from his time in the army. My mother used it when she read on the hammock.

I pull it from the box and lay it on my lap, the cool material whisking me back to childhood, when Mom would spend countless hours reading to me on the hammock beneath the pines.

Below the blanket sits a stuffed animal my father won at an arcade game on their first date. Then a small selection of books—*To Kill a Mockingbird*, *Little Women*, *Anne of Green Gables*. Mom had loved the classics. I pull out each one, my breath catching at the book below them all. Her Bible. I reach for it and thumb through its well-loved pages, skimming over the notes in the margins. How many mornings had I woken to see Mom poring over some section, pen in hand? She'd underline passages, put question marks alongside others, draw flowers and birds in the margins.

I flip through it now, landing on the book of Romans. At the bottom, I glimpse words in blue pen, Mom's neat printing causing a lump to form in my throat.

The Holy Spirit is God's deepest self, loving our deepest self.

I sit back, meditating on the words, and then skimming the eighth chapter, try to figure out what verse or paragraph prompted Mom to write those words. Were they from a sermon, a Bible study, or did she come to that revelation on her own during one of those early mornings?

Wherever they came from, I sit with them now. They almost feel like a message from my mother to me—a part of herself she found important to record for one moment in time. And although I haven't given God much thought of late, I find them beautiful. I'm drawn to them, to finding out the secrets hidden within them, to unearthing deeper truth in the words that sparked their writing.

I shake my head as I continue to flip.

No doubt, going through Mom's things are going to drum up all kinds of foreign emotions.

I land on the book of Matthew and catch several notes near the Lord's prayer.

This prayer is a humble dependence on the grace of God.

I run my fingers over the letters and read the prayer aloud, its familiar cadence taking me back to childhood when Mom would come into my room, hold my hand, and recite the prayer with me.

Where was Dad all those times? His fishing job required him to be out early in the morning, so likely he was already sleeping. Or maybe he was relaxing in front of the television. For whatever reason, he'd never been a part of our nightly prayers. In fact, there were a lot of daily rituals he wasn't a part of. Soccer games and dance lessons, school plays and field days. I'd never felt his absence, just accepted it. And he was usually around for holidays, his jolly laugh seeming to make up for the times he wasn't around.

I flip more pages, catching Mom's handwriting on nearly every page, taking in snatches and snippets. After a while, I set the Bible aside, vowing to read a little every day to learn more about Mom.

I'm reaching the bottom quickly, and I don't know whether to be relieved or disappointed. A colorful picture of a snail lay at the bottom—a piece of artwork I'd made at school and gifted to Mom in elementary school—along with a framed Mother's Day card she'd hung on the wall. I wonder if it had been too painful for Dad to walk by it every day and if so, was it painful because it reminded him that his wife was no longer a mother on this earth or that his daughter was no longer around?

A small photo album lies on its side. Pictures from my parents' wedding and honeymoon.

With a bittersweet ache, I think of Dad marrying someone besides Mom, displaying their wedding album proudly on the coffee table.

I flip through the album, taking in the young, smiling faces of my parents in front of a gushing waterfall, on a tour bus, barefoot on a white-sand beach. Had my father kept his secret even back then? How long had he known it was a secret to keep?

A handful of anniversary cards lay at the bottom. *To My Husband* or *To My Wife* on the front. I can't bring myself to read them.

Why aren't these things in Dad's attic? Why are such personal belongings in Charlotte's possession?

At the bottom lay a slew of small camcorder tapes, blue-inked handwriting on the tops. I don't remember either of my parents with a camera in hand, so I'm surprised to see so many tapes.

I scoop one up. My breath catches in my throat.

For Scout, Love Mom—Tape 2

I pick up another one.

For Scout, Love Mom—Tape 4

They are marked with dates, all in the year Mom died. Was this . . . my hands begin to shake as I fumble for another tape.

For Scout, Love Mom—Tape 5

I scoop the remaining micro-tapes from the box and sort them on the floor. There are five in total, neatly numbered one through five. They can't be anything but what I think they are. But if that's true, then why wouldn't Dad have told me, texted me even, about them right away?

And what's more, how will I watch them?

I search the box but don't see any camera. I release a grunt of frustration. I'm finally facing my past and now that I very much want to, technology is stopping me. Unless someone else has a video camera from the 90s, I won't be watching whatever's on these tapes anytime soon.

I lean against the bed and dig out my phone, Googling "How to watch old video tapes." One Reddit thread and two sites later, I land on a media company that specializes in transferring video tapes to DVDs. I learn what's in the box are Hi8 Tapes. The company claims it takes seven business days to convert them.

I start the online order. Though I hesitate when typing in the return address, I decide on Charlotte's. Could be cutting it close seeing as my three-week vacation will likely be coming to an end by the time the tapes are returned, but it feels important to watch them here, in Maine, not in my lonely apartment back in Swansea. I pay the fee and screenshot the address I am to send the videos to.

The only thing left to do is to get to the post office, less than a mile walk away.

I pack up Mom's box, keeping the tapes and the Bible on the floor. When I come down the stairs, Reagan is nowhere in sight. I round the corner to the kitchen to see Charlotte taking out baking soda, flour, and sugar.

I blink, check the clock. Twelve-thirty? I must have spent more time than I realized going through the photo album and Bible.

"How's it going, honey?" Charlotte opens a cabinet and reaches up to the top shelf for the vanilla.

"Time got away from me, but I finished."

"Oh, good. I just poured Zack some lemonade. Would you mind taking it to him?"

Although I think to protest, I don't want to be difficult. "Sure." The post office will still be open by the time I bring Zack lemonade and help Charlotte make cookies.

"I poured one for you, too. Take it on out there."

"Charlotte . . ."

She holds up her hands, as if defending herself. "I'm just being considerate, honest. No designs on setting you two up. I've vowed to keep my nose firmly out of any romantic hokey-pokey."

I roll my eyes. "Hokey-pokey, huh? Well, when you put it like that . . ." I place the Bible and the tapes on the hutch in the corner. "Where's Reagan?"

"Laney had to run some errands and asked her to go along."

Good. Laney seemed to have a good head on her shoulders. Another woman around to speak into Reagan's life and predicament could be a great thing.

I scoop up the two glasses of lemonade, finagle the screen latch with my elbow, and walk across the sunshine-strewn yard toward the guest cottage.

I breathe in the briny air, but just as I place the two glasses on the small table outside the cottage, I hear Zack scream followed by a "Hey! What do you think you're doing?"

Chapter Twenty

LILLIAN

I've gotten used to shocking statements the last couple of years.

You have cancer.

It's just a tax deduction, Lillian—you need to drop it.

I'm afraid it's terminal, Mrs. Swift.

This new statement, coming from my husband, shouldn't be too much of a shock, especially since deep down, I suspected it for a while now.

"I'm sorry, Lillian. I'm so sorry. I couldn't bear to tell you for so long, and now . . ."

"Now that I'm dying, you need to clear your conscience." The soft tone of my voice doesn't align with the bite of my words.

"When you say it like that, I realize what a scumbag I really am."

If I had enough strength to stand from the couch, I would. Stand far above his penitent form on the living room chair. But all of a sudden, the anger drains from me.

I'm dying. This is disturbing news, but clinging to my anger won't help. Besides, I hadn't pressed him, didn't investigate the money coming out of his checks.

I knew. But I'd turned a blind eye to that knowledge.

"Tell me. When . . .?"

I think of the many times he's been out on the boat over our years of marriage. Had he been having an affair?

"Before we met. A drunken one-night stand when I was a teenager."

"A son?" I don't know why I assume that. Maybe because it's the one thing I've never given Bud that I know he wanted.

"A girl." He doesn't say *daughter*.

"Have you been in contact?"

He shakes his head, hard. "I never met her."

The news sinks in, both a relief and a sorrow. "Oh, Bud."

We're silent for another moment. My mind races. "How old is she?"

"Just turned twenty-one on the sixteenth. Court ordered child support until twenty-three."

The sixteenth. I remember how he'd mistaken the date of our anniversary two years ago for the sixteenth. Whether or not my husband realized it, his estranged daughter must matter to him.

"You need to go meet her."

He snorts. "No."

"Bud, it's the right thing to do."

"Lillian, you have no idea what you're asking me."

"I do know what I'm asking. I'm asking you to be a man, Bud." I wince at the words that slip out.

"There you go, when all else fails, question my manhood—isn't that right, Lillian? I'm trying to protect you, and you emasculate me."

"Don't you dare blame this on me. I don't need protecting from a fatherless child. I need you to do the right thing."

I think of Doug, and I hate myself for it. He's kept his distance after I rebuffed his attempt to spend time with me. When I got sick, I felt him pull farther away. No doubt losing his wife would have made him think twice about whatever feelings he developed for a married, terminally sick woman.

Still, I can't help but think that Doug would have done the hard thing. The honest thing. And that thought alone makes me realize I can never forgive my husband if I'm clinging to an idealized version of someone he will never be.

"I never should have told you." Bud stands, swipes a hand through hair that began to turn salt-and-pepper after my diagnosis.

I lower my voice. "Maybe there's a reason you did."

He lowers himself back to the couch. His head falls in his hands. "I don't care about anyone else, Lillian. I care about you. You and Scout. You're my family. You mean the world to me. Back then was one stupid drunken mistake. And I am sorry. But I am not allowing my mistake to take away from us now. Especially now."

My heart breaks with the sobs that rent the air. The only time I've ever seen my husband shed a tear was after the birth of our daughter. But these sobs? They are saturated with emotion. And I *do* feel for him. But how can he choose one life over the other?

I place a hand on his arm. "That mistake you made is a young woman without a father. And while she might have nothing to do with your choices, she needs your love."

He sniffs. "I'm sorry, Lillian. Don't ask me to do it. Not now. We'll get you through this first, then we'll revisit the situation."

Get me through this. Get me through dying? He'd deal with it after that? I couldn't imagine such a scenario.

Out of the corner of my eye, I notice a form. Scout. I thought she was at work.

Lord, help me hang on just a little longer.

I've prayed the prayer more times than I can count. I want to see Scout graduate. I want, impossibly, to finish our lighthouse quest together.

My chest aches.

"What—what are you talking about?" our daughter asks.

Bud wipes his eyes and clears his throat. When he looks at me, I nod.

"I didn't want you to find out this way, Scout," he says.

"How did you want me to find out?"

She heard us, then. She heard everything.

"I was a teenager. Young and stupid and drunk. I know that's not an excuse, but I didn't even know until a few years ago that—that she was mine."

"You . . . you're a small, small man." And then she leaves, taking all the air in the room with her.

Looking at my husband, shoulders hunched, I can't help but feel bad for him. He loves us. His love may cause misguided choices, but it's all he knows to do.

"She'll come around. All of this is a lot on her."

"It's a lot on all of us." He slides his hand into mine. "Lillian, I know I don't have a right to ask, but I need to."

I lift a weak hand to his face. "Shhh. I forgive you, Bud."

Forgiveness is the way of my God. It's not the easy or convenient way, but with my time incredibly short, there can be no room for grudges. What's important is Scout. And if I don't forgive Bud, neither will she.

Chapter Twenty-One

ZACK

I lower the bathroom fan vent from the ceiling of the cottage, climb down the four-foot ladder, and place it on the floor. The leak from the kitchen had spread to the bathroom. Spots of mold appeared around the vent in the ceiling—the whole thing had to come down.

I grab my hammer, ascend the first two steps, and give the ceiling a firm blow, tearing down large chunks of sheetrock. There's no insulation, so the white board cracks in large pieces and crumbles with a hollow sound that echoes through my hammer. I give it another blow, but this time, something furry and brown sweeps down past my arm. I yell and watch the rodent—a squirrel —scurry with loud clacks over the vent on the floor and skirt the walls before scampering out of the bathroom.

"Hey! What do you think you're doing?" I jump off the ladder and dive out of the bathroom, searching the living area. A flash of a tail behind the couch. I lunge for it, landing partway on the couch and partway on the floor.

Behind me comes a feminine "Ahem."

I crane my neck to see Scout in the threshold. "Oh. Hi."

"Hi." She grins. "Watcha doing?"

"There's a squirrel. You didn't see him, did you?"

She raises an eyebrow. "No, but—" She lets out a small shriek as the fast little rodent darts from beneath the couch and into the open door of the bedroom.

"You didn't close your bedroom door?"

"I didn't know the contractor was inviting in the woodland creatures today."

"It was in the ceiling."

"So how do we get it out?"

"You go in there and scare it out and I'll try to point it toward the door."

"Uh-uh. There is no way I'm crawling around on the floor and poking my face under the bed to get my nose bitten off by a squirrel."

"Fine, I'll go in. That okay?"

She gestures toward the room she's been staying in. "Be my guest."

I enter the bedroom. The first thing I notice is its orderliness. There is nothing to indicate a person is staying here. No clothes, no bottles on the dresser, no shoes, not even a suitcase. The bed is made without a single wrinkle. The only hint of Scout is a faint scent of flowers.

Shouldn't be hard to find a squirrel in this place.

I bend down, tapping my finger along the wall. No movement. I peer beneath the bed to see three pairs of shoes in a neat line. No squirrel.

I stand and continue along the perimeter of the room. Where could the rodent be? "Come on, Mr. Squirrel, we're just trying to get you to a safe place."

"You see him?"

"No. Maybe—" I spot a lump at the foot of the bed beneath the covers. "Found him." I try to calculate how difficult it would be to scoop the sheets off the bed with the squirrel inside. The comforter's fairly thick—I don't think I'd get scratched.

"Well, where is he?"

"In your bed."

"*So* not funny." Scout's voice comes closer.

"Not trying to be funny."

Scout makes a sound of despair. "No, no, no . . ."

"It's okay, stand back. I got it."

I raise my arms to my sides and bring them down on the comforter, scooping it into a ball in an attempt to bring the blankets around the animal. "I think I have it!" I walk briskly toward the door with the blankets in my hand, but I trip on the corner of the comforter. "Watch out!"

Scout's soft body breaks my fall, but I take her down with me, comforter and limbs landing on the hard wooden planks of the living room. Something scurries around my leg and races past me out the open door. "He's out."

With the squirrel gone, I prop myself onto one elbow. Scout is beside me, the length of her body alongside mine, only a corner of comforter between us. She's rubbing her head.

"Oh man, are you okay? I didn't mean to—"

She shakes her head. "To be fair, you did tell me to stand back."

I nudge her hands from her head. "Let me take a look."

"I'm sure I'm fine. Just a bump." She lowers delicate fingers from her head.

I push aside a few locks of shiny hair above her temple. An angry red mark shouts up at me. "No blood, but you probably should put some ice on that."

I lower my fingers, but they seem to have a will of their own, taking their time as they brush the side of her face. Realizing what I'm doing—I stand up, but my legs get caught in the comforter and in my haste, I fall flat back on the ground at Scout's feet. My head knocks against the floor and this time, I'm the one rubbing a knot.

Beside me, Scout giggles uncontrollably.

I swat at her, continuing to rub at my head. "Real nice. Way to show compassion, Swift."

I try to rise again but my legs are still tangled in the blanket. I kick them off with gusto. She's still laughing, which causes me to finally crack a smile. But by the time I make it to my feet, she's in near tears.

I cross my arms over my chest as I stand above her. "You about done here?" I attempt to instill urgency into my voice. I feel like a complete idiot.

She shakes her head. Finally, she seems to compose herself. "Is he gone?"

"Saw him scoot right out the door." I hold my hand out and she grabs it, allowing me to pull her up.

Her hand is small, but her grip is firm. When she doesn't release my hand immediately, I don't release hers. We stare at each other, our palms pressed together, an electric current passing between us.

"Scout? You in—"

Scout rips her hand out of mine and whirls. I look up to see Reagan at the threshold of the cottage, staring at us. Her gaze falls to the blanket at the floor and her eyes widen.

I rake my fingers through my hair.

"Reagan . . ." Scout's eyes follow that of her pregnant friend's. "This is *not* what it looks like."

Reagan holds up her hands. "None of my business. I'm sorry to interrupt. Charlotte told me you were taking a walk to the post office, and I wondered if you wanted company." Her blue eyes flick to mine. "But maybe you don't need any . . ."

I clear my throat, point to the bathroom. "I'm going to get back to work. Make sure you get some ice on that head, okay?"

Scout's hand flies to the bump I examined as if she's already forgotten about it. "Yeah, thanks." She picks up the comforter, starts to bring it back to the bedroom, but seems to think twice and decides to bring it with her. "Oh, there's some lemonade outside from Charlotte."

I grin at her. "Still stuck on bringing me lemonade, hey, Swift?"

She rolls her eyes. "Keep dreaming, *Garrison*. I'm not a twelve-year-old with a silly schoolgirl crush anymore."

I tilt my head to the side. "You had a crush on me?"

Though I hadn't given much thought to the skinny preteen girl hanging around at Charlotte's, I was starting to give some thought to the grown woman right in front of me. One side of her hair is tussled, and for a moment, I consider what it would be like to belong with her.

She rolls her eyes as she follows Reagan outside. "Goodbye, Zack."

"I think you forgot where the blanket goes," I call after her.

"No, I didn't. Who knows what sort of diseases that rodent was carrying. This is destined for the wash."

I can't stop myself from taking the few steps to the door. I grab the top of the frame with one hand and study the two women as they walk away. The pale-skinned girl who's beginning to walk with the heavy burden of pregnancy and the short, dark-haired beauty with a crumpled quilt beneath her arm—the one who has no business intriguing me as she does.

My phone vibrates, and I dig in my pocket. "Hello, Zack speaking."

"Zack, hi. Brad Whitman, your father gave me your number."

The West Street guy? I sink into one of two chairs outside by the table. A glass of lemonade, ice nearly melted, sits on the metal tabletop.

"Hi, Brad. Dad mentioned you had a pretty extensive project you're looking to complete."

"It's extensive all right. But he seemed to think you could take it on. He's drawing up the plans now. I was wondering if you'd come by and take a look. I'm getting estimates from a couple other companies, but figured I'd throw you into the mix."

Throw me into the mix. Turns out a simple recommendation from Dad was far from clinching this job. Well, good. I wanted to earn it.

We spoke a few more minutes about what he had in mind—a complete restoration of a thirty-five hundred square foot Victorian with the priority of keeping the historical structure intact.

It would definitely run Brad a pretty penny and rake in a hefty amount for the contractor. More than that, if I won the job, it would earn my business a solid reputation in town.

No more gutters.

We set up a time for Thursday and I hang up, my thoughts on potential plans and subcontractors and timelines. I'd have to hire some full-time guys.

I return to the partially deconstructed bathroom sheetrock and take my hammer to the ceiling once again. I wonder about Scout, wonder if she might stick around long enough to see me win the West Street job.

I scowl at the thought. Why do I care? What about her is getting under my skin?

Whatever it is, I better keep up my guard. There is no way any good can come out of me thinking more than I have to about Scout Swift.

Chapter Twenty-Two

There's a part of childhood we can't get away from—a part of us that is truer than anything we're living as adults.

~ SCOUT SWIFT'S JOURNAL

As we walk toward the main house, Reagan whistles low. I give her a sidelong glance. "What?"

"You know what."

"Just to be clear, what you saw back there was not how it looked. *At all*. There was a squirrel in my bedsheets, so he grabbed them up and—"

"Uh-huh . . ."

"Reagan!" I stop walking. For some reason, it's incredibly important she understands this. As much as I'm hesitant to admit it, I have an inkling Reagan admires me, respects me even. What does it say about my morals if she thinks I'm ready to jump into bed with the first hot guy I see?

She looks at me, one side of her mouth hitching up in a smile. "Yes?"

"You need to listen to me. We weren't *doing* anything."

"Oh, I know."

I blink. "You do?"

"Yeah. It's what you weren't doing that says it all."

"What?"

"It was that smoldering look he was giving you, like he very much *wanted* to do something."

Intense heat rolls over my skin, making the back of my neck and the spot in the middle of my breastbone hot and damp. I remember those intense green eyes gazing down at me, as if trying to puzzle me out.

She's right. He looked like he wanted to kiss me.

Not that it meant he would have. Or even that he thought it was a good idea.

And what did I think?

My head aches where I banged it.

"So, you had a crush on him when you were young?"

We continue our traipse toward the house. "Yeah. I'm surprised he didn't know. He was the cool high school guy getting his driver's license and doing yard work. I was the awkward, spindly preteen trying to get his attention with a glass of lemonade."

"Well, I think it's safe to say you've got his attention."

Before my imagination can run away with romantic thoughts, I sober. "Even if something could eventually happen, I'm not the type of woman to rush into things. It's important to take things slow, to—"

She raises a dark brow. "To not end up like me? Don't sweat it, Scout, I got it." She jogs up the steps.

"Reagan, that's not what I meant."

But it was, wasn't it? Not that I was trying to separate myself from her. I was only trying to be the role model she deserved. Yet maybe I didn't have to turn our conversation into an object lesson. Uh, so frustrating. It wasn't as if I asked to be saddled with this responsibility. Couldn't she see I was doing my best?

I think of Lexie's tears across the table of the restaurant. I think of Charlotte's confession of how much I hurt her. I think of my dad getting married without sending me an invitation.

It shouldn't come as a surprise that my best hasn't been enough.

The Holy Spirit is God's deepest self, loving our deepest self.

The words Mom had written, now engraved in my head, come to me in that moment. Is this my deepest self, then? Trying, but forever failing?

When I enter the kitchen, Reagan is nowhere in sight, and Charlotte is greasing a cookie sheet with a plastic sandwich bag and a can of shortening. "Everything okay, dear?"

"It will be."

She glances down at the glass in my hand, the comforter beneath my other arm. "You didn't drink your lemonade."

"I got sidetracked. Could I throw this in the wash? We had a squirrel invader."

"Of course."

After I run a small load and wash my hands, I'm measuring out flour, baking soda, and salt into a bowl and mixing it together with a spoon.

"Charlotte, can I ask who packed up that box with Mom's things?"

She pauses, broken eggshell hovering over the mixing bowl. The yolk and whites drop in and she sets the shell aside. "Your dad did that. Took him a long time, too."

"Then how come you have it? And how come it's your writing on it?"

"Bud gave me the box a few years back when he sold the house. He wasn't sure if I wanted to go through any of it."

I stop stirring. "Did you?"

"I took out a photo album, but seeing your mom and you as a little girl . . . I was surprised the pain could still be so fresh. I tucked it away, put Lillian's name on it, and forgot about it until the other day."

"There's home video cassettes in there." I walk to the hutch, show her the labels with my name on them. *For Scout, Love Mom.*

Her breath hitches. "Do you think . . ."

I lower the tapes, reading her mind but also scared to speak such a hope—such a fear—out loud. "I don't know. I don't have the video camera and no way to play them. I'm going to send them off to a company to have them transferred to a DVD."

Charlotte presses her lips together. "I'll be anxious to hear what you find. And I'll be praying those tapes stay safe on their journey."

"Thank you." We're silent another minute, the only sound the mixer on low speed as it creams butter, sugar, mashed banana, peanut butter, and eggs. When Charlotte shuts it off, I gather the nerve to ask what's on my mind. "Why do you think Dad would have packed the tapes away when they're so obviously meant for me?" Sure, we aren't close by any means, but we texted every now and then. He could have snapped a picture, sent a text. *Found these. Just wanted to let you know they're here when you're ready. Thinking about you.*

Was that so hard?

Charlotte scrapes the side of the mixer with a silicone spatula. "Honey, I'm afraid I can't answer that question for you."

I bite my lip and think back to the secret I found out weeks before Mom's death. I think back to me confronting my dad and my stomach curdles. Suddenly, I'm very much dreading dinner tonight.

I help Charlotte spoon dough into pans and while the cookies are in the oven, she makes us tea. The kitchen possesses a cozy warmth, the scent of sweet banana and peanut butter goodness wafting through the room.

After the cookies cool in the pan for a few minutes, we sit at the island and munch on a couple as we sip our tea. Charlotte reminisces about meeting Mom at a church barbecue years earlier.

"She was my best friend, though I ended up thinking of her like a daughter. And you, my granddaughter."

"You were always like family to us, Charlotte." I point to the cookies. "Can I take a couple of these to Reagan?"

"Absolutely. That girl is working much too hard." She hesitates only a moment. "What can I do to help her?"

"She has family somewhere nearby, but she doesn't know where they are." Or she doesn't want to find them.

"Well, let me know if you need any detective legwork. I have some connections in this town, even if I don't get out as much as I used to."

I give her a wink. "Will do." I raise the cookies, wrapped in a napkin. "Thanks for these."

"Don't mention it, honey."

I leave the kitchen and walk through the sitting area. Reagan sits in the same cross-legged position I found her yesterday.

I wave the cookies in front of her face. "If you take a walk with me to the post office, these cookies are yours."

She doesn't look up from flipping through a copy of *East of Eden*. "I'm sure Charlotte will give me cookies free of charge."

I flop down next to her on the green and blue area rug. "Reagan, I'm trying to be a good friend and I'm doing a lousy job."

She closes the book. "I really appreciate what you're doing for me. I understand how huge this is." She waves her hand around the historic room. "But I have to tell you, it's tough to feel like a charity case. I get that I messed up. I get I'm in a predicament. I was stupid. I didn't think. And yet . . ." She places her hands protectively over her abdomen. The mature gesture somehow makes her look even younger than she really is. "I can't make myself regret this life growing inside me."

A soft smile forms on my mouth. "Can I tell you a story on our walk?"

"You should have started with that. Cookies can be resisted. Stories, not so much." She struggles to her feet. "I need to use the bathroom first."

Five minutes later, we walk toward downtown Bar Harbor, the sun warm above us, a slight breeze caressing our skin. Reagan munches on cookies while I tell her how I ended up in Swansea. How I gave a guy I thought loved me my money, my body, my life. How it was only by chance that I wasn't pregnant when he drove away.

"Wow. You were almost as stupid as I was. Maybe more so."

"Gee, thanks."

She elbows me. "Why'd you tell me that? You could have let me go on thinking you were this perfect adult."

I wrinkle my nose. "I still don't feel like an adult. And I'm far from perfect. I guess I was tired of feeling fake around you, pretending like I've always had it together. And as far as Zack, what I said is one hundred percent true. I'd take things slow. Not that there's anything to take slow. I'm leaving in two weeks. My home isn't here anymore."

"Why can't it be?"

"Because I have a job, a life, back in Massachusetts. My entire adult life has been there. What am I supposed to do—throw it all away on a childhood crush?" I laugh aloud at the preposterousness of the idea.

"Okay." Reagan says the word as if she is not convinced.

"Which brings me to a different topic, you. I don't think Charlotte minds us around for a couple more weeks, but Reagan, you need a plan."

We pass a forested enclave on our right with a dirt parking lot. A father lowers his toddler daughter off his shoulders and guides her to the car. The way he holds his daughter's hand as the girl climbs into her car seat is so sweet and simple, it causes a lump of longing to form at the base of my throat.

"I'm trying to track down my sister."

A sister? Okay, this is progress. "Any luck?"

She shakes her head. "She hasn't answered my texts or calls."

"Do you want help trying to find her? I bet we can run a ton of searches on the—"

She rolls her eyes. "I know how to run a Google search, Scout. She seems to have fallen off the face of the earth."

"Huh. Could she have gotten married? Changed her name?"

"If she did, I didn't find an announcement."

"Okay, well anyone else you could try to find?"

"I've been thinking. Give me a week or so, okay? Things with my family can be . . . tricky. I want to make sure I get in touch with the right person."

"Let me know how it goes, then?"

She rubs her side. "So, why the urgent trip to the post office?"

I tell her about the tapes I found, and she looks off toward the beginning of shops and crowded streets, a wistful expression on her face. "How neat to have a mom who thought of you like that, even when she was facing death."

"She was special, that's for sure." We walk in silence for a minute. "What about your mom? What was she like?"

Reagan shrugs. "We didn't have much of a relationship. My sister used to tell me what an amazing mom she was, but then she had back surgery, got hooked on pain meds. The doctor kept giving them to her. I think that's what wore out her heart—the meds." She sighs. "Or maybe it was the aching for the drugs. From what I remember, it was intense."

Again, I realize I have no idea what this girl has been through. I've judged her for living in a camper with her druggie boyfriend when I should have been applauding her for staying clean herself, for breaking away from the cycle and wanting something better for her child.

"What happened to you and your sister?"

"Ashely's older than me. You actually remind me of her a little. Only you're more responsible. Cleaner. You would have been a great older sister."

I laugh, try to shrug off the sweet compliment. "There's not many people out there cleaner than me."

Reagan smiles. "She had a boyfriend she lived with when Mom died. He didn't want me around. Besides, he gave me the heebie-jeebies. I was sent to foster care."

"And your sister let that happen?" An extreme dislike for this woman I don't even know rolls over me. If I'd had a little ten-year-old Reagan sister, I would have done everything in my power to make sure we weren't separated, that she was taken care of.

"I don't blame her. She took Mom's death hard. Grief can make us do crazy things, right?"

Her meaningful look puts me in my place. I had no authority to pass judgment on Reagan's sister after all the people I disappointed in my own grief. "You're right," I whisper.

She stops suddenly and points at a sign above our heads. "Wait! This is the place Laney was telling me about—Back of Beyond Bookstore! It's where they have their writer's meetings. Mind if I check it out?"

"Sure. I'll meet you back here."

Reagan practically skips into the store. I go to the post office, pack up the tapes, and pay Priority before handing them over to the clerk behind the counter. When he tries to take them, I can't let them go. My heart beats fast, pulsing all the way to my ears.

For some strange reason, I think of Reagan and wish she was by my side.

"Ma'am, you want to mail this, correct?" The clerk, a young man with a tattoo of a lion on his forearm, tilts his head to the side, as if assessing me.

I blink, release the package to his care. "Yes. Um—that includes tracking, doesn't it?"

"Sure does."

"And when will it get there?"

He places the white and blue envelope on the scale and taps out something on his keyboard. "Looks like . . . Tuesday."

I swallow. Tuesday. Only a few more days. But if the company takes the full seven to transfer them, I might be cutting it close. I imagine asking Elise for more time off. There is no way that will fly —Sherry has already texted me repeatedly saying how much she misses me. Although I'm not sure it's me she misses exactly, or the workload I lightened.

I decide to pay for Priority Express and next-day shipping, because, suddenly, I can think of little else than seeing what's on those tapes.

When I walk out of the dim post office into the bright sunshine, I say a prayer that the tapes will be safely delivered and transferred back to me. Such a small thing, really. I think of Reagan losing her drug-addicted mom at ten years old, of her older sister allowing her to go into the foster care system.

There are so many more important things God must deal with than overseeing the safety of my little tapes. Yet, those tapes are now tangled up in my mind with Mom's memory. Just as true, just as precious.

I can only hope I'm not disappointed.

Chapter Twenty-Three

I don't know why it surprises me that my father has aged. It's been almost eight years. But there's something else that's changed about him, something I can't quite put my finger on.

~ SCOUT SWIFT'S JOURNAL

The HELP WANTED sign catches my eye as I push open the Back of Beyond Bookstore door. A merry bell above my head jingles and the comforting scent of paper and ink, cedar, and sea, greets me. I close my eyes and know instantly that Mom would have loved this place.

The plentiful bookshelves allow space enough for an introvert to browse. A display at the front boasts everything local—lighthouses and blueberry farms and haunted islands and harbor cruises and historic inns.

Reagan waves to me from where she stands at the counter. "Scout! Isn't this place amazing?"

I tap my chin. "I have an inkling that you think any place with books is amazing."

She shrugs and glances at the pretty Asian girl across the counter. "Guilty. See, I love books! I'd be perfect for this place."

I'm trying to piece together what she means when the girl walks out from behind the counter, thrusting out her hand. "You must be Scout. Laney's told me all about you."

I place my hand in hers and squeeze. "She has?"

"Of course, she has. I'm Kiran."

I'm drawing a blank. Reagan elbows me, as if I'm being rude. "Remember Laney told us Kiran was going to be her maid-of-honor?"

"Um . . ."

Reagan shakes her head. "Never mind Scout. She's had a lot on her plate and she's too busy making googly eyes at the hot contractor at the B&B."

I shoot her a glare that could cut glass. "And you better be careful or there'll be no more room for you at the inn."

She bites her lip, but her eyes don't lose their twinkle. "Oops. Sorry." She turns to Kiran. "I have trouble monitoring my mouth, especially when I'm excited. But I know a lot about books and I'm good at recommending them to people, too."

Kiran tilts her head. "Okay. I come into the store and say I'm looking for a book for my eleven-year-old niece who loved Harry Potter."

Reagan snaps. "I'd recommend the Land of Stories series by Chris Colfer or Dust by Kara Swanson."

Kiran raises her eyes, clearly impressed. "Good picks. Hmmm . . . I come in looking for a book for my dad who loves Clive Cussler."

Reagan scuffs the toe of her tennis shoe on the ground as she thinks. Not a minute later, she meets Kiran's eyes, triumph in her gaze. "I'd point you to James Rollins or Steve Berry."

Kiran claps, clearly delighted. "That's amazing. Very impressive."

"So, am I hired?"

I flash Kiran a smile. "Excuse us." I pull Reagan to a corner of the bookstore.

"What are you doing?" she says through clenched teeth. "I'm in the middle of a job interview."

"I hardly think you'd be talking about my googly eyes at a job interview. You are not thinking this through."

"What are you talking about?"

"Bar Harbor is one of the most expensive places in Maine to live. You have no idea if your sister or any of your family are close by. You're about to give birth in a matter of weeks. Do you really think finding a job right now is the wisest idea?"

"You're the one who told me to make a plan, Scout. That's what I'm doing. Besides, I belong here. I feel it in my bones."

I want to ask her if it's the same feeling she had when she decided to hook up with an addict or sleep on sacks of bird seed at a Walmart, but I've done too much harm with my words of late. Who am I, anyway, to take ownership of this pregnant teen? What right do I have to tell her what to do?

But it's not a right. It feels more like a responsibility. A responsibility I really do not want.

"You do what you want to do. I can't stop you."

She brushes her hands together. "Thank you."

I trail back to the counter, where Kiran slips a book into a brown paper bag for a middle-aged woman. The bell jingles as the customer leaves.

"Sorry about that, Kiran. As I was asking . . . am I hired?"

Kiran gives her a soft smile. "I'd hire you on the spot. Unfortunately, the decision's not mine."

Reagan seems to deflate where she stands. "It's not?"

"I'm not the owner. But I'll pass on your application and be sure to tell her about your impressive recommendation skills."

Reagan's smile flickers. "Thanks. You have my number. It's on the application."

"I'm sure you'll hear from us soon. And I can't wait to see you both Monday night."

"What's Monday night?" I ask.

"Writing group. Remember, Laney invited us?"

"I do remember her inviting. I don't remember saying yes."

"Don't you want to go? Writing is a great way to unload."

Kiran watches our exchange with an amused smile dancing on her lips.

I rub my temples. "We'll talk about this later. It was nice to meet you, Kiran."

"You, too!"

The bell above our heads announces our exit. I have no strength left on the walk home to rebuke Reagan for signing me up for something I didn't commit to. Maybe it's the hormones. Maybe she wants me to go and convinced herself I agreed. Maybe she truly couldn't fathom why anyone wouldn't want to sit with a bunch of strangers and pour out their innermost thoughts on paper. Crazy, but who knows.

Not for the first time, I entertain the notion that Reagan is some sort of test in my life. And the only reason she's frustrating me is because I'm coming to care about her as one might care about a little sister—entirely too much.

I MAKE it a point to be in the bathroom when the doorbell rings at five o'clock. I brush out my hair one last time and glance at myself in the full-length mirror on the back of the door. I'm wearing capri jeans and a black T-shirt with a wood-bead necklace and matching earrings.

I hate that I care about what Dad thinks, but I do. After all these years, I want him to think well of me. I want him to be proud of me.

Even if I never believe I can feel any of those things for him.

I emerge from the bathroom to hear Charlotte and my father talking politely about the good weather, the start of summer, the restoration of the Beacon. I round the corner and stand just over the threshold.

It's been eight years since I've seen him—eight years since I came home for that cold, lonely Christmas that sent me running back to Swansea. His hair is thinning now, more gray than brown. He's packed on weight around his middle, but he looks happier than the last time I saw him.

"Hi, Dad." But I don't move closer. It's as if my feet are stuck in jam.

"You're beautiful," he says, as if surprised. "You have her eyes."

My bottom lip trembles and I clamp my teeth over it to subdue my emotion. This is not what I expected.

"Hug for your old dad?" He holds out his arms.

With effort, I force my feet off the floor and push them forward. I put my arms around my father, keeping my body well away from him and hugging with tense arms. He squeezes me, but pulls back only a moment later, no doubt sensing my reluctance.

"Ready for dinner? I was thinking The Terrace Grille."

My old workplace. The place I first met Greg. But Dad doesn't know any of that, and refusing him would be weird, maybe weirder than going back to the restaurant. "Sounds great." I bid Charlotte goodbye and follow my dad outside, where we take the short drive in his GMC Sierra to downtown Bar Harbor. We park not far from where Lexie and I parked the other day and begin walking past historic homes and then shops, hotels, and waterfronts. He asks about my job, about how I handled the pandemic working at the pharmacy. He inquires where I live, if I go out with my friends a lot.

Surface stuff, but I'm okay with surface. For now.

When we reach The Terrace Grille, an oceanside patio restaurant at the base of the historic Bar Harbor Inn, the hostess leads us to a table adjacent to the water. The green forest of Bar Island sits down the bay from us and a red, four-masted schooner floats by with little kids on the deck waving in our direction. Adjacent to where I sit, the mounds of the Porcupine Islands rise out of the bay like scoops of mint chip ice cream.

I order a ginger ale and Dad does the same. I try to hide my surprise. Guess I don't do that very well because he gives me a sheepish grin when the waitress walks away. "Quit drinking five years ago. Realized I had a problem. Found some AA meetings. I've been sober ever since."

"That's good." I scan the menu, perusing the homemade clam chowder, lobster bisque, and fresh blueberry salad.

"Get whatever you want. Actually, let's order the charcuterie to start. You have to taste their wild blueberry jam."

I stare at my menu, but really, I want to ask what this man has done with my father. The gruff and tough fisherman, beer always in hand. The man who loved to hunt, play poker with the guys, and didn't care a whit about AA meetings or wild blueberry jam.

Instead, all I manage is, "Okay."

Dad taps the back of his menu on the table. "Think I'll get the burger."

Nice to see some things haven't changed.

I place my menu to the side. "Lobster roll for me."

We sit in awkward silence until the waitress comes to take our orders. As soon as she leaves, the quiet resumes. Dad's gaze flicks to the building beside us, the Reading Room Restaurant and Bar Harbor Inn. "You know this place originally opened in 1887 as the Mount Desert Reading Room? They wanted to promote literary and social culture." His face reddens. "Of course, you probably know that having worked here and all."

"No, actually. I never paid much attention to the history. That's interesting." Mom would have thought so. Reagan, too. Far as I remember, though, Dad had never broached the subject of history. "How do you know so much about it?"

His ruddy face turns redder. "Brenda and I got married here. Took a tour at some point."

"Must have been a nice wedding." My words come out unintentionally sarcastic. Or maybe, if I'm honest, there's just a little intention in them.

Dad shifts in his seat. The waitress brings our drinks, and he rips the paper off his straw and dips it into his soda, guzzling it like a runner after a marathon.

I sip my drink, test out words in my head. *I'm happy for you.* I can't push them past my lips.

"Thought it was better I didn't invite you. Thought you wouldn't come anyway."

There is no way he's getting off that easy. "I would have come."

He looks at me above his half-drained glass. "You would have?"

"Maybe not. But it would have been nice to be asked."

"I didn't think you wanted anything to do with me."

I force myself to take a bird's-eye-view of the last twelve years. All the texts and phone calls I ignored. When I didn't flat out snub them, I'd resorted to pithy one-word answers.

I can't keep brushing it all aside. My hurt, but also my actions. This is why I've come to Maine, after all.

"I decided to finish the lighthouse project Mom and I started."

His blank face tells me all I need to know.

With much effort, I imagine my anger draining into the boards at my feet. "We were trying to see all the lighthouses in New England. Started when I was thirteen. We . . . never finished."

His brown eyes flicker with light. "I remember you taking a trip to West Quoddy and wishing I could have gone with you."

I squint at him. "Really?"

"Yeah."

The waitress brings the charcuterie board and it's a delight of color with an assortment of crackers, meats, cheeses, honeycomb, fruit, and wild blueberry jam.

I take a cracker and a piece of goat cheese, layer it with jam, my tastebuds bursting with appreciation at the unusual but sweet combination. "Tell me about Brenda."

His entire body relaxes and a jolt of jealousy funnels through my body. Are these feelings on behalf of my mother's memory, or are they welling up from my own pride?

"She's fantastic, Scout. She's a middle-school teacher, loves to cook and quilt. We started taking an improv class together, and it's hilarious. I've never laughed so hard—" He stops short, seeming to understand the effect his words have on me. "Sorry, honey. You probably don't need all the details."

My breaths come fast, the point in the middle of my breastbone tight. I order myself not to have another panic attack and begin humming, "This Little Light of Mine" to try and ward it off.

"Honey? You okay?"

I nod. "Just . . . need a minute."

Dad flags down the waitress and asks for another ginger ale for me, even though my glass is three-quarters full. I gaze out at the Porcupine Islands and think about making banana peanut butter cookies with Charlotte. Slowly, my breathing loosens. Air enters my lungs.

Another few minutes and I sit up straighter, give a firm nod of my head. "I'm . . . better."

"What's wrong?"

"Small attacks . . . I've had them before. No worries. Um, you were saying?"

"I should have invited you to the wedding. Shouldn't spring all this on you now. I should have done a whole lot of things differently."

He's never said that before. "You've changed."

"I'd like to think I have. Still a flawed man, but . . . you and your mom deserved better, Scout. I'm sorry for that."

"Does Brenda know about . . ."

He stares at me blankly.

He's got to be joking, right? How is it not at the forefront of his mind? I lean back and cross my arms over my chest. "About your other daughter?" I can't hide the ugly sarcasm in my words.

He clears his throat. "Yes, I told her when we were dating."

"And . . .?"

He looks around, as if searching for an escape or for the waitress to come with our meals. Finally, he meets my gaze. "I'm not sure what you're looking for here, Scout."

"She doesn't have a problem with you ignoring her very existence?"

For the first time, I see a hint of my old father jump to the surface in his expression. It's defensive, in the slight tilt of his chin, the narrowing of his eyes. "That was a long time ago, and no, Brenda does not hold it against me."

I stare out at the harbor. It's not the answer I expected or wanted to hear. To me, the choices he's made are so plainly wrong. But he doesn't see it that way, it seems. Maybe never did.

How do two people standing on entirely different moral truths ever see eye-to-eye, ever put aside those blockades to come into relationship with one another?

I think of Mom and suspect that she and Dad never did come to the same conclusions on this topic. If she hadn't been sick, could she have gone on living and honoring a marriage built on untruths?

I remember the day I overheard Dad and Mom arguing about his "other" daughter. It was the first time I found out about the girl. I'd been shocked, betrayed. *I* was his only daughter. *I* was his girl.

"Mom thought you should find her."

That's what they'd been arguing about. Mom had insisted on a restoration between my father and this daughter. A daughter of another woman, a daughter who had been born several years before me. After a day or so of the new information planting itself within my spirit, I realized she was right. How could my dad just abandon this other young woman? What's more, how could he foist this news on Mom when she struggled for her life?

Dad shifts in his seat. "I know very well what your mother wanted. But my decision was to protect both you and her from all of that. Can't you see I did what I did out of love for you both?"

I can't stop a sarcastic laugh from escaping my mouth. "No. You did what you did out of self-preservation." Because if his real motivation was to protect me and Mom, why hadn't he sought out this other daughter when we were both out of the picture?

"Scout, I'm not sure we'll ever see eye-to-eye on this. It's your choice what you want to do. You can run away and ignore me again, or you can leave this burden to me. We can still have a relationship. A relationship I very much want."

I want to make stipulations. I want to tell him if he wants a relationship with me, to do the right thing. But in the end, I can't. In the end, I can't control my father.

For the first time in a long time, I realize *I* can seek out my half-sister. I might not be able to control my father, but I can control my own actions. Would such an introduction be welcome at this point? Helpful? Or would it be more hurtful in the end? I try to imagine myself a woman without a father—would I welcome the news that he wanted nothing to do with me, but that my half-sibling did?

I wasn't sure.

The waitress brings our food, and we sit in silence. I pick at my lobster roll. Light mayonnaise, celery, and spices I can't name coat the thick pieces of lobster. It really is good. If only I had an appetite.

Dad asks about work. I force myself to answer in polite tones, but beneath the effort, anger brews. Mom had been in the trenches of her sickness during that massive argument. Deep inside, I blame Dad for wearing on Mom, for contributing to her downfall. I have no proof, it may be illogical, but I can't help the gnawing suspicion that, if it weren't for my father and his stubborn ways and past mistake, Mom would still be alive.

I breathe in a large breath and force it out to release my anger. I did not agree to this dinner to pour salt in old wounds—either mine or my father's. I did not come to Maine to play out an old story, but rather, to make a new one.

I clear my throat. "I found some old camcorder tapes in a box of Mom's things. Charlotte said you packed it up."

He sucks in his cheek, biting it no doubt, and nods slowly. "Yes, I remember."

He doesn't volunteer more. I press my lips together before speaking. "Why, Dad? Those tapes were clearly meant for me. Why wouldn't you tell me about them?"

"You walked away, Scout. If you were so interested in anything your mom left for you, you would have been here, helping me go through her things. You would have been here, and we could have gone through our grief together."

I blink. It's the first time he's ever hinted at the hurt my absence caused. And yet, I can't help but doubt even that, wonder if he's reflecting off my actions to avoid *his* actions.

"You should have told me about the tapes." I push my plate aside.

We don't say much through the rest of dinner. He pays the bill and drives me back to Charlotte's in tense quiet. Inside, I fume, though I'm not sure all my anger is aimed at my father or a portion at myself.

For one dinner, I could have tried more. I could have avoided the topic of my father's secret. But it all bubbled to the surface. How could it not, after simmering there for so many years?

When I push open the door of his truck, I thank him for dinner.

"Maybe . . . maybe we could try this again before you leave?" Dad rubs the back of his neck. "You could come over for dinner.

Brenda would love to meet you, and I'd love for you to meet her."

He wants to bring me into this new life of his without taking account for the things of the past. Can I do it?

"Maybe," I manage. "Text me?"

He nods, seems to want to reach in for a hug but settles for a squeeze on my hand. "Thank you, Scout."

I leave the warmth of the truck cab and step into the cooling night. I slip inside the Beacon, a haven from the past. A haven from hurtful memories.

One thing is clear from this night: my dad has not changed as much as I initially thought. He's still clinging to his stubborn pride.

The question is, am I doing the same?

Chapter Twenty-Four

This place, more than any other, chases me down with memories of Mom.

~ SCOUT SWIFT'S JOURNAL

Some places cling to our memories more tangibly than others. Bound up with emotions and time and significant moments, they tuck themselves away in the recesses of our mind, only to come out when stoked to life by a place, a person, a scent, a time of year.

The old church in town is one of those places for me.

The sky drizzles as Laney and Jason lead us inside. Through the old wooden door and into the small foyer where a rope for the steeple bell hangs, I walk alongside Charlotte and Reagan. Laney had introduced us that morning to her fiancé, a man a few years younger than me with eyes as deep as an ocean. We follow them into the sanctuary where Charlotte sits in the same wooden pew she sat in my entire childhood. The same pew I sat in, always beside Mom.

Now, I sink into it and close my eyes. The wood is cool along my back and arms and the scent of mustiness, fresh lit matches, and old hymnals surround me. How many Sundays had I sat in this very pew? How many Christmases and Easters? If I reach my hand out, I can imagine Mom taking mine.

"You okay?" Charlotte leans in to whisper in my ear.

I open my eyes. It is not Mom beside me, but Charlotte on one side, Reagan on the other, beside a large window that looks out onto a lush green lawn. I nod.

Just as the service begins and the congregation stands to sing, "Bless the Lord," Zack slips into the space at the end of the pew next to Jason. He catches my eye and smiles. I force myself to return the gesture, but my stomach recoils. My brain can't seem to recalibrate itself, to recognize that I am here as a grown woman with an older Charlotte and her newfound granddaughter, with a young pregnant teenager I found at Walmart, with an older Zack who is the farthest thing from the cute boy who used to mow Charlotte's lawn.

We sit, and a woman reads scripture about the Holy Spirit coming at Pentecost. The pastor preaches a short sermon, but I can't focus on his words for the dizziness that settles over me. I think of the dinner I shared last night with Dad and my stomach sours. I think of the tapes I sent away, potentially vulnerable in the hands of the U.S. postal service.

The congregation stands and the band begins the familiar tune of "Amazing Grace." I grip the back of the pew in front of me until my knuckles whiten. Mom used to sing this very version when cleaning the house. The house my dad sold, the house where they had that terrible argument, the house where she died. We sang this song the last time I was here—that terrible last time, with Mom's closed coffin in the front of the church, a picture of her healthy and full of life sitting on the mahogany wood that sealed her off from me forever.

I sway where I stand.

Reagan elbows me. "You want a drink?" She holds out a water bottle, but my vision blurs, and I can't tell if it's been opened yet. She wouldn't offer it to me if she already drank out of it, would she?

The thought causes a new kind of desperation to spin within me. I am *so* messed up. Why am I so messed up? I hate to be like this, weak and dramatic. My chest tightens. I think about Mom's lighthouse scrapbook, how I haven't made any progress on it since returning home, and how my broken car will ensure that I don't make more progress for at least another several days. By then, I will have to think about returning home.

I will have failed.

I can't breathe. These panic attacks are becoming a new enemy. They'd never been so frequent back in Massachusetts, where my life is neat and orderly and controlled, where I built my own way and past memories fail to chase and haunt and prick and prod.

Black spots float before my eyes and suddenly, I will do anything to get a fresh breath of air.

"Excuse me." I fumble past Charlotte, then Laney, then Jason, then Zack. I stumble out of the sanctuary and through the wooden door. A path leads to the parking lot and a single bench. I fall onto it, not caring about the droplets of water. I lean over my knees, close my eyes, and try to calm down.

I want to go home. My real home. If my car wasn't broken, I could be there by nightfall. But it is broken. I'm trapped here.

The thoughts only cause the pinch in my chest to tighten, so I force it away, imagine Reagan's voice singing, "This Little Light of Mine."

"You okay?"

I glance up to see Zack. I want to tell him to go away. He does not need to see me like this. Instead, I nod and hold up a hand, gesturing for him to give me a minute.

He uncaps a fresh bottle of water and holds it out to me. I shake my head. Somehow, though, his mere presence serves as an anchor for reality. Another minute and I take the water, gather my breath for what seems an eternity, then take a small sip, swishing the cold water around in my mouth before swallowing. Finally, my body starts to calm, the tension beginning to drain like it might after a long cry, where the hiccuping leftover sobs of breath leave a remnant of peace.

"Thank you."

He sits on the bench beside me. A ray of sun breaks through the clouds.

"You feeling better? I promised Charlotte I'd make sure you were okay, and she'd boil me alive if I didn't follow through."

I smile, strangely touched by their concern. "I'm a little messed up right now." The depleted strain in my body has left me caring little about pretenses. What do I have to hide?

He gives me a lopsided grin. "We all have our moments."

"This is the first time I've been to this church—any church, actually—since my mom died. I think I should have mentally prepared myself."

He doesn't say anything. No trite, "I'm sorry," or mutter of sympathy. I appreciate his silence and the space it leaves for me to say more. I'm surprised I want to.

"I have a lot of baggage this town's stirring up. I thought I was ready to face it, but . . . maybe I'm not."

Zack leans over outspread legs, stares at the cement walk in front of us. "Not that I'm an expert, but some things might not get easier the longer we put them off."

He's right. Ugh, he's right.

"I think the problem is knowing what you're fighting for. What's worth the hassle, you know?" I'm not making sense, but I'm thinking of my dad. Is hashing out old problems going to accomplish anything? Will we ever have a real relationship again? Did we ever have one to begin with?

"Love—real love, not just the flighty romantic kind, is worth fighting for."

I blink and glance at his handsome profile. The strong lines of his nose and mouth beneath day-old bristle. He looks like he's somewhere else, battling his own demons. Who is he thinking about when he talks so adamantly about love?

I prop one foot up beside me on the bench and wrap my arms around my leg. "What about love for a person who's no longer alive?"

He leans back on the bench, contemplates my words. "No one expects you to ever stop loving your mom, Scout. That would probably be impossible."

I sniff. "I came up here to finish a project we started together—to see all the lighthouses in New England. We were making a scrapbook when she got sick. I thought, maybe if I came back home, made peace with my dad, and finished our undertaking, I could finally put some of my past behind me."

How am I not farther along on the path to healing after twelve years without my mother?

"That sounds like an admirable thing. A healthy thing."

"Only patching things up with my dad is proving harder than I thought and my car's broken, so . . . you know what, Zack? Could I take you up on that offer to bring me to the rental place?" I should have done this as soon as my car failed me. So, it was a little extra money. Wasn't my peace of mind worth the price tag?

"Of course. But if you want to save yourself the price of a day of renting a car, I'd be happy to be your chauffeur today, drive you around for the afternoon. I don't have any plans and I've been meaning to see a few lighthouses myself."

I cock my head and study him. "You have?"

"Well, not like I've been meaning to see them this summer, but I'd like to see more in my lifetime, anyway."

I laugh. Am I guessing wrong, or is he wanting to spend time with me? And why does that both thrill and frighten me?

"I'd like to ask Reagan if she wants to come. She really loves history and was a big help getting through some of the list on the way up here."

"No problem. Which ones are on your list?"

His quick answer causes me to slash the idea that he wants to spend time with me. No doubt, he's just being nice.

"Are you sure?"

He points to the sky. "It's brightening up. I have no other plans except hanging out with Atticus."

I blink. "Atticus?"

"He's a little slobbery. Do you think he'll bother you and Reagan?"

Oh, his dog.

I smile, somehow the fact that this man has a dog—a dog named *Atticus*—endearing him to me all the more.

"I'd love to meet Atticus."

Be careful, Scout.

I did not come to Bar Harbor to rekindle a schoolgirl crush.

"I think you probably should meet him, considering your name."

"What made you name him Atticus?"

He shrugs. "*To Kill a Mockingbird*'s a great book. Charlotte introduced it to me when I was in high school, and he seemed like an Atticus."

I wonder what other books this handyman enjoys.

"So which lighthouses are on your list?" Zack shifts in his seat.

Some of them will be tough to see without a boat, but I try to think of one that's somewhat close and easy to get to. "When I was leaving the other day, I was headed to see Winter Harbor."

"That's on the east side of Acadia, right? It's beautiful over there. Quieter, too. Not so many tourists."

People begin to spill out of the church, and Charlotte and

Reagan walk toward us, Laney and Jason close behind. When the older woman reaches me, she touches my arm, looks at Zack. "Everything alright?"

"I feel better. Just got a little claustrophobic is all." I can't meet her probing eyes but can't lie either. "A lot of memories in there."

A soft smile forms on Charlotte's lips. "Oh honey, I'm sure. If Lillian could peer down from heaven, I'm sure she'd be touched to see you back in there." She turns to the small group. "What do you say we head back to the inn? I have a big ol' batch of potato salad in the fridge, cornbread cooling on the counter, and chicken drums ready for the grill."

Jason rubs his stomach. "I am not turning that down." He glances at Laney. "Unless the wife-to-be has other plans?"

Laney elbows him. "I made plans with Reagan to go over the books she found, but other than that, I'm free."

Charlotte glances at me.

"Zack's going to take me to Winter Harbor Light, but I'm willing to bet he'd love a good meal first." I raise my eyebrows at him.

"Sounds good to me."

"Good. I would, too."

"It's settled then." Charlotte heads toward the parking lot, beaming at Zack. I fall beside Reagan.

"You want to come with us to see Winter Harbor and explore some history?"

"Um . . ." She glances from Laney to Charlotte. I can't decipher her thoughts. "Well, Laney and I are going to go through the books I've gone through so far. I'm feeling a little crampy, so if it's okay with you, maybe I'll just stick around the inn."

"Of course." I'm surprised she doesn't jump at the chance, but I'm not actually disappointed over the fact that I'll spend time alone with Zack.

And Atticus.

Reagan grabs my arm and slows so I'm forced to hang back

with her while the others walk ahead. "You scared me back there. It was another panic attack, wasn't it?"

I nod. "I think so."

She bites her lip. "Not that I'm an expert or anything, but maybe you should get some help, you know? Talk to someone."

I try not to be offended at her suggestion. It's not that I'm against the idea of therapy or even medication if needed, but getting help now means putting down more roots in this place than I intend. "If it keeps happening after I get back home, I will. But I have a feeling once I'm in Massachusetts they'll disappear."

Reagan shrugs. "Whatever you think."

"You hear from your sister yet?" I almost wince at my attempt to toss the ball of conversation back to her problems.

She shakes her head. "No."

I consider pressing, but don't. May be better to get through the weekend. There will be plenty of time to worry about renting a car, seeing more lighthouses, and what to do with Reagan, tomorrow.

Chapter Twenty-Five

ZACK

"Man, I am stuffed. Charlotte sure knows how to make a meal." I force out the friendly tone to disguise the fact that I'm more than a little angry at myself for offering this afternoon trip. Just because Charlotte hinted yet again last night that it would be nice for me to help Scout out didn't mean I had to comply. I owed Scout nothing. Charlotte, however . . . sometimes, I felt I owed her everything.

I open the passenger door of my truck for Scout. She climbs up. No use doubting how much I enjoy the sight of her perched in my seat. That thought, however, stirs up fierce resistance. I will not be swayed by a pretty face. I have too much going on. What's the point when she doesn't even live around here?

I walk around to the driver's side and climb in. Scout's looking down at her feet, then at the console. "It's really clean in here."

"Thanks." She's inspecting the cab from top to bottom, running her gaze over the windshield to the floor. "Is that . . . important to you?"

She reddens, and I study her, try not to care that I'm making her uncomfortable.

"Let's just say I have some neurotic issues when it comes to cleanliness."

I raise an eyebrow. "How neurotic?"

"I'm not sure I know you well enough to disclose how neurotic I am." She chuckles.

"I don't remember you being neurotic as a kid."

"I would say most of my neurosis occurred after I left home."

I rub my chin as I turn onto Route 223. "Hmm .. why do you think that is?"

"Are you trying to psychoanalyze me?"

I shrug. "Just curious, is all."

She looks out the window. "Hey, what about Atticus?"

"I was going to stop at my house and grab him. That okay?"

"Absolutely. I can't wait to see how clean it is."

"Oh boy, don't let the truck ruin your expectations. I *love* my truck."

"And you don't love your house?"

"Sure. But Atticus is home alone while I work and sometimes, he gets bored."

I don't think I imagine the look of horror that passes her face. Oh, this is going to be fun.

She shifts in her seat. "What does he do? Like, tear your couch up or something?"

My mind scrambles, unable to resist the opportunity. "He's developed this peeing problem, actually. Tried to break it, but seems he's got this bladder issue. Pees everywhere. I tried doggy diapers, but he just tore them off. I've learned to live with it. Just be careful where you step when you come in."

I almost regret what I'm doing when I see her pale a bit.

"Oh. Well, I can stay in the truck while you get him. It's not a problem, really."

"Oh no, I totally think you should come in. Atticus can show you his toys."

She swallows. "Are they . . . does he . . . mark them?"

My lips twitch. I almost can't hold in my laughter. "Now that would be gross, Scout."

I pull into my driveway, try to see the neatly landscaped Cape through Scout's eyes. I'm proud of it, I decide.

"Nice place," she says, but I can see she's still hung up on Atticus's fake bladder problem. Maybe I'm pushing this too far. She did say she was overanxious. Am I being cruel?

"Thanks." I hop out of the truck and come around to open the door for her.

She doesn't unbuckle her seatbelt. "I'm good here, but thanks."

A pinch of regret spirals through me. "Scout." I wait until she looks at me. "I was joking. Atticus doesn't have a bladder problem and while I am a busy bachelor trying to do my best, I consider my house reasonably clean."

Her jaw falls open. "You're rotten!"

I turn away, unable to keep the grin off my face. "Come inside. I'll only be a minute."

I unlock the door, and Atticus runs to greet me, but after seeing I have company, regards me as chopped liver. I give him the hand signal for "sit." He does, his tail brushing along the tile in the foyer with vigorous strokes.

"He's well-trained."

I give Atticus the release command and he jogs up to Scout, sniffing and wagging his tail a mile-a-minute. She rubs behind his ears and the bridge of his nose and it's the second time that day I'm caught unaware by the lurching in my chest as she seems to fit into the small places of my world.

Am I getting sentimental in my years or is it simply the sight of her planting one knee on my tile and grinning at Atticus flopping onto his back for a tummy rub? She pats his stomach, and he wiggles with contentment.

Scout giggles. "I think he likes me."

"I think so."

He wasn't so fond of Priscilla. But neither was Priscilla fond of him.

I watch my mutt of a dog completely give his heart to the enemy in ten seconds flat. I think of Scout's prolonged grief over her mom, of her good-natured way of taking my Atticus joke.

Scout is not Priscilla. Scout is also not the same person who left all those years ago. That didn't mean I needed to ask her out or anything, but maybe I should give her the benefit of the doubt, after all.

"I just have to grab a few things. Thought I'd take the kayak too—we won't be able to get too close without it."

Scout stands and Atticus whimpers a protest at the halt of her tummy rub. "That sounds like more trouble than I intended."

"No trouble. Unless kayaking's not your thing?"

It wasn't Priscilla's. Come to think of it, she hadn't liked much of anything I liked. Why did I think we were a good match?

"I've actually never been kayaking, but I think I'd love it."

"I have an extra lifejacket. The water can get a little choppy out there."

She bites her lip. "You know what you're doing?"

"I like to think so."

She scrunches up her face. "How reassuring."

I let Atticus out, grab a couple water bottles, and load the double kayak, paddles, and lifejackets into the back of my truck. Scout uses the bathroom, and I try to remember how clean I'd left it that morning. But she must read my mind, because when she emerges, she gives me the thumb's up sign. "Surprisingly clean for a bachelor."

"Phew. Glad I passed."

A few minutes later, we've returned to my truck, Atticus sitting in the back seat and panting.

"He likes to be on the water?"

"Loves it."

"Thanks for doing this, Zack. It means a lot to me. And maybe on the way back to Charlotte's, you might be able to drop me off at the car rental place?"

"I can. Or if you wanted to borrow my truck, I use my work van during the week. It's just sitting in my driveway."

I don't fully think the words before they're out, but what's the harm? It's a perfectly good truck not getting any use during my workday.

"This truck?"

"Yes. My very clean truck that I love."

"I'm sensing some hesitation in your offer," she teases.

I grimace because she's spot on. "It's just an automobile," I ground out.

She laughs. "This is hard for you, isn't it? Never mind, don't answer that. It's sweet that you offered."

She thinks I'm sweet. Swell.

"You probably wouldn't want to drive it, actually. It can be a little intimidating, much bigger than Chunky."

She scowls. "*Chippy.*"

"That's right, my bad. *Chippy.*"

"If you can just drop me off at the rental place later, that would be awesome."

I feel like an absolute heel.

"No, really, you can borrow the truck. On one condition."

"What's that?"

"No nicknames. It's a truck. Rugged. Manly. Understood?"

She laughs. Apparently, she doesn't know how serious I am. "Got it."

We drive another minute before she speaks.

"So why are you offering now?"

No one could accuse her of being vague.

What had changed my mind? I'd been ready to dislike this woman who waltzed back into Charlotte's life after hurting her all those years ago. I'm still half ready to dislike her. But something had changed. What?

I think of her standing at the top of the Beacon, like some sort of angel. I think of her tangled in her comforter on the floor of the guest house, frantic over a squirrel. Of her vulnerable form outside the church, of her rubbing Atticus's belly.

I sigh. "When you first came here, I thought for sure you'd hurt Charlotte again."

When she speaks, it's just above a whisper. "The last thing I want to do is hurt her. I didn't realize what an impact my leaving had on her the first time. Then again, I was young, totally wrapped up in myself. I'm trying to be better, you know?"

"I think I do."

There are so many reasons not to trust people. I think of Priscilla leaving without warning. I think of my dad brushing off thirty-five years of marriage to be with another woman. People could be horrible. Scout had left Charlotte twelve years ago. Was I foolish to think she wouldn't do it again?

Only this time, Charlotte might not be the only one to get hurt. I glance at Atticus sticking his head over Scout's shoulder. She grins and obliges him by rubbing the bridge of his nose.

I can't afford to get close to this woman. Whatever I'm beginning to feel toward Scout, it's just that—the beginning. Let her borrow my truck, fine. Let her bond with my dog. But when it comes to letting her past the walls of my heart, I'd have to think twice.

Chapter Twenty-Six

It's been a long time since I've tried something new. It ignited a passion within me, a passion I want to know more intimately—the fierce desire to not just be a spectator in my own life, but to live it wholeheartedly.

~ SCOUT SWIFT'S JOURNAL

"I thought you said the water was calm!" I clutch my kayak paddle as if it has the power to give me stability, but a smile is on my face, laughter is in my throat.

I feel *amazing*. The thought catches me off-guard, but I don't dwell on it for fear I'll decipher it away.

"You kidding? This is calm for Acadia. We're almost there. You're not going to get sick are you, because the wind's blowing downstream and that wouldn't be a good look on me."

I laugh again. I'm sitting in the front of Zack's kayak, and I am the farthest from sick I can imagine. I'm invigorated. Foreign joy and enthusiasm are tugging me onward. I'm alive.

Atticus sits between me and Zack, and I turn around to see his tongue hanging from the side of his mouth, his gaze on a loon several yards away. The rocky cliffs and ledges of Acadia surround us and directly before us is the white brick pillar of light alongside a tidy white keeper's house. I know from the little bit of research I did on the way here that the lighthouse is now privately owned. But the words I'd read to Zack from an online source on the way here, written by Bernice Richmond, who had bought the lighthouse in 1934 with her husband, echo across my heart.

In each life there are but a handful of great moments and I knew this was one of mine. I could not look hard enough or deep enough. I was dreaming of something I had lived, or living something I had dreamed. . . .

She went on to describe the island and her real love—the tower, describing it with such tenderness and affection, I could hardly wait to see it myself.

Now, as I look at the light perched on Mark Island, I understand Bernice's meaning. She saw the lighthouse as a beacon of safety and, for the first time, I understand. I understand why my mother was fascinated by lighthouses.

"How close can we get?"

"Not too much closer. Too many rocks."

"Will you take my picture?"

Zack opens the waterproof compartment of the kayak and fishes out his phone. The kayak rolls gently with the waves, and he gives an expert twist with the paddles to position me directly in front of Winter Harbor Light. He raises the phone, and for once, I forget to be self-conscious in front of the camera. I want to remember this moment—not just to record it in a scrapbook to check off a stop on a list, but to record it for the sake of this memory.

"Can I get one of you and Atticus?" I ask.

With a little bit of effort, he turns the boat so the lighthouse is behind him. He hands me his phone. "I'll text them to you after."

I raise it and position Zack and Atticus in the frame, the picturesque lighthouse shining in the sun behind them. I snap it, feeling I will remember it forever. This entire experience makes me feel outside myself, as if something this simple and beautiful—taking a kayak ride with a guy and his dog—cannot be happening to me. I hand the phone to Zack. Not until it's back in the watertight compartment does it strike me that I hadn't wondered how clean his phone was when I took it from him. That might seem like a small deal to most people, but it leaves me mulling over the moment, rolling it around in my head again and again.

As we row parallel to the island to get a closer view, I still can't shake the small event from my thoughts. Is it that I'm distracted with something more important—not dying at sea on the Maine coast? Is it that I have seen the inside of Zack's house, and it met my rather high expectations? I don't know.

"I don't remember you being neurotic as a kid."

"I would say most of my neurosis occurred after I left home."

The thought that home could be connected to my mental well-being is a new one. And yet, what if it was the act of leaving home, or even Mom's death, that made me start trying to control every little thing? Things such as germs and cleanliness?

It's a new thought.

"Tide's coming in. I think we should head back."

I glance at the small, choppy waves and then back at Winter Harbor Light one more time. I nod. We navigate the minor swells around the coast until we reach Zack's truck. He hops out, bare feet in the shallow water at the shore, and pulls in the kayak with me and Atticus in it with little effort.

The kayak rocks on the wet sand. He extends his hand to help me out. I take it, and he brings me to my feet with one pull. I grin up at him, reminded of the squirrel incident. "Thanks. That was really amazing."

"You're a pretty brave woman, Scout Swift."

I cock my head.

"I didn't want to say anything when we were out there, but those waves near the island were making me a little nervous. You handled it like a champ."

I laugh. "And here I thought that was all normal and we were perfectly safe."

He clears his throat and releases my hand but doesn't stop gazing into my eyes with those green orbs. "Don't get me wrong, I've handled swells like that by myself before, but not ever when I've had important cargo."

I press my lips together, can't meet his gaze any longer. "Atticus *is* pretty important."

He gives me a lopsided grin before seeming to censor himself. He clears his throat and looks away. "Right, Atticus."

At the sound of his name, our four-legged companion whines and jumps out of the kayak with a splash. He wriggles his body between us, forcing us apart. Zack leans down and pats him.

Whatever moment lays between Zack and me dissipates beneath Atticus's demands, but I can't bring myself to resent the dog even a little. He is so adoringly affectionate I wonder why I never thought to have a dog before.

But I know. They take over an orderly house with their demands and toys, dribbles of water and sometimes copious amounts of hair. They get dirty and smelly and, despite Zack's attempt to joke, they do indeed pee on the floor or vomit now and then.

I look at Atticus, following faithfully at Zack's heels as he places the paddles into the bed of the truck. And despite all the reasons to not have a dog, I see why one might want one like Atticus. For his companionship and loyalty might be worth cleaning up some dog puke every now and then.

Zack takes our phones from the compartment in the kayak and hands me mine. I help him to lift the kayak into the bed of the truck, though I wonder if I am more a hindrance than a help. We unzip our lifejackets, and I hand the bright pink one back to Zack. Who was its previous owner?

On the way home, Zack talks about his business, how he went to see a big job in the historic district downtown.

I sense him loosening up to me as he speaks, letting his guard down. I have to admit, I am, too. Call it the sea air and sunshine, but something inside me feels incredibly free.

"It's a huge deal," he says. "It has the potential to grow my business in ways I can only imagine. I don't know . . ." He bites his lip and winces.

"So, what's the problem?"

He pulls to a stop sign and raises an eyebrow at me. "Problem?" After completing a full three-second stop and ensuring no cars are crossing, he presses the gas.

"There's something in your voice. Like you're doubting yourself."

He clears his throat. "You're pretty perceptive."

I shrug. "One of my gifts. So . . . what's the problem?"

He sighs, long and deep, seeming to vacillate on how much to share, if anything. "I don't even have a crew yet. Not that I couldn't get one together quick enough. Also . . . my dad gave the owner my number."

"And you don't like people to recommend you?"

"No, normally I do."

"I see. You don't like your *dad* to recommend you."

He rubs the back of his neck. "Well, when you put it like that it sounds silly."

"Zack, you did an amazing job restoring the Beacon. I remember what it used to look like, and I'm sure it only got worse in the twelve years I was gone. Why doubt your ability? You clearly know what you're doing."

He shifts in his seat. "Thanks. That means a lot."

"It's the truth."

Another minute of silence. "The actual truth is that I'm kind of mad at my dad right now. He told me and my mom last week that he was leaving her for another woman. I think this recommendation is his way of trying to butter me up."

The news isn't shocking exactly. People get divorced all the time. But Zack has always seemed to have it together—first, as a teenager who lent a hand to the older couple grieving their daughter, then as a man fiercely protective of Charlotte, running his own successful business, faithful dog by his side.

"I'm sorry." I look out the window at an inn with a large farmer's porch on our left. "That's rotten."

"It's against everything my dad stands for, you know? He's always been about integrity and faithfulness, both in business and family."

I grapple for something meaningful to say but come up short. The truck sinks into silence.

After another few minutes, I open my mouth, then close it. Open it again. "I think people forget themselves sometimes."

His brow furrows. "What do you mean?"

I think of how I left my dad and Charlotte and Lexie for the promises Greg made me, spoken and unspoken. A promise of a better life, one without memories and grief. "Like, we get distracted by something that comes along promising to fill the broken parts of us."

"Even if it goes against everything we stand for?"

"Yeah, I think so." I lick my lips. "And just for the record, I think dads—parents, really—have been disappointing the expectations of their children since the beginning of time. Probably the other way around, too. It's the forgiving that keeps the relationship intact, and truthfully, I'm struggling with that myself right now. So, I think I know how you feel."

"Struggling to forgive your dad?"

I blow out a breath, fanning the hair at the side of my face.

"Yeah. Long story, but I came back home to . . . not fix things I guess, but find closure? It's harder than I thought."

"So, you're saying I'm not the only one having trouble dealing with things."

He flashes me a sad smile and for a split-second, our gazes connect across the console of the truck. A jolt of electric pleasure scampers through me, settling low in my belly.

Zack clears his throat. "Is it okay if I get Atticus home to feed him and drop off the kayak before taking you back to Charlotte's? Unless you want to stick around for dinner? I could grill some burgers."

I don't think before I answer. I don't want to ponder the logistics and what my attachment might mean for my future.

"Sounds great." I try to pull off a casual tone, but my voice sounds awkward and high-pitched, even to my own ears.

"Awesome. I'm not much of a cook, but I'm pretty sure I've mastered the burger."

Chapter Twenty-Seven

I haven't felt like this in a long time, and it's scaring me more than anything—more than facing my dad, facing Lexie, facing my grief, or coming back home.

~ SCOUT SWIFT'S JOURNAL

After Zack rinses off the kayak and stores the paddles and lifejackets away, we enter his house. I fill one of the dog dishes with filtered water from the sink while Zack digs around in the pantry closet for Atticus's food.

My new four-legged friend spins in excited circles as he anticipates his meal, but Zack makes him sit before releasing him to eat. Zack then washes his hands in the kitchen sink, opens the fridge, and pulls out a package of hamburgers.

"What can I do?" I scrub my own hands in the sink.

"Want to cut up the veggies while I throw these on?"

The simple act of teamwork in preparing dinner sits warm and comforting inside me. How many times in the past decade have I been inspired to cook a lasagna or chicken alfredo only to sit down at my table and feel the palpable notion that something is missing?

Being at Charlotte's, even being with Reagan, had filled that hole. And now, with Zack handing me veggies, a knife, and a cutting board, I'm feeling it again—that notion of completion. Our fingers brush, and I can scarcely think what the pleasant lilt in my insides means.

Zack goes outside to start the grill. I cut with a precision that startles me. After I'm done, I open the cabinet to see the plates arranged neatly by size and the ever-increasing warmth spreads to my lungs. I grab a plate and arrange the slices of lettuce, onions, and tomatoes.

What is happening to me? Clearly, my girlhood crush is being stoked to life. I should stamp it out, of course. Snuff it out before it has a chance to further root within me. But as I look up and see Zack sliding the screen door open to come into the kitchen, I know I'm already a goner.

Was this how I felt with Greg all those years ago? If so, I needed to be crazy cautious. Otherwise, I had learned nothing in twelve years.

I shake my head free of the notion. No. Zack is not at all like Greg. I've known him since childhood. Charlotte knows him. He's dependable, with a business and a house and a dog and roots. Greg was a blip on my radar, full of seduction and promises and adventure and lies.

"What?" Zack turns from the trash bin.

Too late, I realize he saw me shaking my head. I repeat the gesture. "Nothing."

"Oh, come on. I bare my soul to you in the truck and you're not going to return the deed?"

"Nope. Not up to embarrassing myself tonight."

He leans a hip against the counter, those green eyes penetrating. "Was it about me?"

Is he *flirting*? My face blooms, and I preoccupy myself by

arranging red onions on the plate alongside ripe tomato slices. "Stop it."

"It *was* about me, then." He flashes a self-satisfied grin. "Now, to read your thoughts."

I roll my eyes. "They're not worth reading."

"I beg to differ."

I laugh, trying to brush off the topic, but he can't seem to let it go.

"I hope it was a flattering thought."

"Zack . . ."

He snaps his fingers. "I got it."

"What?"

"You ask me something—anything—and if I answer honestly, you return the favor."

I roll my eyes. "Are we in middle school?"

"Live a little, Scout."

I remember the swirling joy I felt on that kayak. The joy of stepping out of the norm and *living*.

"How will I know you're answering honestly?"

"If the question's good enough, you'll know."

"Fine. But give me some time to think about it, okay?"

He holds up his hands. "Fair enough."

When I go outside, I take in the warmth of a fire in the round pit off the patio. The scent of grilled meat drifts through the yard. When the hamburgers are done, he places thin slices of American cheese on top and brings them inside on a plate.

"I don't have any wine. It's beer, water, or ginger ale."

"Ginger ale is great." I might have confirmed that Zack is nothing like Greg, but that still doesn't mean I trust myself around him. I don't need to add alcohol into the mix.

"Two glasses of ginger ale coming up."

We arrange our burgers inside, adding mayo and pickles and veggies. Zack brings out an already-opened bag of potato chips clipped shut with a clothespin around a neatly-folded edge.

We sit at the outside table. The fire crackles and pops, the cozy camp-like feel of it reminding me of a tenting trip I took in the White Mountains with my parents when I was little. The burger is juicy and delicious, the chips satisfyingly salty.

Zack asks about my life in Massachusetts and listens carefully to my answers. It's unnerving but nice at the same time. I've gotten used to feeling invisible. I think of Tom, the customer at the pharmacy that I crushed on for years. Had he ever seen past my blue Walmart smock?

Maybe I'm being unfair. What did I expect from him?

Halfway through my burger, I deflect the conversation from myself. "Charlotte seems well. I'm really glad Laney found her."

"You and me both." Zack pops a chip into his mouth. "It wasn't always smooth sailing. Miriam and her book made it a big challenge, actually."

"Her book?"

"*Locked Light*. You haven't heard of it? She was on all the morning shows for a while."

Locked Light. "Wait, the book about the woman whose parents locked her in a lighthouse?"

"That's the one."

"That was *not* Charlotte's daughter." But my words come out in an unbelieving question.

"It was. Took some time, a lot of stress, and a *Timeline* interview gone wrong, but it all got straightened out. The book's been pulled from the shelves, almost a year ago now."

I sit back in my seat. "Wow. I had no idea." Then again, I had no idea my father had remarried. No idea the Beacon had been renovated. No idea about anything that happened in my hometown the last several years. "I should have been here."

Zack doesn't push back on my words or try to make me feel better, which I appreciate.

"It was a tough time," he says. "The business suffered. The lighthouse was vandalized. Charlotte even had a brick thrown through one of her windows. No one was hurt and it all worked out okay in the end, thank God."

I stare at my half-eaten burger, thinking of what could have happened if Charlotte got hit with that brick. My bottom lip trembles.

"You couldn't have known . . ."

"I made it my business not to know. Not to know anything around here. And then when I need healing and I need something from this place, I crash back into everyone's life."

The raw honesty of the words sit between us.

I mean, of course on some level, I knew what I'd done. But exactly *how* selfish I'd been hadn't hit me fully until now. Until I pictured Charlotte hurt. A *brick* thrown through her window. Are you kidding me?

"I can understand why you hated me when I showed up."

He bites his lip. "I didn't hate you, Scout. I was scared, though. Scared for Charlotte."

I sniff, his vulnerability not making any of this easier. "I get it. And I don't ever want to hurt her again. But Zack, I *will* have to leave soon. I can only take so much time off work."

He stares at the table, seems caught up in another thought. But then he blinks. "Of course, I realize that. But it doesn't mean you'll write her out of your life again, does it?"

"No," I whisper. "Of course not. This visit . . . it's changed everything."

He holds my gaze before clearing his throat. "How's your burger?"

I glance at my half-eaten sandwich. "Oh, it's amazing. Really." I take a hefty bite as if to prove it.

We finish our dinner with polite, meaningless conversation. How the winters have been the last couple years, if the ice cream at Jordan Pond Ice Cream and Fudge is still the best ice cream around. When I've finished my burger, we take the dishes into the house. Zack loads the dishwasher, and I put the condiments in the fridge.

He pours soap into the appliance and closes it. A soft whirring fills the kitchen.

He pulls graham crackers, marshmallows, and chocolate from the cabinet. "S'mores?"

Wow. He must be warming up to me. "Absolutely."

We pull two patio chairs closer to the fire pit.

"Hope you're ready with your question." He wiggles his eyebrows.

"I've been too busy mulling over my past mistakes to be thinking about what probing question to ask you."

"Oh, no you don't. You are not getting out of this one. Time to face the music." He hands me a long metal roasting stick and offers me the bag of marshmallows.

I take a marshmallow and stick it on the end of the pointed metal. I extend it toward the hot flames.

"Whoa, you'll burn it like that."

I jerk my marshmallow away from the fire. "What do you mean?"

"Hold it just at the edge of the coals if you want it lightly toasted. Unless you prefer it charred, of course."

"Um, no, I don't think I do." I follow his lead in holding the end of the stick several inches above the glowing coals.

"You never roasted marshmallows?"

"We did go camping once, but that wasn't a normal family activity. My dad was gone a lot of the summer. He fishes for a living. I don't think s'mores were on mom's radar."

"But lighthouses definitely were."

I grin. "Yeah."

"Which ones are next on your list?"

"Dice Head and Prospect Harbor Point. I have to do some research on how to get out to the farther ones at sea—Saddleback Ledge, Isle au Haut, and Matinicus Rock."

He raises one eyebrow, and it makes him ten times more endearing, if possible. "Matinicus Rock, huh? Laney and Charlotte have some interesting history with that one."

"What do you mean?"

"There was a famous female lighthouse keeper who spent time at the Beacon in the 1800s and lived on Matinicus for years. I think Laney and Charlotte have thought about going out there before. They might want to go with you."

"That's good to know. I'll ask them."

We twirl our marshmallows in silence. I consider asking Zack what books he likes to read. I've been curious since he told me he named his dog after Atticus Finch, but there's another question that probes me. I decide I might as well get as much bang for my buck since I'll likely embarrass myself revealing my own inner thoughts.

"Okay, I have my question."

"Shoot."

I swallow. "Who's the previous owner of the lifejacket I wore today?"

I can't be sure beneath the darkening sky, but I think he pales.

"That's the question you choose, huh?"

"That's the question."

"And what if I tell you it came with the kayak when I bought it off Facebook Marketplace?"

I raise an eyebrow. "You said you'd be honest."

"I did." He props his marshmallow stick against the cobbles of the fire ring and reaches for the graham crackers. He offers me the opened package and I take a rectangle slice.

He reaches for the package of chocolate, hands me a wrapped square. I follow his lead in breaking the cracker in half and laying the unwrapped chocolate on one side. He positions the two halves of the cracker sandwich over the marshmallow on his stick and presses, sliding it off the stick with ease.

Talk about stalling.

Still, I try to follow suit to make the s'more, but my coordination is not up to par. He reaches out then hesitates. "You okay if I help you out? My hands are clean—I promise." The remark is probably the most considerate, touching thing he could have said. When was the last time someone, especially a guy, understood my inner struggles?

I nod, and he manages a perfect s'more, handing it to me with a napkin. "Thanks." I bite into it, the sweet crunch and marshmallow softness tantalizing in my mouth. "That's good," I manage through a full mouth.

He laughs. "I'm honored to be part of your first s'more experience." He bites into his own sweet treat, chews carefully. "Her name was Priscilla."

I perk up. "Was?"

"Is. But 'was' in my life." His bitter tone catches me off guard.

"She hurt you."

"It was over a year ago. We were a terrible match. I see that looking back on it. But still . . ."

"Where'd she go?" Maybe a pointless question, but it's the only one I can think to ask.

He sighs. "Back to New York."

"How'd you meet?"

He gives me a long sideways glance. "I think you're getting more than one question in here."

I laugh. "But I'm only getting three-word answers."

He shoves the rest of his s'more in his mouth and leans back in his chair, chewing with care as he stares at the first stars beginning to lighten the twilight sky. At my feet, Atticus thumps his tail on the stone of the patio. "Her dad hired me to replace some windows. We spent the summer together. I thought she was the one. I don't know, maybe we moved too fast. One day in early September, she just up and left."

I take all this information in, separating it in my mind as one might rake stones from sand. I can't deny the twinge of jealousy I feel imagining Zack kayaking with this woman in a lifejacket he bought for her. What else did they do? Did he teach her how to roast a perfect marshmallow? Did Atticus curl up at her feet in this very spot?

Then I think of her blindsiding him by leaving, seemingly without warning. I think of his heart breaking.

"I guess if I'd had more than a text, I could have worked it out, healed better. But in the end, it was apparent she didn't take me seriously. Didn't take us seriously. I was just a handyman who installed windows and kept her company for a summer. She had better things waiting in New York."

"You never spoke to her again?"

He shakes his head. "I tried calling a few times after she left, but no. I'm not a social media guy, so I have no idea what she's up to. Probably better that way. And I really am over her. It's the rejection I sometimes can't shake." He blows out a long breath. "There you go. The most honest answer I've ever given, probably even to myself, about my former love life."

"I'm honored. And I'm sorry you were hurt so badly." I think about what he told me about his dad leaving. I think about the cold shoulder he gave me when I arrived. I think of Charlotte. Lexie. Even my dad. Am I any better than this Priscilla character who left this considerate man high and dry?

I reach out my hand but change my mind at the last minute and tuck my fingers securely into my lap. "And Zack, I hope you see yourself as more than a handyman. I haven't known you long but you're kind, considerate, talented, and . . ."

He tilts his head. "Go on."

"Super clean."

He lets out a loud guffaw. "Coming from anyone else, that might not be such a compliment."

I smile and finish off the last bite of my cracker.

He holds out another marshmallow, but I shake my head. He rolls up the package and snaps a clothespin on the end. "Thanks,

Scout. You know, I grew up with a genius of a dad. He always seemed to expect more from me." He laughs a small pathetic sound, that lacks humor. "Now I'm the one expecting more of him."

This time, I don't hold back, or think. I reach out, lay my hand atop his. It's warm and foreign, his knuckles thick and worn from working outdoors.

He surprises me by turning his hand over so our palms meet. Somehow, the gesture becomes a thousand times more intimate. His fingers close around mine, and I release a shuddering breath that I hope he doesn't hear.

"Thank you," he whispers, voice husky.

We sit that way another minute, hands entwined, fire popping, before he seems to remember himself and jerks his hand from mine. "Okay, my turn. What were you thinking about earlier in the kitchen?"

My hand is empty and cold. But better this way. There's no way I can bare my soul with our skin pressed together.

I brace myself as if about to be sprayed with freezing water. "I was comparing you to the guy I ran away with back in high school, trying to convince myself you're not like him."

"Okay . . . and did you?"

"What?"

"Convince yourself?"

Should I share more? I think back to telling Reagan. It had felt good, right. And Zack had opened himself up to me. Was this sharing of myself part of what I'd come home to find?

I prop a foot up on the chair and hug my knee to my chest as I stare into the fire. "I think so. He was a real piece of work. Took me to a town six hours south of here and dropped me off at a Walmart. Never returned."

"What?"

I shrug. "I was stupid. I gave him all mom's life insurance money."

"And you didn't come back home?"

"I was too ashamed. And I didn't want to face my dad."

He breathes long and deep, his broad chest rising and falling in the light of the fire. "That sucks, Scout. What a lowlife. I'm sorry that happened to you."

"Like I said, it's my own fault."

He meets my gaze. "So, I hope it goes without saying, but I am not like that guy, Scout."

I can't help but think he's also telling me he's not like his dad, that he'd never abandon the woman he loves. A flutter works its way up my spine where it settles, tingling, at the base of my neck.

I stay another twenty minutes before I hint that I should return to Charlotte's. Zack puts out the fire. We bring in the graham crackers, chocolate, and marshmallows. Atticus curls up on the dog bed in the living room.

When we reach Zack's truck, he opens the door for me. I climb in, but he stands beside the passenger's seat. "I had a good time today."

I grin. "I did, too."

"Maybe we could do it again sometime?"

"I'd like that."

"You would?"

He's surprised? Is he not aware how completely disarming he is? "I mean, I'm leaving in another week, but yeah . . . I would."

He hangs an arm over the frame of the door. "Can I be honest with you about one more thing tonight?" His voice is low, husky.

I swallow, his nearness and the scent of his aftershave doing strange things to my body. "Yes."

"I really want to kiss you right now."

My mouth grows dry. Zack Garrison, the boy I fell asleep dreaming about all my middle school years, the man I now am privileged to know as kind and decent and considerate, wants to kiss me?

Part of me loves that he's asking. Another part wants him to lean in and swallow me whole.

"Why don't you, then?"

He drifts a hair's breadth closer, and I inhale the subtle scent of cinnamon and spice and woodsmoke. "Because you're dangerous."

I draw back to better look at him beneath the faint light of the front door. "How so?"

"Because I'm a little emotionally unstable right now, and I vowed to never let another woman get close to me who might leave me again."

"And I'm leaving. In a week," I whisper.

He straightens, sending us both back to reality. "Right. In a week." He rakes a hand through his hair. "I'm sorry about that."

I try to laugh off his apology, though I don't find it funny in the least. "We're both a little drunk on fresh air and marshmallows."

He smiles at my pitiful attempt to lighten the mood. "I heard sugar and corn syrup can do crazy things to your brain."

"Absolutely."

He gently closes my door and walks around to his, leaving me in a pile of confused mush.

Chapter Twenty-Eight

Sometimes you don't know you've needed something until you actually have it.

~ SCOUT SWIFT'S JOURNAL

I'm not sure what made me finally give in to Reagan's badgering about the writing group, but once I agreed, I decided to go all in. The day after my kayak ride with Zack, I texted Lexie.

Scout: I'm going to a writing group tonight at Back of Beyond. You interested?

Lexie: Wait. You're not trying to resurrect The Adventures of Milton and Minny, are you?

I SMILE AT THE MEMORY. Milton and Minny had been our collaborative creative writing project in fifth grade. Inspired by a smattering of fairytales, we managed about forty handwritten pages before our enthusiasm for the project fizzled out.

Scout: Not unless you want to. It's supposed to be casual. I don't even have anything I'm writing, but they said that's okay.

Lexie: Dogs allowed?

Scout: Hmmm . . . not sure.

Lexie: What time?

Now, I walk with Laney and Reagan into downtown Bar Harbor. Parking's crazy this time of year, so we decided to walk the three-quarters of a mile to the bookstore. I see Lexie's shiny car when we draw closer. Somehow, she managed to snatch a spot close by.

She opens the door of the car and waves, sticking out a skinny jean-clad leg and a high-heeled shoe. When she straightens to her full height, she does a small shimmy, pulls her jeans up, and shakes out her hair. Then she reaches into the seat for Gumdrop, who wears a red and black vest that pronounces him a service animal.

Huh. I think of Gumdrop running ahead of us on his leash the other night. I wonder if he's actually a certified service animal.

As if to prove he is not a sufficiently trained service dog, Gumdrop wiggles out of Lexie's arms and then runs around her legs until she's wrapped in his leash. "Gumdrop!" she squeals.

A twinge of regret—or is it embarrassment?—pinches me. I'd been trying to connect with Lexie again before I go home. Trying to restore what I'd broken all those years ago. But was that even possible?

Looking at Lexie tangled up in her tiny dog's leash, teetering on her high heels, I wonder if inviting her tonight was a poor decision.

I drag in a breath and jog over to her, offering my help. She hands me the leash, and I unwind it from her legs. When she's sorted, she scoops up her little dog. I introduce her to Laney and Reagan, who both greet her warmly.

We head into the store.

"Hi!" Kiran says when we enter. Laney reintroduces us. I don't miss the hopeful look Reagan gives Kiran, but the friendly sales-clerk in the overalls doesn't seem to notice. "Feel free to take them up, Laney. I think we're waiting on one more before I can lock things up down here."

Laney leads us to a staircase at the back of the store. The room on the second floor is large with windows overlooking downtown Bar Harbor and beyond that, glimmering Frenchman's Bay.

Only one woman is upstairs. She's arranging paper plates and napkins alongside a plate of cookies. Laney gives her a genuine hug and then introduces the forty-something woman.

"Emily is a fantastic writer," Laney says.

Emily blushes, her pale skin showing red beneath strawberry blonde hair. "I don't know about that, but I love trying."

"Like we all do." Laney smiles and gestures to the table.

We each take a seat and a moment later, Kiran ushers in a woman about Laney's age. "John and Roger couldn't come. Looks like it's just us girls tonight."

"Good," Lexie mutters, just loud enough for me to hear.

Kiran welcomes us, tells us that they usually critique one another's work but that no one sent anything the month before. "Anyone want brainstorming help?"

Laney shakes her head. "I'm too distracted to write lately."

Kiran gives her a knowing smile. "With your *lobster*?"

Laney rolls her eyes. "More like *marrying* my lobster in four months. Wedding plans are no joke."

"You haven't made any progress on your story, then? I'm dying to know what happens next."

"It's in my head. I just need to get it on paper."

"No time like the present," Kiran says with a sly smile.

"That's why I'm here."

Kiran turns to Emily, who reports that she's written five-thousand words. Kiran and Laney seem to get excited at that and pepper her with questions.

"It's really flowing, and I see the end in sight. It's exciting. But Penelope's starting to resist her naps. Once that's done, my writing output's going to suffer."

"All the more reason to finish the book." Kiran wiggles her eyebrows. It's clear she's the persistent encourager in the group, a natural leader.

"What about you, Kiran?" Laney asks.

Kiran smiles. "Well, I heard back from the agent I queried."

I almost hear Laney and Emily's synchronized, sharp intake of breath. I guess this is a big deal.

"Well . . .?" Laney draws the word out.

"She asked for a full!"

The three women are squealing and stomping their feet, leaving me, Reagan, and Lexie to give each other amused, confused smiles.

After they calm, Laney turns to us. "A full manuscript request from an agent is a big deal. It means they're really interested."

"That's great." If it weren't for Reagan and Lexie, I'd definitely feel out of my element. "So, did you send it?"

Kiran nods. "This afternoon. Now, nothing to do but pray."

Laney claps her hand. "I'm so excited for you!"

"Me too, but enough about that. I want to hear from our new friends. What do you all write?"

Reagan and Lexie look at me, so I swallow back my hesitation and open my mouth. "I haven't written much until lately. And only journaling at that." My skin heats as I think about my entry last night, about the words that seemed to solidify my day with Zack, that surreal moment in his truck where he admitted to wanting to kiss me.

What did it mean? In my heart, it was such a big deal—the guy I loved my entire young teenage life had some sort of feelings for me—but in my head, it's nothing more than a missed chance. He acknowledged that we shouldn't get involved with me leaving so soon. In many ways, we've been doomed from the start.

Had anything from my life in Maine ever flourished? I sincerely doubted that a relationship with a great guy like Zack would be the first.

"Journaling is how I started writing." Laney grabs a cookie from a plate. "Nothing wrong with that. Even if you never go beyond journaling."

Reagan clears her throat. "I'm not sure journaling is something you need to get beyond. It's its own creative art form. It helps us process our lives. That's a pretty worthy use of writing."

The table grows quiet before Kiran speaks. "You know what? You're absolutely right, Reagan."

I look at Reagan as if I'm seeing her for the first time. She has surprised me in the past, but with the distraction of being home, going through that box of Mom's, and whatever blossoming romance with Zack I have going on, I haven't given as much thought to her as I should. I have to leave in six days. Where does that leave her? In some ways, she is mature beyond her years. In other ways, she is hopelessly helpless and young. But can I really turn her in to social services?

"What do you write, Reagan?" Kiran takes a swig of her bottled water.

Reagan's face glows. "I'm writing a baby book for my baby."

Her expression, and the words, serve to break my heart. I'm not even sure why.

Laney tilts her head. "That's a beautiful idea. What kind of things do you write in it, if I can ask?"

"Right now, it's about how excited I am to meet him or her, how I want to be an amazing mother but how I'm a little nervous I might fail."

My heart splits in two.

Laney squeezes Reagan's fingers. "I have a feeling that's nearly every mother's worry. You're going to be amazing."

Reagan looks down, bites her lip. "There's a lot I need to figure out." Her gaze flicks to me. "But I'm determined to do this right."

Another moment of silent smiles before Kiran turns to Lexie. "What about you, Lexie? What do you write?"

Lexie shifts in her seat. For the first time since we've been here, Gumdrop whimpers, and I wonder if he senses some sort of distress from her. "I haven't written since middle school. I'm probably a worse writer now than I used to be. But Scout asked me to come, and I usually do anything Scout asks me to do."

Huh. Weird statement, considering we haven't hung out for the last dozen years. Though not an entirely untrue statement, since she did always do what I asked her to do. Study. Run cross country. Go see a movie she didn't particularly care about.

She'd been such a good friend. And I'd been such a crappy one.

"Oh, okay." For once, Kiran seems like she doesn't know what to say. "Well, it's nice you're open to exploring new things."

"That's me. Always open to exploring new things." Lexie gives a forced, fake smile.

What is with her?

Kiran shifts in her seat. "We usually take some time to write."

Kiran, Laney, and Emily pull out their computers. Reagan takes out the notebook I bought her, and I reach in my bag for a notebook. No way I can journal my most private thoughts with all these people in the same room with me. I'll figure out something else.

Lexie opens the Notes app on her phone. Gumdrop whines. "He has to go out. I'll be right back," she whispers.

Thirty seconds after she leaves, I have the distinct feeling she will *not* be right back. She has not left her purse. The seat beside me seems heavy with her absence.

"Excuse me," I whisper to no one in particular as I slip out of the room and down the stairs into the empty bookshop. I push open the door to the front sidewalk and round the corner to see Lexie backing out of her parking spot, Gumdrop on her lap, pawing the window when he sees me.

"Lexie!" I raise my hand, race to the side of her car.

She stops, unrolls the window. "Sorry, Scout. Not feeling the greatest."

"Don't go. Let's talk."

Her shoulders slump. She nods and pulls back into her parking spot.

I climb into the passenger's seat. "What's up? Spill it."

"I don't know why you invited me to this thing."

"I'm leaving in six days. I didn't want that time to pass without seeing you."

"So you try to squeeze me into something you were already doing with your other friends?"

Gumdrop whimpers, nudging Lexie's hand with his nose. She obliges by petting his small head.

"That's not it. We used to write together. I thought—"

"You thought wrong. I keep trying to tell you I'm not the same person. But you're not listening."

I bite the inside of my cheek, hard. "I'm trying, Lexie."

"My therapist said I should forgive you, but it's hard."

She talked to her therapist about me, so my presence must be bothering her. I open my mouth, close it, then try again. "I can understand that. And maybe forgiving isn't as easy as doing it because your therapist tells you to."

She rolls her eyes. "You're telling me. I can't make my heart and my head act a certain way. And I've had a lot of forgiving to do the last half of my life. Just telling you now, I don't have a great track record for it."

I lean my head back. Outside, a sparrow pecks the asphalt then flies away, reminding me of my birds in Swansea. "I understand more than you know. I'm having a hard time forgiving my dad."

She looks at me, eyebrows raised. "What for?"

I realize that I never told her all that transpired before I left, in the last months before Mom died.

"A couple of months before Mom died, we found out he had another daughter."

"Oh. Wow."

"Mom thought he should make amends—have a relationship with this other girl. He disagreed, said all of his time and attention should go to the family right in front of him. His real family."

Lexie doesn't say anything, so I continue. "I didn't know how I felt about it at the time, but I know the entire ordeal put a new kind of stress on Mom. She went downhill quickly after that. I've never been able to forgive my father for forcing her to deal with that as she was dying."

"I'm sorry, Scout." For the first time, she sounds like the Lexie I once knew.

"Thank you."

"Why didn't you tell me?"

I shrug. "Towards the end, I was wrapped up in all things Mom. I didn't want to make her last days any more humiliating for her than they already were. I didn't want anyone else to know about our family drama."

"I was your best friend. I wouldn't have told anyone."

"I know," I whisper. "I just wanted to ignore it, make it disappear."

After a moment of silence, she turns to me. "I'm not sure I can go back in there again."

"Okay."

"You can go, though."

"I think I'll hang out with you, if that's okay."

"Don't you want to be with your new friends?"

It was such an immature question, one that reeked of a lack of self-confidence. But my heart went out to her. "Maybe we can go for a walk on the Ocean Path, then ask Laney and Reagan if they want to get ice cream when they're done?"

She wiggles her feet. "I have sneakers in the back."

"Great."

In a few minutes, we're soaking up the ocean breeze, walking along the paved path, historic Bar Harbor Inn on one side, the vast expanse of the sea on the other. Lexie relaxes and even opens up about the verbal abuse she took from her husband in her former marriage.

Each sentence seems to cost her something and I listen, not offering any platitudes. It seems to be what she needs. I tell her more about my life in Massachusetts. She's surprised to hear I'm a bit of a loner, that I haven't dated much and spend my time hiking and visiting beaches. I tell her about my almost kiss with Zack the night before, how I can't stop thinking about him but how I'm hesitant to start anything.

"You've loved him forever, Scout." She tugs Gumdrop away from a signpost. "And while I'm leery of most guys right now, Zack always seemed genuine. Not that I'm the best at reading men, mind you."

We laugh and it feels good. Right. Like healing.

When we meet back at the bookstore, Reagan excitedly tells me that Back of Beyond has hired her and she starts tomorrow. Lexie, suddenly her outgoing self again, suggests we celebrate with ice cream. I trail Laney, Kiran, and Lexie toward Jordan Pond Ice Cream and Fudge. Reagan hangs back with me.

"I know this isn't a permanent solution." She moves her fingers over her bulging abdomen. It seems to have doubled in size since we arrived.

"Reagan, I leave in six days. I know Charlotte didn't say, but I would definitely assume that's the end of her offer to host us for free. What are you going to do?"

"I have an idea."

"Okay. Feel like sharing?" I realize my sarcastic tone as soon as the words are out.

"Not yet, but I will. Soon." She points to the others waiting in line outside the shop. "Let's just enjoy the ice cream."

I nod, but my stomach sours. What idea does she have? And how can she be so certain that everything will work out?

If only I had that same confidence when it came to my own life. But if I have no big goals or aspirations for myself, what would having confidence gain me?

Maybe I needed to figure out my own plans before worrying about poking holes in Reagan's.

Chapter Twenty-Nine

I'm not ready to see Mom again.

~ SCOUT SWIFT'S JOURNAL

The package comes sooner than I expected. The morning after writing group, I'd helped Reagan sort books for a few hours. Then I walked downtown on a mission to find a few art supplies—nothing crazy, some paints and paper, a few brushes.

While being at writing group around women excited about creativity didn't make me want to write a story, it did get me thinking about painting again, about what it would feel like to dip a brush into paint, to watch color form on a page. I was on vacation, after all. I hadn't yet taken up Zack on his offer to borrow his truck to explore more lighthouses. Yes, I was stalling. But somehow, this felt right. Painting.

I'd come back from my walk, brown paper bag in hand, when

Charlotte handed me the white Priority envelope. She squeezed my arm. "This is a good thing, honey."

I nodded. She set me up in her bedroom, the only room in the house with a DVD player.

Now, my hands shake as I tear open the thick, bubble-wrapped package. Charlotte hovers at the threshold. "You good?"

I drop the package in my lap and nod. Charlotte walks over to me, gives me a hug and a quick peck on the head, then leaves me alone, shutting the door behind her.

I look around her bedroom. A yellow paisley comforter and matching curtains. On her night table sits a picture of her, Laney, and a woman I assume to be Charlotte's daughter, Miriam. I know things were not always good between them, but seeing that picture now is like a beacon of hope. Maybe broken things can be fixed, after all.

My trembling hands fumble with the package until I pull out two DVDs.

That's all. The tapes had made it seem like so much more.

I put the first one in and hit play on the remote. And then, there she is.

Mom.

My bottom lip shudders.

"Hi, honey! Hmm . . . is this thing working, you think? One second . . . " She moves the camera around, then sits back in front of me. "It shows it's recording, so I think we're in business." She looks straight into the camera. "Hi, Scout."

A sob slips from my throat, and I hit pause on the screen because I'm not going to hear anything she says if I don't get my tears under control. But instead of trying to contain them, I let them flow free. Once I give them permission to come, they don't stop. Seeing her in front of me, her dark hair short from the rounds of chemo, but her eyes bright and smiling above dark circles, I finally allow my body a release it's been holding in for years.

I take in everything about the still picture in front of me—the familiar shirt she's wearing, sea-green with small buttons in front, the bedroom comforter we curled up on together for hours in those last few months, the window looking out to the pine tree where we'd hung the hammock. I take in all of it while a flood of pent-up emotions spirals through me. Like a waterspout, it funnels up and wrings me thoroughly until finally, it runs itself out. When I've used all the tissues by Charlotte's bedside and there's nothing left inside me except trailing, hiccuping sobs, I push play again.

"So, it's Mom." She shakes her head and rolls her eyes. "Of course, you know it's Mom. I guess I'm a little nervous. Feels so strange talking into this thing . . . but I thought it might be good for you to have it, you know, after I'm gone."

I glimpse her Bible on the nightstand behind her, the same one I retrieved from the box. I'd kept it with the scrapbook, had been reading a little bit every morning, finding comfort in the memories and stories and words they contained.

Mom's smile flickers, but she continues. "I'm having a good day and you're at school. Dad's on the boat. We had a difficult night two days ago. An argument you overheard. Anyway, I'm getting ahead of myself. There's so much more to say, more important things to say. Like *you*, Scout. You. Fabulous, beautiful you. Honey, you know how proud I am of you—how proud both me and your dad are of you—but just in case you need to hear it again. Here it goes. We love you and are so proud of the young lady you're becoming."

I blink back more tears as Mom smiles that radiant smile at the camera.

"And I'm not proud of you because you're smart or because you earned a scholarship or because you're beautiful and love all the same books as me"—she gives me a wink—"I'm simply proud of you because you're my daughter and I love that you're my daughter. That you're *you*."

I pause the recording again to wipe away more tears. This is way harder than I thought, and yet I can't shake the sense that it's a necessary part of dealing with my remaining grief. That maybe even the tug I felt to come home was not just because of the light-houses, but this, these tapes. Had God or Mom known I needed to find these?

"I can't believe you're graduating this year." Now, it's Mom's turn to wipe away tears. "How is it even possible that my little girl's graduating? I'm praying so hard I'll get to be there. Only a few more weeks. You looked gorgeous at prom last week. So grown up. I remember the day your dad and I brought you home from the hospital. He couldn't say anything for two straight days except, 'Isn't she beautiful? Isn't she beautiful?'" Mom laughs at the memory, a memory I've heard many times before but I've managed to block out the last several years.

"Honey, your dad's not perfect and he's made some mistakes, like we all have, but one thing is certain—he loves you so much. He loves both of us so much. Never doubt that. And never be afraid of loving, Scout. It's the bravest thing you can do, okay?"

She goes on to reminisce about memories she has of me as a child. The time I woke up in the middle of the night, as a four-year-old, to try and hang a Happy Birthday sign for her on the eve of her special day, the time I called my mom to come and get me from my first sleepover at Lexie's house, the time I came home with a broken heart from an eighth-grade dance.

She went on and on, sharing her treasured memories, some I knew and some I didn't. She gave me advice about being an adult, advice about college, about money, about dealing with difficult people and relationships.

"Don't give up on God, honey. Even when I'm gone and you're angry. Even when people let you down. Even if people from the church let you down, do not give up on God. Jesus is always holding out His hand. He understands you when no one else does, and He might be the only one who can set you straight when no one else can. But don't block out people, even when you're hurt. That's a lesson I had to learn some time ago. Relationships are messy. Love is messy. But it's worth it."

Her words are getting jumbled and slurred. She's obviously tired.

"Okay, we have to talk about your father, but first, I want to check in on how you're doing on our little project." She holds up our lighthouse scrapbook and a peanut-sized lump lodges in my throat at seeing it in her hands. "You didn't think I'd forgotten, did you? Now, I vacillated on this back and forth for some time and let me be clear, Scout, I never want to pressure you into finishing our trips. I know it will be painful. I know it will be hard. But something tells me it might be just what you need when I'm gone, you know? And don't go it alone. Take Lexie, take your dad, take Charlotte—who knows, maybe you'll have a boyfriend or even a husband by the time you're watching this. Savor the journey. And I'm praying and trusting it'll help you heal."

She stares at the camera. "If that seems difficult, maybe start with the one we were saving for last." She nods. "Yup, Bass Head. I know we used to go all the time, and I know we've been saving it for last, but truth is, I'm not sure I'll be able to make it with you again. I think you should go now, honey. I think . . . I think there's something there for you. And when you come back, keep watching these videos and maybe I'll be able to give you some insights into your dad, things maybe you should know to better understand him."

She stares into the camera another few seconds, places her hands on her hips. "I mean it, Scout. Go. For me. I'll be here when you get back."

I stop the DVD, drag in a deep breath. The last hour has wrenched every emotion possible from me. I'm left with a strange sort of empty fullness, and yet I'm not sure how to feel about Mom's insistence that I go to Bass Head Light.

We had been keeping it for the last on our list. A sort of

bookend to celebrate our accomplishment. What does she think is there for me? And what if I find nothing?

But there is no way I can continue playing the DVD while ignoring her request. That is out of the question for sure.

I look out Charlotte's bedroom window to see Zack walking toward his work van. I wonder if he's up for another lighthouse trip.

Chapter Thirty

ZACK

"Zack!"

I turn at the sound of Scout's voice. It seems like I summoned her with my thoughts, because I'd just been thinking about our time the day before. But of course, that can't be true, because I've thought about her day and night for the last two days and she didn't appear out of thin air any of those times.

Much to my dismay.

Only a few days left, and she'd be gone for good. Would I be able to cast her from my thoughts then?

She jogs lightly out the front door of the inn toward me, her long ponytail slapping her back. Her eyes are red and puffy, and a fierce swell of protection mounts inside me.

"What's wrong?"

She stops short in front of me. "Nothing. Why?"

"You look like you've been crying."

"Oh." Her fingers flutter to her face. "I was watching a video my mom left for me." She shakes her head. "It's a good thing."

"Glad to hear that."

"I wanted to thank you for the other day. It meant a lot. Not just the lighthouse, but the conversation."

"I enjoyed it, too. And I hope I didn't scare you off with . . . you know."

A soft blush crosses her nose and cheeks. My throat grows dry.

"No. The opposite in fact."

Oh, man. How am I going to stay away from her these next few days? She's successfully tearing down any barriers I've tried to erect with just a few words and a blush. "Would you let me take you to dinner tonight?"

"That sounds really nice. Actually, I was wondering if you'd take me to another lighthouse? Then maybe I can pay you back by taking *you* to dinner."

I raise an eyebrow. "I see. You're using me for my wheels."

She laughs. "No denying your wheels are a perk at the moment, but I enjoy you, Zack Garrison. The lighthouse is a request, from my mom."

"Ah, gotcha." That definitely explains the tears. "Yes, then. For your mom, anything. Where we headed?"

"Just to Bass Head."

"Not much of a chore. I'm surprised you guys didn't knock that off your list first thing."

"We were saving it for last. She seems to think I need to see it now, though. I'm not sure why."

"I wish I could help you figure it out."

"Taking me there is help enough."

I look at her, the long ponytail draping over one shoulder, the smattering of light freckles across her nose and beneath puffy eyes. What could happen between us if she stayed?

I think of Priscilla. Had I ever had a conversation—a real, meaningful conversation like I'd had with Scout on Sunday—with Priscilla? Looking back on my time with my ex, everything felt surface-level. I thought we were right for each other, but maybe I'd been too eager to find the right girl, too many years past thirty and feeling like my time to find my special person was running out.

Kind of like my time with Scout. But no, I can't think about her leaving. Not right now. Right now, I have a work van to unload, a shower to take, a lighthouse to see, and a night with a woman who is confusing the living daylights out of me.

I'M PULLING out of Charlotte's drive when my phone rings. I answer it on my Bluetooth.

"Hey, Mom, how's it going?"

"Good, honey. You home? I was wondering if I could stop by for a minute?"

"Um, heading there now, though I wasn't going to be around long. What's up?"

"I'd rather talk to you in person. Can you spare fifteen minutes?"

Dread coils in the pit of my stomach. "Yeah, sure. See you soon." I hang up and drive the rest of the way home, the coil winding tighter and tighter. She sounded good. Better than a woman whose husband was leaving her for another woman had a right to sound. What was I missing?

Of course, I'm glad Mom isn't drowning in misery, but wouldn't there be a better chance of Dad coming to his senses if she were? Maybe I misread her voice. Maybe she even heard from Dad. Maybe he realized what an idiot he'd been and wanted her back. Maybe she wanted to talk it over with me so I wasn't surprised.

By the time I put my turn signal on to go into my driveway, I was sure that was it. My world slid back into place. Things wouldn't be easy, of course. Mom had a lot to forgive. Shucks, I had a lot to forgive. But we would. Mom and Dad would find a marriage counselor. They'd rekindle their love and maybe even be stronger for it.

Mom's sitting on my doorstep. I give her a hug, apologizing for the white powder of sheetrock coating my shirt and skin. She smiles, and it looks genuine. Though I don't think I'm imagining the new lines around her eyes, there's something in those eyes that wasn't there last time.

"Thanks for letting me come over, honey," she says.

"Anytime, Mom." I gesture toward the door, where Atticus is barking excitedly inside. "I better let him out. We can talk in the backyard?"

"Sure."

Two minutes later, I'm throwing Atticus a tennis ball. Mom stands beside me, the fire pit with the leftover coals from my time with Scout on the other side of her.

"How are you?" I ask, since she doesn't seem to be taking the initiative to begin this conversation.

I wait for her words, can practically anticipate them. *Your father came by this morning. We talked for a long time. He changed his mind, Zack. He asked me to forgive him.*

"I'm well. I've been doing a lot of thinking, actually. Talked to your Aunt Susan." She meets my gaze, and in that moment, I know she's not going to tell me that Dad came to see her, or that he changed his mind.

My heart sinks, and I kick myself for being so naïve, so stupid. This was not a fairytale, or even a book that needed a happy ending. This was life. My life, now. A life where I had to deal with my dad making crappy decisions.

"I think I'm going to move down south."

Down south. I blink. "To Florida?"

She nods. "Susan says the house is unbearably empty since your uncle died last year. The kids are gone. She lives in a nice community and there's a lot to do. Pickleball and yoga and such.

She loves her church, tutors kids, runs food drives. I need a new start, Zack."

My mind isn't comprehending. Atticus drops the ball at my feet, nudges the knee of my jeans with a wet nose. The action spurs me into focus. I pick up the ball and throw it.

"Florida. Wow."

Mom swallows. "I'm not sure I can stay here, honey. Not knowing I could walk downtown, turn a corner, and see them at any moment." Her bottom lip quivers and my heart melts for her. Of course, she doesn't want to stay in our small town. And while she has plenty of friends, none of them are likely reason enough for her to stay. But what about me?

"I've always hated the long winters here. I miss your aunt. The only reason I'm even hesitating over this decision is . . . you."

I breathe, long and deep. There will be no solid family connections any longer. It will be Dad, up here with a woman I will have a very hard time not hating, and there will be Mom, many hours away, building a new life for herself in Florida.

"If you don't want me to go, I'd seriously reconsider. But you're a grown man. I know you don't need me. And me being around is only going to be a burden on you. I know you, honey. You'll worry over me, feel you need to check in on me every day." She gives me an amused sideways glance, as I have indeed checked in on her every day since Dad dropped his bombshell.

"I think my moving will actually be a healthier decision for all of us."

I don't want her to go. Truth is, I want her here, where I can keep an eye on her. But she's right. There is a better option for her, and it isn't Maine.

"You could never be a bother, Mom."

She raises her hand to my face. "You were always such a sweet boy. You've turned into a beautiful man. And I love you so much, honey."

I wince, stoop down to give her a hug. "I love you too, Mom.

And if moving is what you think you need, I'll fully support you. I'll load up a U-Haul and drive it to Florida myself. But please, if we could tone down the beautiful man talk, I'd sure appreciate it."

We laugh, and it releases some of the sad tension in the air.

"Thank you, Zack. It means a lot to me that you support me in this."

"I'm here for you. I'm always here for you."

She stays a few more minutes. I promise to call her tomorrow and talk over the logistics of such a move. She and Dad have already put the house on the market. They'll split the proceeds.

It all sounds so foreign, so unlike anything I've ever imagined for my family.

But, I'm learning, that's life. And a big part of it, at least in mine, seems to be about the people I love, leaving.

I think about Scout and her scheduled departure in only five days. Something desperate mounts inside me as I usher Atticus inside, feed him, and strip off my dirty clothes to hop into the shower. As the hot water hits my back, I play out a possible future in my mind's eye. A future that involves Scout.

Chapter Thirty-One

I don't know what to think about Zack's words. I know what my heart thinks, but my head is thinking something altogether different.

~ SCOUT SWIFT'S JOURNAL

Despite my mother's advice to include those in my life on my lighthouse quests, I doubt asking Zack to come as soon as we park at Bass Head Light. We don't know one another that well, and this visit is super personal.

I close the passenger door, and we walk down a steep, paved hill to the right. The real view is down the stairs to the left of the parking lot, but it's neat to see the lighthouse and bell up close.

I think there's something there for you.

What did Mom expect that to be? Surely, she hadn't hidden something for me to find somewhere on this property. Was it the experience itself? Did she think I'd connect with the memory I had of our first time here together?

I'd been ten, maybe eleven. It had been a clear but cold January day, a rare week when the snow had melted. I think there'd been one other car in the parking lot. We'd navigated the many steps to the water with care and climbed on the rocks to see the iconic image of Maine's most photographed lighthouse.

Bass Harbor Head Light.

I don't remember anything more than that. I don't remember anything she said to me or showed me. I don't remember what she was wearing or even if I particularly wanted to be out on that cold day.

Would I need to be alone to remember? To take in whatever my mother had been certain was here for me?

But the simple fact of the matter was, I didn't want to be alone. I wanted Zack here. In fact, I wanted to be with him until I had to leave.

And after that . . . well, I had a feeling I'd still want to be with him.

I groan. I was falling too fast—like I told myself I shouldn't.

"What's the matter?"

"Just realizing how not ready I am to go back home."

He bumps me gently. "I'm not ready for you to go back home, either."

A smile tugs at the corners of my mouth, but I tame it as we near the rail above the cliff.

We look over the placard displaying the history of Bass Head. We admire the closeup of the keeper's cottage, the lighthouse, and the bell. There are informational signs that tell us Maine boasts over seventy lighthouses, most dating back to the 1800s. Today, these lights guide lobster boats, tour boats, cruise ships, and schooners. A Coast Guard family currently lives at the Bass Head lighthouse.

"That's neat." I point to a sign. It says that each Maine light has a different light pattern and color for sailors to recognize their "fingerprint"—Bass Head's light is red, occulting, or darkening, every four seconds.

"I didn't realize that." Zack tilts his head, as if deep in thought. "That each light has a different pattern and color to help them be recognized."

"It's like a mark of their identity." I take in the sturdy white-washed lighthouse with the black catwalk at the top and its black-capped roof. I try to imagine the lighthouse keepers of the past that made their homes here. This light has seen many a storm but stood solid and firm and still, shining its constant red light every four seconds. "I wish I knew what my mother wanted me to find here."

"Don't pressure yourself. Just soak it in. Remember your mom. Maybe that will be enough."

"Maybe. Can we walk around the other side? That's where the real view is. I remember that much."

"Of course."

We make our way back toward the parking lot, and although I'm more than a little preoccupied with my own thoughts, I sense I'm not the only distracted one. "You okay? Work on Charlotte's place seems like it's going well. The sheetrock looks great."

He nods. "I'm ahead of schedule, at least."

"You hear anything from the owner in the historic district?"

Another shake of his head. "Not yet."

"Can I ask what's on your mind, then?"

He stops walking, turns to me. "I . . ." He seems to change his mind. "I'll tell you at the bottom."

We walk the many stairs that lead us down the steep cliff toward the massive rocks at the edge of the ocean. A handful of people climb over the rocks and pose for pictures in front of the squat lighthouse, shining in the setting sun.

I inhale a sharp intake of breath at its majestic beauty. I can understand why it was Mom's favorite. "Take a picture with me?"

He nods. I ask a couple to take our picture, and we stand with our arms slung over one another while the woman snaps a photo. We return the favor and then stare at the lighthouse a few more minutes before finding an out-of-the-way rock to sit and admire the view. The sky darkens, the clouds shine pink and purple above the horizon. When the light turns on, its red beacon indeed flashes on and off every four seconds.

I close my eyes, pray that God would give me a sign, or some knowing. What if I sensed nothing but Mom's absence, a feeling that I'm disappointing her?

When I open my eyes, Zack is sitting beside me, the setting sun splashing orange and red hues across his handsome profile. Behind him, the red light of the lighthouse beckons.

It's breathtaking. He's breathtaking. If I didn't know better, I could fool myself into thinking that he's what my mom told me to find here—that in some weird, time-bending way, she knew he was in my future. She knew I needed him.

I kick the thought from my head. More than likely, I'm hallucinating. I haven't eaten much today. I probably need food.

But first. "You going to tell me your deep thoughts now?"

One half of his mouth hooks up in an irresistible smile. He turns to me. "I was thinking about you."

Warmth stirs beneath my breastbone. "Oh."

"And the other night."

I can't stop the blush that works over my face and neck. "Oh." Is he wishing he kissed me? Has he imagined it a hundred times since that moment as I have?

"I don't want you to leave."

His words hang between us. I don't know what I expected, but it wasn't this. This is more than just fanciful wishing or musing. He's pondered this, maybe even spent a lot of time tossing the thought back and forth in his head.

A nervous laugh escapes me. "I don't want to leave, either."

"Then don't."

"What?"

"Don't leave. You have so much here. You said yourself you

were lonely back home. Why not stay a little longer? Or, a lot longer?"

"Zack, I have a job, a life, back in Massachusetts. And yes, it might be work and might even be lonely from time to time, but it's mine. I built it myself." Maine was a place of panic attacks and broken dreams. Even my body rebelled against it—how could I settle here? "What is it you want from me, exactly?"

I'm daring him to name it. At the same time, I'm angry that he would ask me to give up so much when we're little more than old acquaintances who share an attraction for one another.

No matter if I loved him as a girl, I'm not a girl any longer.

He rakes a hand through his hair. "I want a chance, Scout."

"A chance?"

"To figure out what could be between us if you stick around."

"So I need to give up everything over a chance?" Sounded more like a gamble. I'd only gambled once in my life on a man, and I wasn't doing it again.

"I know it sounds crazy. But I have this feeling."

"Yeah, a feeling I'm dangerous. Go with your gut, Zack. You hated me when I showed up a week ago. Now, you're asking me to rearrange my entire life around a hazy feeling?"

And God help me, something inside me wanted to rearrange my life around that almost kiss, around this feeling. Around this man. But I'd been hasty before and I'd gotten burned.

"Will you at least think about it, Scout? I can't stand the thought of you driving away again. Only this time, I won't be sad for just Charlotte. I'll be sad for myself."

I stand up on the rock, but it feels no more solid than shifting sand. "This is crazy. You don't really know me. I'm messed up. I'm broken. Sometimes I wonder if everything I touch is doomed to destruction." My breath catches on my last few words as the truth of them hits me with full force. I think of my relationship with my father, with Lexie, even with my mom. I think of my ambitious attempts to keep everything clean and orderly to create meaning out of what I can control.

I look at the lighthouse, sturdy beneath rains and storms and wind. A constant, despite its surroundings. That's what I had to be. Constant. Control what I could—the world I'd built, my sense of security.

"All I'm asking for is a chance. Maybe we could be great together."

I breathe deep, the waves coming higher up the rock.

The words make me dizzy. I want to fall into his arms, profess that I've thought the same thing since middle school, but a hitch in my spirit stops me. This can't be for me. This man is too good. This life is not what I deserve and maybe not even what I want.

I open my mouth, close it. Fumble for words. "'Maybe' is not a good enough reason for me to come back here. I'm sorry, Zack."

He gives me a sidelong glance, exhales a long breath. "Would you be open to getting to know each other better over the phone, then? Like talking?"

"People still do that?" I inject humor into my tone, but it comes out flat.

He forces a laugh, stares out at the water. Several long minutes pass between us. "I didn't mean to hijack this moment from you and make it about us. I should have waited until dinner."

I shake my head. "It's okay. I'm actually not feeling so great. Do you think you might be able to take me back to Charlotte's?"

I'm a horrible person. He probably assumes I've only used him for his truck.

"If that's what you want." He starts toward the stairs that lead to the parking lot. A twinge of regret climbs my insides.

What am I doing?

Zack is a good guy. A *great* guy. And I like him a lot. But after Greg, I told myself if I ever got involved with a guy again, it would be slow and methodical. I refuse to allow heady emotions to overtake reason and logic.

Agreeing to his request to stay is too much of a risk. Like touching the germ-infested door of a store and not washing your hands before eating. Too many bad possibilities. Too much risk.

I draw in a deep breath and look back at the lighthouse one more time. "Sorry, Mom. It doesn't look like I found what you wanted me to."

In fact, I may have indeed lost something she'd have wanted for me.

Chapter Thirty-Two

ZACK

"We can still go out to dinner, you know. We could talk. Or just eat. Whatever you want."

I park my truck in front of Charlotte's house. It's empty and dark inside, as if no one is home. I glance at Scout, my gut twisting and turning. What I wouldn't give to go back an hour when we were just two people hanging out, watching a gorgeous sunset. Simple, hopeful. But I'd ruined it. I'd let fear get the better of me. Didn't want to trust that a possible budding relationship could handle distance.

"I think I need some time to think. Can we talk tomorrow?"

I nod, and she slips out of my truck. I watch her enter the front door of the bed and breakfast, where she closes herself inside.

I can't make myself put my truck in drive. Is it selfish that I can't leave her? Or is it fear? Like if I leave now, I'll never get back what was almost ours?

I pull forward to turn my truck around but catch Scout's dark head as she walks out the side door of the inn and toward the lighthouse. I press the brake and watch until I see her tiny form emerge on the catwalk. She stands straight against the setting sun and once again, I'm captivated.

She belongs here.

She belongs here, with me.

The thought stops me. I'm not a creepy stalker. I'm not a narcissist. Why then does this notion hit me so strongly?

I lean back in my seat. "God, give me some guidance here." It hits me then how long it's been since I spoke to God, how I'm coming to Him now because I'm looking for something. I blow out a long breath. "I'm sorry. I'm lost. If she leaves, I'll have to survive. But I don't think she wants to leave. I think she's scared."

Suddenly, out my open window, I hear a scream. I'm out of my truck faster than Atticus at top speed. I'm racing toward the lighthouse, searching for Scout, but I don't see anything. There's not a doubt in my mind that scream came from her. But why aren't Charlotte or Reagan or even one of the guests rushing to see what's wrong?

I run over the footbridge and through the open door of the light. All I can think of is Laney's mother near toppling from the catwalk last year. I imagine Scout plummeting to her death and my heartbeat ramps up, my throat tight. I race up the concrete steps but they might as well be a mile long for how slowly they are taking me to Scout. Finally, at the top, I reach the lamp room. I search the catwalk and breathe a tremendous sigh of relief when I see her standing, whole and healthy.

"Scout," I call from the lamp room, not wanting to scare her. I again think of Charlotte's daughter during her television interview. I know what it is to frighten someone up here unintentionally.

She looks back, her mouth parted in surprise, strands of dark hair flying in front of her face.

I straighten from where I'd been catching my breath. "I heard a scream. I thought—you scared the living daylights out of me. Are you okay?"

She bites her lip, looks guilty. "I thought I was alone. Charlotte and Reagan aren't here. Ever feel like you just need a good scream?"

My chest drains of pressure. "Not exactly, but it's a relief to see you're okay." I look back at the stairs. "I guess I'll leave."

I don't want to leave. I also don't want to force my presence on her when she so obviously doesn't want it.

"Don't." A beautifully vulnerable tear meanders down her cheek. "I'm sorry. Please, don't leave."

I take two great strides toward her and sweep her up in my arms. I press her to me, as close as I can up against my chest until I'm not sure if hugging her any harder will be painful. "I won't leave, Scout. I'm not leaving."

Her sobs wet my shirt, but I stand steady, supporting her in my arms for as long as she needs. Truth is, as much as I hate to see her sad, I'm glad I'm the one here for her in this moment.

The wind from the ocean pushes against us, but I brace myself on the floor of the catwalk, as if daring it to try and unsteady my grip on this woman. I inhale the scent of flowers mixed with sea, a scent I know is distinctly Scout. I never want to move on from this moment. The golden heat of the summer sun ebbs away at the horizon. I could stay here forever, battered even by storms and rain, if it means I can hold her.

I realize then I could fall for her in an instant if she opened up to me. That realization cements my hunch from two nights before —Scout *is* dangerous. I think of my parents, of Priscilla.

Am I wrong to offer something I might not even be good for? To ask Scout to change her entire life for me?

She pulls away. The cry of a gull sounds overhead, haunting in the rush of the sea. She claims she's broken. But aren't we all, in some way?

I pull her close again, whisper against her temple. "Broken things can be made whole." I squeeze her hand. "I want to be a part of making you whole. Will you let me help? Please?" My words are quiet, barely competition for the surge of the ocean below us.

Please let me in.

Her phone vibrates. She reaches for it in the back pocket of her jeans and pulls away from me to answer.

"Hello?"

Her face pales. I think I recognize Charlotte's voice on the other end, but I can't be certain.

Scout sways where she stands. I place a hand on her elbow to steady her, my own nerves at attention at the thought that something could be wrong with the older woman.

"Is it Dad?" Scout asks.

The waves quiet, and I can clearly hear Charlotte's voice. "No, it's Reagan. The baby's coming, but something's wrong. She needs you, honey."

"I'll be there as soon as I can."

She hangs up and for a split-second, our gazes tangle. There's a lot left unsaid, but it can wait.

"Let's go."

She rushes down the stairs of the Beacon ahead of me. For the second time that night, I pray. This time, not for me, but for the teen girl and her baby.

Chapter Thirty-Three

LILLIAN

There is nothing left to be done.

That is all we can really hope for in the end. That we've loved the best we could, that we've given our all for our God, for our family, for those who exist in our tiny worlds.

Bud's warm hand encompasses mine, and I fight a hazy sorrow that we could have been more had we had the opportunity to get through this.

He prayed for me the other day. For the first time, he prayed for us. It was the best gift he could have given me.

He still hasn't gone to see her, his other daughter. But he promised me he would.

I believe him.

The only reason I can't leave this world in peace is Scout. We have peace between us, but she clings to her anger. Maybe her anger toward God for allowing this to happen, but also her anger toward Bud for dumping the truth about his other daughter upon us in these last hard months.

I think of the videos I left for her and pray they will make a difference. One of my last thoughts is a memory I have of Scout at Bass Head Light. Somehow, I know she will find what she needs to find there.

I leave this world knowing I will understand complete wholeness soon.

I leave this world knowing I have forgiven and knowing I have loved.

I leave this world anticipating the arms of my Savior.

<h1 style="text-align:center">Chapter Thirty-Four</h1>

Sometimes you don't realize how much someone means to you until you're within a breath of losing them.

~ SCOUT SWIFT'S JOURNAL

I don't remember the ride to the hospital, but I do remember racing into the emergency room, finding Charlotte, and throwing my arms around her.

"What happened?"

"She was having pains over dinner and then her water broke. She panicked, poor girl. I called an ambulance right away. I tried calling you multiple times, but you didn't answer."

"I forgot to turn the volume up on my phone this morning. I didn't hear it until that last call." I rub my face. "Can I see her?"

"They won't let anyone in who isn't family. I tried to tell them of the circumstances, but . . ."

A fierce surge of protection comes over me. I stride to the nurse's station and calmly ask to be allowed to see Reagan. "Sorry, ma'am. Only family." The nurse doesn't look up from her computer.

"I am family. I'm her sister." I'm not in the habit of lying, but it doesn't feel like a lie. What is family, anyway? Are they not the people you love and live with, the people you go to in hard times and forgive after arguments? They're the people you go to when you have no one else.

Reagan has no one else.

And there is absolutely no way I'm going to let her deliver this baby by herself. So, I decide right then and there, that she will always have me.

I will be her family.

"Very well, then." The nurse prints me out a badge, and I hug Zack and Charlotte, promising to give them more news as soon as I am able.

"We'll be out here, praying. You tell her we're praying, okay?" Charlotte grips my hands and looks deep into my eyes. I can see how much she's come to care about Reagan, too.

I assure her I will let Reagan know, and then I'm being led through a maze of corridors until finally a curtain is swiped aside to reveal a pale, panting Reagan lying on her side in a gown that makes her stomach look the size of three watermelons.

I rush over to her and squeeze her hand. The shell she'd shown me on our car trip, the one from Jaden, is clamped tight in her grasp. My heart breaks a little as I sink into the seat pulled up next to the bed. "I'm here, Reagan."

She lifts her head off the pillow, leaving a damp tendril of hair plastered to the case. "Scout?"

She looks exhausted, nothing like her peppy self. Not to mention the fact she seems to question my presence. It's not that hard to believe I'm here, is it?

I rub her hand, trying to instill calm and peace into her. "You're doing great, honey."

"No, I'm not," she groans. "It's too soon. It's too soon!" She wails the words, her desperate moans dissolving into hiccuping sobs.

"Try to keep her calm," a nurse with bold-framed glasses instructs me as she looks at the monitors beside Reagan.

I run my hand over Reagan's sweaty head. "Reagan, listen to me. It's going to be okay, understand? Babies are born early all the time. You're in good hands. And Charlotte and Zack are in the waiting room praying for you. It's going to be okay."

She's quiet for a moment. "Did you pray for your mom, Scout?"

My throat swells. "Yes."

"Prayers . . . prayers don't always work like that. Sometimes, things go wrong." She's crying again but then her tears dissolve into something more difficult—pain. She curls around herself as a contraction tears through her.

I have never felt so helpless in my life. I've never seen someone have a baby before. I've heard it's painful, of course, but this . . . I don't know if I'm ready for this.

I consider escaping back to the waiting room and transferring my name badge to Charlotte. If it could be that easy, I'd do it in a heartbeat.

Finally, the intense pain seems to release the girl, and she falls back on the bed.

"I can ask Charlotte to come back here. They might let her."

But Reagan's shaking her head back and forth on the pillow. "No."

"She knows more about having babies than I do. I don't know how to help you, Reagan."

"I want . . . you here."

I swallow. Why? Why does she want me? What if something goes wrong?

I want to argue with her. My presence didn't stop my mom from dying any more than my prayers did. Not that I think Reagan's going to die, but her baby . . . it is several weeks early.

"Don't leave." Her whispered words scarce make it past her lips.

I tighten my grip on her hand, decide in that moment I will be strong for her. "I'm not going anywhere until this baby is safe in your arms, okay?"

A wan smile tilts her lips. "Thank you."

Another contraction comes and goes, seeming to drain my young friend of energy.

"You're doing great," I assure her, although in truth I have no idea if she is handling labor well or not. "You're a strong woman. And now, you're going to be strong for your baby, too."

"It's too soon for it to come. It's too early. What if it's sick? I don't have a plan. You told me I needed to have a plan and . . . you were right. Now, it's too late."

"Reagan . . . Reagan, look at me."

It takes her a minute, but finally, she focuses on my gaze.

"We will figure this out, okay? Together. I promise, I am not leaving you alone. You hear me? You are not alone."

She sheds more tears, but they are different tears. Not desperate and fearful, but accepting. Maybe even hopeful. She nods. Another contraction comes, then another and another. I hate seeing her in such pain.

A nurse comes in and checks her progress. Five centimeters. It is going to be a very long night.

"Could you give her something?" I ask.

"We could. She said she didn't want anything, though. You change your mind, sweetie?"

Reagan shakes her head.

I shimmy closer to her. "You have nothing to prove, okay? There's nothing wrong with a little help."

"I have to do this, Scout."

I don't question her. If I know one thing about this girl it's that when she's determined, she means it.

The night wears on with Reagan making little progress. She

seems to weaken throughout the night, but the medical team assures me this is normal. Apparently, delivering a human is a heck of a lot more work than I realized. They monitor the baby closely and assure us the little one is doing okay.

I update Charlotte and Zack periodically. At some point, Laney shows up and Reagan brightens when I tell her this news.

She's seven centimeters at around five the next morning. That's when she reaches for my hand.

"I'm here," I say, scooting my chair closer to her bedside.

"I have to tell you something. In case I don't make it."

I laugh. "You're delusional, honey. You're a young, healthy, strong woman. People like you don't die in labor."

"Scout . . . please." The gravity of her words meet me with their seriousness.

"Okay. Whatever you need."

Another contraction comes and when it releases its grip on her, she swallows, asks for an ice chip.

"I met you on purpose." Her hair is plastered to her forehead, and I wipe her skin with a cool cloth.

"What?" I'm functioning on no sleep, and I can't make sense of her overtired words.

"I was looking for you at Walmart."

"I don't understand." Why would she seek me out?

Her face contorts before she continues, but I don't think it's from the pain of labor. "I knew about you. I searched your name online and saw an employee-of-the-month article. That's how I found out where you worked."

"But why?"

She rides out another contraction by gripping the bedrail. When it eases, I know we don't have a lot of time before another comes. I hope she starts talking sense soon.

"It had your picture. You looked just like her. It's how I knew."

"Like who? Like my mom? Did you know my mom?"

But aside from our eyes, I look nothing like my mom.

Everyone always said I got the entirety of my genes from the other side of the family.

Reagan moans. "My sister. My half-sister. Ashley."

All the blood drains from my face. Still, I doubt her meaning. She can't be saying what I think she's saying. "Reagan . . ."

A nurse comes in and checks Reagan's progress during the next contraction. "Almost there," she says. "You'll be able to push this little one into the world in no time."

"How's my baby?" Reagan asks in a breathy whisper.

The nurse glances at the monitors. "You have a strong one, young lady. He or she's small, but a fighter. You keep up the good work."

Reagan nods, her face still contorted in pain as the contraction takes its time releasing her. When it does, she licks her lips, panting between words. "I'm only telling you in case—in case something happens to me. We're not related by blood, but I had to find you. I thought we could be . . . a family."

Her words swirl in a ball of incomprehensive muddle between us. I look like her half-sister, Ashley.

"How did you . . . " But the words die on my lips.

"Your dad contacted Ashley once. I was seven or eight, I think. I re—remember because she was supposed to meet him, and it was a big deal. But she didn't go. Didn't even cancel, just didn't show up."

All at once, everything makes sense. Ashley. Reagan's sister. Half-sister. *My father's daughter.* My half-sister.

Me meeting Reagan at Walmart was not a coincidence.

I blink fast, trying to make all the pieces fit together but failing miserably. "You never introduced yourself. You never said anything."

"I was scared. I met Jaden, thought maybe I could forget about you and make a life for myself. When you found me that morning behind the bird seed . . ." Another contraction makes it impossible for her to speak. This time though, she screams and machines start beeping wildly.

"Help!" I jump out of my seat and shove aside the curtain, but a nurse and a doctor are already running in our direction.

They check vitals, but Reagan's eyes flutter, head limp against the pillow. Hands push aside blankets to examine her, to study the monitors.

"Let's prep her." A woman doctor with skin the color of walnuts finally makes a call.

They begin to wheel Reagan away, but when I move to follow her, a nurse holds me back. "We'll let you know as soon as the baby's born."

"But I promised I wouldn't leave her until she was holding her baby."

The nurse gives me a sympathetic look. "We're going to take good care of her, honey. And I promise you'll be the first to know when the baby's born."

I nod, shoving aside the fierce wave of protection surging through me. Reagan is unconscious. They are taking her to surgery. They are going to cut the baby out of her.

Reagan had been so protective of her unborn child. She'd be furious to know she was unconscious during its birth. Furious even with me that I broke my promise.

I run after the nurse. "Please, take good care of her. She's— she's my sister."

And though I meant it before, this time there's a different element of truth to my words.

She pats my arm. I turn with blurred vision toward the waiting room. When I push through the double doors, I search the room for Charlotte, Zack, and Laney. But I only see Zack.

He rushes toward me when he sees me and I fall, exhausted, into his arms.

Chapter Thirty-Five

I've been building my life on certain truths only to find most of them crumbling down around me.

~ SCOUT SWIFT'S JOURNAL

Once I'm in Zack's arms, he ushers me out the doors of the waiting room. I gulp in fresh morning air through exhausted tears.

I really need to stop making it a habit of crying in his arms.

"You didn't leave." He's been here all night.

"How's Reagan?"

I pull back from him, the cool morning serving to cleanse my senses. "She passed out. I don't know what happened. They took her in to do an emergency C-section. Wait. Where's Charlotte and Laney?"

"Laney went back to make breakfast for the guests at the inn. Charlotte went to scout us out something to eat."

I want to tell him more. About how Reagan's half-sister is my

238

half-sister. I want to puzzle out the logistics with him, understand Reagan's motives. Fit it all together.

My dad had contacted Ashley. His daughter. Why hadn't he said anything?

I remember that horrible argument I overheard between my parents a few months before Mom died. I can still hear their voices.

We didn't speak of it again the next few months. We both turned our attention to Mom. But inwardly, I fumed over his awful timing, over his poor decisions.

When Mom died, it wasn't hard to push my father further away. And when Greg came along, I was more than ready to leave Dad. To deprive him of any daughter. To hurt him how he hurt me.

Now, as Zack and I walk back into the hospital, I let the news sink in that Dad tried to connect with his first daughter. A long time ago. Before Mom died?

No, Reagan said ten years. But how accurate are memories of an eight-year-old? Especially ones from a young woman deep in the throes of labor?

The nameless, faceless identity of my half-sister begins to take shape. And I'm not going to lie—that scares me. It was one thing when she was only a hazy image. Now . . . she's Reagan's sister. She's my sister.

I try to remember what Reagan said about Ashley.

She had a boyfriend once. Something about drugs. Ashley had allowed Reagan to go into the foster care system after their mother died. Now, Reagan can't locate her.

I hadn't liked Ashley for releasing Reagan to foster care, and I liked her even less now, knowing we shared the same blood.

But could I really judge her? I knew so little of her story, other than her mother had been hooked on painkillers, her father—my father—had been absent.

And while I'd harshly judged my father for not trying to be a part of his other daughter's life, even for Mom's sake, in all the years I'd known about my mystery half-sibling, I'd never made an attempt to find her, either.

Because she wasn't my responsibility.

I think of Reagan, unconscious and about to have a baby. Reagan isn't my responsibility, either. But it doesn't seem like a chore to be here for her, to support her, to do everything in my power to help. She had quite purposefully and effectively wheedled herself into my heart.

"Honey." Charlotte, face drawn and pale, walks toward us with a brown bag. "How's she doing?"

I tell Charlotte what I told Zack, again leaving out the part about Ashley. Right now, we need Reagan to deliver this baby. I'll worry about complicated logistics later.

Charlotte hands me a blueberry muffin, which I eat with gusto.

"Zack, you should take Charlotte home. There's no point in us all being here. I can call as soon as I have news."

Charlotte nods. "First though, let's pray."

I don't argue with her. Praying might not have helped my mom, but I can't deny the urge to draw near to God, to someone bigger than myself, in this moment.

As Charlotte prays softly for Reagan and her child, though, a sense of satisfaction—peace, even—winds through me. I listen to Zack's steady voice beseeching God for Reagan's baby, and something bends inside me.

Whether or not God hears us or intends to answer us, there's no doubt in my mind that this small action of prayer has brought me closer to these two other people as we join in begging the Creator of the universe for her health and safety. He is here with us, whether or not He answers our prayer how we want.

When we finish, though I haven't uttered a word, I'm surprised to find a knot of emotion lodged in my throat.

Zack kisses me on the top of the head, the gesture only serving to expand the lump. "I'll be back right after I drop Charlotte off."

I shake my head. "Go. Get some sleep. We'll talk soon, okay?"

"You sure?"

"I'm sure. But thank you, Zack. For everything." I remember our time up on the catwalk of the Beacon, his whispered words near my skin.

Broken things can be made whole.

As if he himself has the power to hold me together. And I wonder as he walks away with Charlotte, if indeed perhaps he does.

Scout: I know this is a HUGE inconvenience, but I'm wondering if there's any way I could have a few more days off?

Elise: Scout! Miss you! Wish I could say yes to that, but we are hurting over here and you've already taken all your allotted days. Sorry. Hurry back.

I STARE AT MY PHONE. Elise hadn't hesitated in her answer, which meant there was absolutely no wiggle room. Not that there was much wiggle room with Walmart, anyway. They'd been generous in granting me all the vacation time on short notice. It seemed I wouldn't be able to get any more without getting fired.

Zack's words, this time from our time at Bass Head, again echo around me, chasing me down.

Don't leave. You have so much here.

I rub my eyes. I need coffee. The strongest coffee money can buy.

"Ms. Swift?"

I sit up at the call of an unfamiliar voice.

It's the doctor who ordered Reagan taken to surgery. I jump up, my pulse knocking against my temples. "How is she?"

The doctor nods. "She's doing well now. Her uterus ruptured. It was a good thing we took the baby when we did."

Spots form before my eyes and my chest tightens. I breathe around the familiar panic. Uterine rupture. That had to be serious. "Is the baby okay?"

"She's doing well. Very well, considering her bumpy start."

My airways open, allowing precious oxygen to rush into my lungs. *She.* Reagan had a little girl.

"We were able to repair Reagan's uterus without a hysterectomy, but her recovery won't be easy. I noticed she's a minor. You're her sister?"

I swallow, give one nod.

"Are you her guardian as well?"

I bite my lip. "She'll be eighteen in two weeks. She's been on her own for some time."

The doctor flips through the chart she holds in her hand. "According to the birthday she gave us, she'll be seventeen in two weeks."

Seventeen . . . meaning Reagan was only sixteen? I look up at the ceiling and groan.

"Ms. Swift?"

I lower myself into the seat behind me and shake my head. "She lied to me."

The doctor raises an eyebrow at me. "She's your sister and you didn't know how old she was?"

"It's a long story. But the short answer is no, I am not her guardian."

The doctor stares at her chart, as if it will give her some answers. "Once she's seventeen, she won't be considered a ward of the state. But that's not for another two weeks. I'm afraid I'm going to have to call social services."

Panic tears through me. "What does that mean?"

The doctor places her hand on my arm. "Likely not much at

this point. But I need to report it. They will probably ask Reagan some questions. She can request an emancipation."

My head spins as I try to think of the legal implications for Reagan and her child. My mouth grows dry.

Have I failed her? Though I've only known the girl for a few weeks, I've made promises to her. I told her I wouldn't leave her. Now, would I be forced to? "You said her baby is well?"

"Strong for one so little. She had to go to the NICU and will likely be there for several days. But she's a fighter and I'm confident she just needs a little time."

I swallow. "They won't take her from Reagan, will they?"

"No. No one will take her baby, no matter if she's a minor or not. As long as she proves herself to be a fit mother, there are no worries there."

I breathe out a long sigh of relief. "Can I see her?"

"She's still a bit groggy, but yes."

I follow the doctor beyond the heavy double doors and back down the hallway to where Reagan lies in a recovery room. Her long hair is tucked beneath a blue cap and a fresh blanket drapes her body. A nurse adjusts an IV drip.

A steady beep on the monitors is both comforting and unnerving. I place my hand on her warm arm. Reagan's eyelids flutter open.

"Hey." I smile as bright as I can, though I fear she will see it's for show.

Her eyebrows furrow. She looks around the room, feels her stomach. "I can't feel . . . my baby."

I glance at the nurse, and she nods. "She's in the NICU. The doctor says she's small but strong."

"She?"

I nod.

Reagan's smile gives way to a happy sob. When she starts to sit up, the nurse places a restraining hand on her shoulder.

"Careful, honey. You're still recovering, too. Your daughter needs her mama strong when she graduates from the NICU."

"I *need* to see her."

"You need to stay lying down for right now. Besides, they're still getting her set up. Could be a few hours."

"A few *hours*? You're seriously going to stand there and tell me I can't see my own baby that I've carried around with me for eight months? What are you people, jail keepers?"

In my attempt to calm the hysterical, half-drugged, new mother, I make a shushing sound.

Wrong move.

"Don't shush me, Scout. I have a right to see my baby!"

In a strange way, I admire her ability to stand up for herself and her child in this medical environment. I'm not sure I would have the gumption to do so.

I look at the nurse. "Can I see if I can glimpse her in the NICU?" I turn to Reagan. "I can tell you how she's doing."

The nurse tells me how to find the NICU and though I have little hopes of them allowing me to see the baby, a friendly nurse points out Reagan's daughter to me. She is sleeping peacefully in an incubator closest to the large window. She is swaddled in a blanket and hat. She is unbelievably tiny.

The nurse from the NICU nods. "She's doing very well."

I take a short video of Reagan's daughter and rush back to find her. When she sees her baby on my phone, she clutches it, blinking back fast tears. "This is her?" She looks up at me, as if unbelieving.

I nod.

She looks back at the phone. "She's beautiful."

I smile. "She is. And they said she's doing wonderfully. She's right where she needs to be, and we're praying she'll be in your arms before you know it."

I have a lot to say to Reagan. I have questions. We have to talk about the fact that she lied to me.

But all of that can wait. Today is a day for celebrating the birth of a healthy baby.

Chapter Thirty-Six

Today has brought more questions than answers.

~ SCOUT SWIFT'S JOURNAL

When I finally wake in the guest cottage at Charlotte's, it's nearly dark. I feel for my phone on my nightstand. Eight-thirty. I click on the bedside lamp and lay listening to the steady sound of the waves below the Beacon.

With a start, I realize I don't even know if Reagan has her phone with her. I scroll past a slew of unread texts to Reagan's name.

Scout: Hey, I just woke up. Not sure if you have your phone. How are you?

Reagan: I'm good. They wheeled me into the
NICU, and I got to be with her for a long time.

Scout: That's great! How are you feeling?

Reagan: Sore, but I'm okay.

Scout: I'll be down there first thing in the
morning.

Reagan: Scout, thank you. For everything.

I PRESS MY LIPS TOGETHER, vacillating over whether to give
her a head's up about social services or not. Maybe better to let her
get a good night's sleep without excess worrying.

Scout: Any name yet?

Reagan: Still thinking.

Scout: Okay. Have a good night. See you
tomorrow.

Reagan: 🩶

I scroll next to Zack's name, where an unread text sits.

Zack: Hope you're getting some rest. Miss you.
Call or text when you can.

Warmth stirs within me. I close my eyes and remember his
words atop the Beacon. But there is so much to figure out. Elise
denied my request for more time off. I have to return home in four
days.

Four days. Would Reagan still be in the hospital? The doctor
said she'd be able to request an emancipation—how long would
that take? And where would she stay? She'd managed to obtain a
job but now, with the baby arriving so soon, she wouldn't even be
able to train or prove herself.

And what good would a piddly part-time job do when it came to paying for childcare? For a place to live?

And why in the world did I feel the weight of all this so heavy on my shoulders?

But I knew. I'd claimed her as my sister, even before I knew about the link we shared.

I groan. I need to talk to Dad.

Instead, though, I tap out a text to Zack.

> Scout: Just woke up. Hope you got some rest too!

The next minute, my phone rings. I smile at the sight of Zack's name lighting up the screen. I *could* really get used to this.

I swipe right and snuggle deeper into my blankets. "Hey."

"Hey, yourself." His voice is deep and gravelly. "How you doing?"

It's such a simple question, but it pulls sweetly at my spirit. "I'm good. A few hours of sleep can work wonders."

"How's Reagan and the baby?"

"They're both doing great."

"Good news."

"Sure is. What about you? I hope you rested today."

"For a little. But I got some good news that kept me up."

"Oh?"

He pauses a moment, as if he's shifting or sitting up. I try to picture him in his living room, Atticus at his feet. "Heard from the owner of the West Street job. I won the bid."

"Zack, that's wonderful. Congratulations."

"Yeah, it is. I have a lot of work ahead of me but I'm all in."

"You're going to kill it."

He's quiet for a minute. "Your car part came in."

"Oh." I was running out of excuses to stay in Maine. "Listen, you have a lot on your plate. Let me call around to some shops, see how quick they can get me in."

"No way, Swift. I ordered the part, I'm fixing your car."

It is nice to be cared for. I decide not to argue. "Thank you."

"I'll start on it tomorrow after work. When do you need it?"

His question hangs in the air. We both know what he's really asking.

"I leave Sunday. I asked my boss for some extra time, but she can't accommodate."

He's quiet. "What about Reagan?"

"I'm not sure. Before she went into labor, she said she had a plan. I haven't talked to her about what that is yet."

He's silent again, this time for a good stretch of time. Then, he speaks, his voice raspy. "What about us?"

"Zack," I whisper. "I like you. A lot. I'm just not sure if upending my entire life is the wisest thing to do right now. I thought we were going to, you know, keep talking."

"Oh, so you're open to talking." I hear the smile in his voice.

"I'm not against long-distance relationships. Are you?"

"Long-term long-distance, yes."

"Then maybe we should try to make it short-term before we rearrange our lives." I'm talking sense, of course, I am.

"What if . . ." He doesn't finish his sentence. "Never mind. Okay. I'll do whatever makes you happy. And when you fall in love with me and decide to move here, I can say 'I told you so.'"

I giggle. "You're awfully sure of yourself."

"Like I said, I have this feeling."

I sigh, deep and content. There's a lot to be worked out in my life right now, but I love sitting in this hopeful place with Zack.

"Can I come over?" he asks.

The words send a million prickles and tingles up and down my spine and over every inch of my body. I imagine him here, in the guest cottage. Alone together. I imagine kissing him, only this time with the memory of us at Bass Head and at the top of the Beacon fresh in my mind. His words.

Broken things can be made whole.

I'm still exhausted and not thinking straight. I'm weak.

And I know what it is to be weak. I know how dangerous it can be.

"I don't think so. I need to catch up on my sleep."

"Can I see you tomorrow, then? Maybe take you out for the dinner we never had?"

I smile. "I think that could be arranged." I try to think what has changed since the night before, but I don't exactly know. Maybe me. More likely, it was the words he spoke on the catwalk of the Beacon.

Broken things can be made whole.

I want to be a part of making you whole.

Who says things like that? Apparently, this construction man I'd had a crush on since the sixth grade. This man I'm coming to care about entirely too much.

And it feels wonderful.

"Oh, almost forgot to send you the picture from the other night."

The text comes through, and I study the image of me and Zack in front of Bass Head Light. "I love it."

"Me, too."

"Hey, I have to make a phone call. Will I see you in the morning?"

"I'll be there. Nothing better than scones and Scout in the morning."

"You did not just say that."

"Oh, I think I did."

We laugh and say goodbye. After I hang up, I sit in the moment, unwilling to contemplate my next task. A minute later though, I force myself to dial my father's number.

"Scout? Everything okay?" His voice is faint and tired. No doubt he was sleeping.

"Hi Dad. I know it's late. Oh, shoot. You probably have to go out on the boat early tomorrow."

He clears his throat. "I don't. I was just dozing on the couch. What's up?"

"I was hoping to talk to you. In person."

"Um . . . now?"

This is stupid. I could have waited until morning. Maybe I should have watched more of Mom's videos first. What has gotten into me?

But I know. Reagan's words have driven me the last several hours. Even in sleep, I dreamt about what they meant for me, for my dad, for Reagan's sister. *My* sister. For my past, for my future.

I need answers.

"We could talk on the phone, if you want?"

But it sounds like he's already moving around. "No, honey. I'll be over. Give me fifteen minutes."

I tell him I'm staying in the guest cottage and fifteen minutes later, he's knocking on the door. That fact alone—that he rushed over here simply because I asked him to—softens my heart toward him.

I open the door to see him in a flannel shirt and jeans and . . . glasses.

"Thanks for coming." I gesture him inside the living area. Zack completed the bathroom two days ago, but the kitchen is still a work-in-progress. "Can I get you some tea?"

"I'm okay. Just a little worried about you." He sits down, leans over outspread legs.

I smile. "I'm fine."

Fine. I hate that word. It's such a brush-off, a cop-out. Inauthentic.

I clear my throat. "I like your glasses."

"Oh." He takes them off, slips them into the front pocket of his shirt. "I use them to drive at night."

"They suit you."

We're quiet for a moment before I work up enough courage to

start this conversation. "I don't think I told you about Reagan when we had dinner?"

His blank expression prompts me to continue.

"She's a pregnant teenage girl I've been helping out. A customer I knew from my job back in Massachusetts."

"That's nice of you." Dad shifts in his seat, clearly trying to see where I'm going with all of this.

I prop one leg up beneath me and reach for a quilt, bunching it in my hands as I continue. "She went into labor last night. It was a bit touch-and-go for a while. She was tired and desperate. Anyway, during labor, she told me that our meeting wasn't a mistake."

He cocks his head. "What do you mean?"

"She's Ashley's little sister, Dad."

I can tell from his expression that he doesn't need an explanation of who Ashley is.

"She knew about you. She remembers that Ashley was supposed to meet you one day but that she stood you up." I pause to catch my breath before diving further. "You contacted her."

He's shifting in his seat again, and then he's up, pacing the length of hardwood in front of the door. "I didn't mean to get you involved in this, Scout."

"I'm an adult, Dad. Please, tell me. Tell me what happened."

He rakes a hand through his thinning hair. "She didn't meet me, and I thought maybe it was for the best. I tried, you know? I did what your mom asked me to do."

"When?" I whisper. His answer could make all the difference.

He blows out a long breath, stares at the area rug beneath the small coffee table. "About six months after your mother died."

I let his words sink in. Half a year. Two months after I left.

So, he hadn't tried to set things right while Mom was still alive. He'd been late. Too late.

Would any of it have made a difference? Would it have given

Mom peace? Would it have changed the course of things in any way? I wasn't sure.

"I spoke to her. Ashley." It's visibly hard for him to say her name. I understand. For so long she was an unspoken curse, a nameless identity. It wasn't right, but that's how it was.

"What did she say?"

"She said she'd like to meet me. But when we set a time and place, she didn't show. I called her once more, just to make sure I had the right day and time. She didn't answer. I decided to respect that."

"And it was easier for you." The honest words are out, naked between us.

My father curses. "I tried, Scout. Isn't it enough? It was my mistake and my decision. I wish to God it never happened and yes, I wish I'd done things differently once I realized they did happen."

If it was simply a mistake he'd made in a bubble, a decision he'd made that didn't affect me or Mom, I could have bought it. But that's not how most mistakes are, are they? They affect those around us. They affect those we love.

"It was the one thing Mom asked you to do before she died. And you didn't do it." My voice is soft. Despite the harshness of his words, I want him to understand. *I* want to understand.

He slumps where he stands. "I made the decision I thought was best for my family. I told your mother that I would contact Ashley, but not while she was fighting for her life. Not while we were standing at death's door. She needed me too much then. And I didn't need a distraction. I followed through with my promise, and I respected Ashley's decision to not invite me into her life. She was an adult by then."

His words circle around me. A glimpse of . . . empathy—maybe understanding?—nudges the corners of my fractured mind. "I didn't know you made that promise to Mom. She never told me."

"I'm guessing she didn't want to bring it up any more than I did. We had enough going on."

"When did you find out you had another daughter?"

He swallows. "On your eighth birthday."

I close my eyes.

"I didn't think it was true. She was already thirteen by then. I thought her mom was just trying to get money out of me. I fought it, but the blood test revealed the truth."

"And Mom never knew until . . . until . . ."

"It was a lousy thing for me to do. Confess that to her when she was in that state. I realize how selfish it was."

I bite the inside of my cheek. "It was selfish. That kind of stress did not help her beat cancer."

He's blinking back tears. "By that point, the doctors had only given her months. Not that I'm defending myself. Deep down, I think she knew. She questioned the withdrawals from my paychecks, never pressed me when I brushed them off. I had to be up front with her in the end."

I let all this new information sink in, but none of it really makes me feel better. "I'm still mad at you."

"I know. And I am sorry for all the pain I caused both you and your mother. But Scout, there's nothing left for me to do besides ask you to forgive me."

The opportunity sits before me, almost like something I've been waiting for that I didn't know I was waiting for. But I can't take it.

Someone once told me that forgiving is giving up our just right for revenge. And that's the thing—I'm not ready to give up that right. I know it's ugly and unflattering, but somehow, some way, deep down, I still want my father to make everything right.

"Reagan was having trouble tracking down her sister. You know her name. Do you still have her information?"

My words visibly wear on him, pulling at his features, tugging on his posture.

"Maybe I could help Reagan reunite with her." I'd meet with Ashley first, of course. If drugs were still in the picture, a reunion might not be the wisest thing for my young friend. "Besides, I think I would like to meet her."

All these years, my dad wasn't the only one to ignore this woman of our blood. I could sit here raining down judgment on him, but I'd ignored her, too.

He rubbed his face. "That might not be a good idea."

"Why not?"

He lowers himself to the chair across from me. "I've kept tabs on her. Actually, I saw her two weeks ago."

My turn to stand up. "What? Why wouldn't you tell me?"

He presses his lips together, folds his hands in front of him. "She's in jail, Scout. Has been for the last six months. Assault and robbery. She won't be out for a good long while."

Chapter Thirty-Seven

I'm learning more about my dad than I ever knew. I'm learning more about myself, too. And it's not all rainbows and unicorns.

~ SCOUT SWIFT'S JOURNAL

"Hi, honey! Did you do it? Did you go see Bass Head?"

I smile at the screen in Charlotte's bedroom, where Mom looks expectantly at me. "Yeah, I did Mom."

"Good. I knew you would. I'm not sure why, but I felt like that might be good for you—doing the thing that was supposed to symbolize the end of our journey, first. Was it? Did it help?" She grows serious. "I sure wish I could have been there with you, Scout. I wish . . ." She shakes her head. "Never mind all that. We need to talk about your father."

I hit pause on the remote and hug one of Charlotte's throw pillows to my chest, my mind replaying my time at Bass Head with

Zack and then at the Beacon, to Dad in the guest cottage the night before, answering questions I thought I wanted answered.

The half-sister I never met is in jail. My father *visits* her every two weeks. He's trying to form a *relationship* with her. He is trying to actually help her.

It's beyond anything I could have thought or imagined from him.

And I'm realizing how very wrong I've been about so many things.

I push the play button. "The thing about your father is . . . " Mom begins. "Well, there's lots of things about your father. Did I ever tell you how we met? I must have. Did I? I can't remember. Sometimes these drugs make my brain so fuzzy. Anyway, I worked at a diner in Bar Harbor. I was still in high school, getting ready to leave for college. But he walked in one morning with one of his fishing buddies, leaned over the counter, and told me clear as rain that he was going to marry me someday. Can you imagine the audacity?" She laughs, almost like a giddy schoolgirl. I can't remember her ever acting this way and for a moment, I question whether the drugs are indeed messing with her. But maybe that's too simple an answer. Maybe now, knowing she will be gone when I watch this, she is revealing a deeper part of herself.

I try to picture my parents young, my father cocky enough to proclaim such a thing. I can't decide if it's creepy or incredibly romantic.

My mom seems to vote for romantic.

"He asked me out six times before I finally said yes. And there was no turning back after that. I did quit school to be with him, but I never regretted it. And then I had you. Honey, the joy of my life was being your mom."

My eyelids prick. Mom swipes at her own cheeks. "Your dad made some mistakes when he was young. I suppose we all do. But his followed him. And I know we might not be able to understand him, but I also know that in his mind, he feels he needs to choose.

Us or this other woman and her daughter. Now you and I both know there's enough room in that big ol' bear heart for all of us, even if it wouldn't be easy. But your dad's convinced himself that letting them in would be a betrayal to us. In his own funny way, he's refusing my request because he loves us."

I let the words sink in, try to make space for them.

She blows out a long breath. "Now, obviously he's scared, too. We all are. This is a lot. For all of us." She averts her eyes from the camera. "I've decided not to pressure him on this anymore. I don't want my last months—weeks, maybe—to be about guilting your father into something he's not sure he should do. Maybe, when I'm gone, he'll see things differently. And maybe not. Regardless, I love him anyway. I do not want to die holding this judgment over him. I hope you understand. And I hope you and your father find comfort in each other, in whatever life has in store for each of you. Honey, please forgive him."

She speaks a little longer, and then, "I guess it's time to say goodbye." She swallows and when she speaks again, her voice catches. "I love you, Scout. Remember that, my girl. Know I'm in God's hands and know that He loves you so much. Even more than I do, if that's possible. You're in His hands, too, okay? Don't forget that, my sweet girl. Until I see you in all the beauty and light of His presence. Goodbye, honey."

And then the screen turns black.

I still as a numbing sensation takes over my body. So many emotions vie for my attention. I don't know which one to feel first.

I stare at the screen. "Mom." My voice cracks. "I miss you. But the pain isn't as sharp as it used to be, you know? I'm sorry for that." I realize then that the biggest thing connecting me to my history and to my mom is Dad. "She's in jail, my half-sister. Ashley. And I've met her half-sister, have actually come to think of her as a younger sister myself." I keep staring at that blank screen as if Mom's somewhere behind there, listening to me. "It's all so messed up. But Dad told me last night Ashley's in jail. He visits her. He said I could come with him next time."

I still can't get over the invitation. He's inviting me in. He's trying to make things better, even in the hopeless mess.

"I've decided I'll go. I want to meet her, even if I'm kind of dreading it." My breaths come out in long, shaky quivers. "Thanks for the videos. I needed them." I raise the remote, turn off the television. "I love you."

I eject the disk and grab the lighthouse scrapbook from where it sits on the top of Mom's Bible. I flip through the scrapbook, going through each picture, one by one, beginning with West Quoddy.

Little River Light, Prospect Harbor Point, Fort Point Light, Owls Head Light, Rockland Breakwater Light . . .

I take in her smiling face alongside my tight-lipped one, an attempt not to show my braces. I acknowledge my grief but here, somehow, it feels different. I realize then that the pain of my grief might never go away, but how I relate to it has.

I think of Mom's voice.

Never be afraid of loving, Scout. It's the bravest thing you can do.

And then Zack's.

Broken things can be made whole.

I ponder my life, my future, the opportunities before me to choose life, to choose courage. I think of all the sturdy, silent lighthouses, of Mom's encouragement to be still in order to hear God's voice. I want that. I want light. I want hope. Maybe, I even want to surrender my control.

My phone rings. I see Reagan's name and sniff back the last of my emotion before answering in an upbeat voice. "Hey, Momma. Have a name for your daughter yet?"

"Scout . . ." She's crying. Hysterically.

I'm on my feet, that fierce wave of sisterly protection once again flowing through me. "Reagan, what's the matter? Are you okay? Is it . . ." *the baby?* I finish in my head.

"She's okay. I—I just got off the phone with Jaden's mom."

Jaden's mom. Jaden, right. The father of Reagan's baby.

"The social worker said I should tell Jaden, but I didn't think..."

"It's okay, Reagan. Calm down. What happened?"

Her breaths come out in hysterical quivers. "I told Jaden. I thought—thought he might be happy. Thought he might want to be a family."

I close my eyes. *No, Reagan.* I think of the camper in the Walmart parking lot, of Jaden unconscious on the laminate floor. Was *this* the plan Reagan had come up with?

"What did he say?" I try with all my might to restrain my judgment.

She's crying again. "He said he couldn't be a father, that we were better off without him."

I exhale a long breath. In my mind, I imagine the similar decision my father made with my half-sister so many years ago. It didn't seem that Ashley had been better off without him, but my father also hadn't been Jaden. "Honey, maybe . . . maybe he's right. You're a strong woman. You love that little girl of yours. You'll get through this together. And you're not alone."

"That's what I tried to convince myself of, but then Jaden's mother called me."

I bite the inside of my cheek as I wait for her to continue. I remember what she told me about how Jaden's parents blamed Reagan for their son's drug problem.

"She said I could never take care of a baby well enough, that I didn't have the means or the support. She threatened to take the baby, Scout."

"What?"

"When I told her I was planning to love my daughter and raise her on my own, she said she'd take me to court, that a judge would see I was an unfit mother in a second, that I had no chance against her. She's right, Scout. I am an unfit mother. I don't even have a home. I barely have a job." Her voice breaks off in tears. "Jaden's parents are rich. They can afford everything I can't. Including good lawyers. What am I going to do?" She's sobbing hysterically now, and my heart breaks for her. In that moment, I will do anything to alleviate her fears.

"Reagan, listen to me."

More sobs.

"Reagan." My voice is firm, controlled. "You need to listen to me."

Another minute before her sobs quiet to a pathetic muffle.

"No one is going to take your baby, okay?"

"How do you know that?"

"I talked to your doctor. The only way they can take your child is if they can prove you're an unfit mother."

"Being a sixteen-year-old girl who ran away from her foster parents and can't provide a home for her baby might do it."

That's right. There's still an entire story Reagan owns that I know nothing about. But I want to. And really, none of it matters at this point. A plan already forms in my mind.

"Do you have the social worker's name and number?"

"Um, yeah."

"Can you text it to me?"

"Scout, I hate to drag you into all this more than I already have."

I press my lips together. "I want to be in this. Besides, we're sisters, remember?"

She releases a half laugh, half sob into the phone. "About that . . . I'm sorry I didn't tell you sooner."

"I understand why you didn't. Text me that number. I'll call you in a little and try to make it in for a visit later today, okay?"

"Okay."

"In the meantime, just worry about healing up and taking care of that baby."

"Thank you, Scout. Thank you."

"Don't thank me yet." This was going to be a long, uphill road.

"Also, I think I have a name."

"You do?"

"Lucy. It means 'light.'"

I smile. "That's absolutely perfect."

I promise to call soon. We hang up, and a minute later I'm looking at the snapshot she sent of the social worker's card. I have no idea what I'm doing, but I know one thing—I have to do it.

Lucy. *Light*.

I feel an impossible bond with this tiny baby I've only met once through the thick glass of the NICU. To think of her as my niece might be a stretch. Or, it might be the very thought that propels me toward the courage to do the impossible.

Somewhere inside me, I feel the deep, urgent whispering of knowing. An insatiable love sweeps through me, along with the words I read in Mom's Bible.

The Holy Spirit is God's deepest self, loving our deepest self.

In an instant, it's as if all my life is sliding into place, leading me to this moment, a moment of both beautiful surrender and amazing possibilities.

"God," I whisper. "I'm here."

And for the first time, I know He is, too. And He will give me the courage to do the impossible.

Chapter Thirty-Eight

ZACK

By the time I'm finished cleaning up and loading my work van, I am more than ready for a reason to seek out Scout. She's been strangely absent all day and after our conversation last night, I can barely get her out of my head. I feel the press of time upon us, and I vow to make our date tonight as perfect as possible.

After I work on her car, of course. The car that will take her away from me and back to Massachusetts. I remember our plan to try the long-distance thing, to talk and learn more about one another across states. It should make me excited and hopeful, but it sours my stomach. People leave when they want out of a relationship. Priscilla. My dad. Even Mom was moving to Florida to get away from my father. How then, were Scout and I supposed to build a relationship so far apart?

I lightly knock on the back door of the bed and breakfast before entering. "Hello?"

Charlotte looks up from a cup of tea, her mouth in a serious line. Scout sits across from her, a mirrored expression on her own face, a scribble of words on a notepad in front of her.

"Hey. Just wanted to say hi."

Scout smiles, but it lacks enthusiasm. "Hey." Her gaze floats to the numbers and words on the notepad.

"I'm going to go work on your car now. We still on for tonight?"

A ghost of a smile crosses her face. What is going on?

"Oh, yeah, sure. Looking forward to it." Her tone is distracted, anything but convincing.

I look to Charlotte, who's staring into her tea, then back to Scout. "Everything okay?"

She clears her throat. "Yeah, just working out a few things. Thanks for taking care of my car, Zack. You're really sweet."

Sweet. Why do I feel I've been demoted?

"No problem."

I retreat through the back door and head to my work van, but I can't shake the uneasiness climbing my insides. Something's up. And I'm not convinced it's only a passing distraction.

Two and a half hours later, the old manifold's out of the car and I'm losing daylight. Wiping my greasy hands on a rag, I again knock on the back door of the house before heading in. I catch Scout rounding the corner, purse slung over an arm. Charlotte grabs her keys.

I cock my head. "You guys going somewhere?" Without a car?

"Zack!" Scout slaps her head. "I am so sorry. I totally forgot about dinner."

My heart sinks. How could she forget? We just talked about it. It's all I've been thinking about all day. We have three days left. "What's going on?"

"Charlotte and I have to meet the social worker at the hospital. I was so involved with . . . I'm sorry. Can I get a raincheck?"

A raincheck.

I realize then that this is all a terrible repeat of Priscilla. Once again, I am way more into the relationship, way more invested, than the person I'm falling in love with. How in the world will a long-distance relationship work when we can't communicate short distance over dinner plans?

"Um—yeah, sure. I'm making progress with your car."

But Scout scoops up the notepad on the dining table, takes a sip of the dregs of her tea.

"You guys need a ride to the hospital?"

"Laney offered. She wanted to visit Reagan."

Another twinge of disappointment.

Just stay here and fix my car, handyman Zack.

I try to brush off the words pricking my mind. "Okay. Can we talk later?"

"Yes, definitely." She strides over and gives me a side hug. Charlotte places a hand on my arm and gives a reassuring smile. Ugh. Not reassuring. It's a pity smile. I got loads of them after Priscilla left.

The next moment, Laney pulls up the drive. I walk out with them and wave goodbye.

No one seems to notice.

AN HOUR LATER, I'm showered, the grease on my hands finally coming off with a chemical wash I bought that's probably strong enough to eat my insides. The scent of bacon lingers in the kitchen, and I bite into my homemade Egg McMuffin, the comforting taste doing little to soothe my troubled thoughts.

I finish my meal, do the dishes, then sit down to work on a plan for starting the West Street Historic District project. I'd been so pumped. Tonight, though, even that has lost the glow of excitement.

Scout leaves in three days. She barely looked at me as she

promised to call and gave me a quick afterthought of a hug. I can't get Charlotte's sympathetic smile out of my mind.

My doorbell rings and adrenaline rushes to my limbs. Scout? But no, she would have called.

Atticus barks once and trots after me, his paws padding softly on the hardwood floor. I peer through the long side window near the door.

My breath catches in my throat, and I stumble back, shaking off what I'm sure is a horrible vision of my own making. Maybe a nightmare?

But when the doorbell rings again and I risk another look out the window, there's no denying who's standing at my threshold. The question is whether to open the door or not.

I sway toward the door handle, then lean back, vacillating over whether to put my hand on the knob. How many times had I dreamed of this moment? Now . . . now, I want her gone. I consider returning to my kitchen, pretending I'm not home. Why is she here? And why now, at the worst possible time?

But that's ludicrous, of course. I'm a grown man. There is no need to be scared of a woman. I inhale a breath of air before thrusting open the door.

"Priscilla."

She smiles at me, her face as flawless as I remember, even beneath the harsh porch light. "Zack. Hi."

We stare at one another while Atticus performs excited circles around her legs. She ignores him.

"I—uh, I hope it's okay I showed up. I was visiting my family and . . . I couldn't stop thinking about you."

I swallow, my throat thick.

She shifts her weight from one foot to the other, drawing attention to her generous curves clad in jeans and a tight zip-up sweatshirt. Her very presence, the scent of her flowery shampoo, pulls memories from me. Memories of a different time, a time when I thought this woman was my future. A time when I prayed about and anticipated our life together.

"I owe you an apology." She licks her glossy lips. Atticus gives up his circling and sits, staring up at her expectantly as he waits for a pat. I know from experience he won't get it. "I never should have left without talking to you. I was scared, Zack. Scared about what you offered, scared about how I felt about you."

I squeeze my eyes shut. "You were scared about how you felt about me?"

"I know it sounds stupid, but . . . " She glances behind me. "Can I come in?"

I stand my ground. "I don't think that's a good idea."

Her bottom lip trembles and she turns bright eyes toward me. "I made a mistake, Zack. A big one. I miss you."

I can't deny that her words and presence test my resolve. I've spent so many nights imagining this exact scenario that it's hard to believe it's happening. It's hard not to be moved by it.

But then an image of Scout standing on the walk of the Beacon comes to mind. I remember the feel of her in my arms. Beside Scout, Priscilla is nothing but a smudge of history. Scout . . . Scout is it for me. She is the one who makes the brokenness inside me feel restored.

But Scout is leaving.

She wants to see how things go over the phone.

A lead weight falls into my stomach. Three more days and Scout is gone.

I stare at Priscilla. Maybe I was wrong to write her off. She's come back. Love can choose to return.

A flash of my parents tears through my mind, but I push it aside. I can't think of anything with the scent of Priscilla surrounding me.

"I'm sorry, Priscilla. You should have called."

Hurt carves her features. "I mean it, Zack. Leaving you was the stupidest thing I've ever done. I had a lot of growing up to do this past year, I realize that now. I just want a second chance. I'll do anything."

The exact words I want my father to say to my mother.

She drifts closer. "Please forgive me."

There is honor in realizing we messed up. Honor in forgiving, even. Maybe she'd felt exactly what I'd felt but had been scared.

She leans in, the scent of her teasing me with the future I once thought could be mine. It would take little effort for me to close the gap.

But I can't, because all I can see is Scout.

Instead, Priscilla pushes up on her toes and attempts to press her lips to mine, just as a set of headlights shine on us. I pull back, but not before the sound of a car pulling into my driveway pulls my attention toward Laney's Honda.

The pale light from the porch shines through the glass of the passenger window. That's when I see Scout's face, etched with betrayal.

I look to Priscilla, then back toward the car. But Laney is already in reverse, pulling out of my driveway. It doesn't matter that I'm running down the two stairs of my porch. Doesn't matter that I'm screaming Scout's name at the top of my lungs.

All that matters is that the woman I'm falling in love with is running away.

Chapter Thirty-Nine

I understand—really understand—why Mom said loving is the bravest thing you can do. Because loving means risking hurt. Risking the most precious thing we have, our heart.

~ SCOUT SWIFT'S JOURNAL

Two hours ago, my life was falling into place.

That's all I can think about as Laney drives me through the dark streets of downtown Bar Harbor, silence coating the inside of her car. I squeeze my eyes shut, try with all my might to push back the hurt.

But all I can feel is the slow realization that I've once again been left, abandoned, betrayed.

"Scout—"

I shake my head against the start of Laney's sentence. "Please, not yet."

I think of the clarity I gained earlier in the day. The sense of God's presence. My long talk with Charlotte. I think of our meeting with the social worker in a private room in the hospital while Laney visited with Reagan and Lucy.

The social worker, Adrianna, had asked me and Charlotte so many questions, my head hurt. What was my relationship with Reagan? What were my plans for employment? What was the shape of my savings account? Did I have any idea how inconvenient living with a baby was?

I'd answered her questions as best I could.

Finally, she'd closed her laptop. "This is just the beginning, Ms. Swift. We have to run background checks and survey your living area. But I can see you have a heart to do this. I can see you both do. With Reagan's history and her lack of options, I'd say this is likely the best possible scenario for her."

I remember nodding. When we walked into Reagan's hospital room after our meeting, her brow furrowed at the sight of the three of us together.

Adrianna stepped forward. "Reagan, I'm hoping to speak to you alone before you all visit. Would that be okay?"

She nodded, slowly, cautiously, her gaze on mine. I smiled my encouragement. Charlotte and I waited outside in the hall as Adrianna spoke with Reagan.

I'd paced the laminate floor outside her room so many times it's a wonder I didn't wear a hole through it. "What do you think she's saying?"

Charlotte placed a hand on my arm. "She's telling Reagan that no one can take her baby but that there are two people willing to help her and invest in her and love her and that little girl if she's willing to let them."

I hugged Charlotte then, the stress of the day finally melting as we held one another. "Thank you, Charlotte. Thank you for doing this."

"Honey, I am beyond excited. This place has been far too lonely for too long now. I have my granddaughter back, now I have you and Reagan and that darling baby."

"We won't be a bother. I promise. We'll help as much as we can."

"You've offered to pay rent. I don't expect extra help."

I didn't remind her that the rental price she quoted me is far less than what she could charge for the cottage. But she assured me the loss wouldn't be so great considering we planned to pay year-round.

I'd called Elise and regretfully informed her I would not be returning, explaining the circumstances as best I could. And although my savings afforded me some time without a job, when she offered a hearty recommendation, I thanked her. Surely, I'd be able to find another pharmacy technician job in the area.

And, if not, maybe it was time to explore other avenues. Twelve years ago, I'd landed in a Walmart because I was stuck and in need of a job. This time—this time, maybe things would be different.

When Adrianna finally emerged from the hospital room and ushered us in, my stomach was in a knot of doubts. Maybe Reagan would refuse our help. Maybe, not knowing Ashley was in jail, she'd try to seek her out. Maybe she'd go back to Jaden or even Jaden's parents.

But the sight of Adrianna's smile and Reagan's fragile form, wilted and weeping beneath the blankets in the hospital bed, pulled hope through me.

Reagan pressed a tissue to her eyes. "I can't understand why you guys would do this for me. I don't deserve it."

Charlotte went to one side of the bed, and I took the other. She laid a hand on Reagan's arm. "That's grace, my dear girl. But don't give me too much credit—it was all Scout's idea."

"What about your job? What about Massachusetts?"

I exchanged a glance with Charlotte. "I think I'm finally ready to come home."

We both wound our arms around Reagan. There was still a lot to work out. It wouldn't be perfect—in fact it would be downright hard at times, but I also knew that this decision was probably the most important, worthy decision of my life.

For the first time, I was giving up control. I was leaning into the whisperings of the Holy Spirit.

This, being light in the unexpected places, this was the legacy Mom had left me. This was what I wanted my life to be about.

Now, as Laney turns on her high beams to navigate the empty road, I let out a slow, quivering breath. I feel my phone vibrating inside my purse, knowing intuitively it's Zack, but don't answer it.

After Laney had dropped Charlotte off at the Beacon, I'd asked her to take me to Zack's. I'd been so excited to tell him I was staying in Maine. Not just for Reagan, but for him, too.

Don't get me wrong, I'd give up everything for the opportunity to help Reagan and her child again if I had to, but a part of me couldn't deny that a very hefty bonus was the idea of staying near Zack. Having the space and time to see if we could build a life together. Sure, there was the matter of a teenager and her baby I'd now be legally responsible for. But Reagan was no slouch. She would do more than her share to pull her weight. She'd matured a lot in the last several weeks.

I had a feeling motherhood could do that to a person.

I'd been so excited to tell Zack. Nervous too, of course. Maybe he'd hate the idea of me giving up some of my freedom. But I didn't think so.

Then, Laney had pulled into his driveway. I'd had my fingers on the handle of the car door, ready to hop out and run up his walk, bang on his door and fall into his arms, tell him I was staying, tell him the entire story while Atticus circled excitedly around us.

But the only part of my vision to come to fruition was Atticus. Atticus near Zack, yes. Zack and another woman.

I couldn't make my brain agree with my eyes. Couldn't understand what was plain before me. Zack on his threshold, about to kiss another woman. "Who . . ." I'd said, my hand still on the latch of the car door.

"Priscilla," Laney breathed, so quiet I could scarce hear her words.

I squeezed my eyes shut, desperate to erase the vision of her shapely form standing on tiptoes to meet his lips, desperate to erase what was sure to come next had we not interrupted.

"Go, please."

"Scout, don't you think you should—"

I squeezed my eyes shut. "Laney, now. Go. Please, please, please." I could not handle such a rejection. I needed to flee, run away, as far as I could.

Do what I did best.

Now, Laney pulls into Charlotte's drive. When she's in front of the house, she puts the car in park. "Can I say something?" Her voice is quiet, guarded, vulnerable, even.

I nod, the small gesture requiring all my strength.

She inhales. "I spent most of my life basing some of my most important relationships on misunderstandings. On thinking the worst of people. I wish I hadn't."

Anger spews up within me. "Laney, you saw them, right? There's no denying . . ." I gulp down the unspoken words.

"All I'm saying, Scout, is that I know Zack. I'd trust him with my life. He's a good guy. Give him the benefit of the doubt."

Again, my phone vibrates in my purse. Again, I ignore it. "I can't unsee what I saw." This is just how it is to be with me, then. I think of Greg driving away with my money while I'm peeing in a Walmart bathroom. I think of Dad keeping the secret from Mom that he had another child. I even think of Tom, the customer at Walmart, flirting with me and asking about my hikes and light-houses, only to show up with another woman flaunting their shared love for hummus crisps. Then, finally, and maybe most painfully, I think of Zack, about to kiss his old girlfriend. The woman he'd thought he'd be with forever.

And I can't.

"Thanks for the ride, Laney. Thank you for being Reagan's friend."

She smiles. "She's a special girl." Her gaze flicks to me. "I've had my struggles too, you know. I think Reagan and I bonded around that. Maybe someday soon we can talk? Get to know one another better?"

"Turns out I'll be around for a while." But while I don't regret my hasty decision, it has dulled to a different color—black and white instead of vibrant, bold hues bursting with promise. What will it be like to live in this town, to see Zack working on Charlotte's house? Ugh, what if I have to see him with Priscilla?

"You'll come to the wedding, right?"

Zack will be there. He's Jason's best man.

"Can I think on that?"

"Of course."

I open the door of the car. "Thanks again, Laney."

"Goodnight, Scout. I'm praying for you and Reagan and little Lucy."

"Thank you."

I shut the car door behind me and walk the path toward the guest cottage. I let myself inside, dump my bag on the couch, slip off my sneakers, and collapse on the nearest chair. On the coffee table in front of me is Mom's scrapbook and Bible.

I drop my head in my hands, utter a wordless prayer to a God I'd been so sure was guiding my steps. Had I been wrong? Sure, possessing His presence didn't mean life would be smooth and easy. Mom's certainly hadn't been. I could only pray that His presence did mean I wouldn't have to go through the hard stuff alone.

I scoop up the scrapbook and start at the back with the most recent pictures, missing her all the more for watching the videos.

Maybe finishing this project isn't doable. Maybe it was never even the point or the reason behind the urgency in my dreams. Maybe it was simply God's way of getting me back here to help Reagan, to make amends with my dad, to draw me back to Him.

Why do I think I need to even give it reason or organize it into neat little compartments? But I know. Because I'm me.

I realize in that moment I didn't wash my hands, the first thing I always do when I come home. A good practice, of course. But this is the first time I can acknowledge this hygiene sin and not be bowled over by it. I'm changing. I think that's a good thing.

Only, perhaps not good enough for Zack.

I remember him asking me to stick around, to take a chance. He told me he had a feeling. All nice things, but nothing concrete. That kiss with Priscilla proved how some things never change. Once again, I'd been fooled by a man.

I groan.

I let the book slip to the floor, lean my head in my arms, and close my eyes. "God, there's so much . . . I don't have words. Give me strength."

Never be afraid of loving, Scout. It's the bravest thing you can do.

I think of Mom, basking in the light of West Quoddy, marveling at the sun's ability to touch every person on earth in a single day, marveling at God's ability to do the same.

"I'm giving it to you," I whisper. "I'm giving up my right to be angry. Maybe even my right to sulk. Help me to focus on Reagan and Lucy, on being a light in this hurting world."

I can't think of anything more to say. I just close my eyes, feel the nonsensical peace that winds through my spirit. When I finally open them, my gaze lands on the open page of the scrapbook.

The first page. The picture of me and Mom at West Quoddy. That beautiful dove-like cloud, like a white cotton ball of perfect fluff, against a cerulean backdrop of sky.

I blink. That cloud. It looks familiar, from something more than this picture. I search the recesses of my brain. Is it just because I watched the videos of Mom that everything seems so much more recent? Where have I seen that cloud? Did I even see it anywhere besides this picture? Did I dream it?

It hits me all at once. The memory comes with a surge of

eureka followed by a quick moment of disappointment. Still though, I pull out my phone, pushing the many notifications from Zack out of the way to go into our text thread. I scroll to the picture he sent me of the two of us in front of Bass Harbor Light. Our smiling faces, the gorgeous rocks, edges smoothed for centuries by crashing waves, the iconic lighthouse in the background, and finally—there, above us in the pink of the setting sun, a cloud identical to the one in the West Quoddy picture.

I close my eyes, open them again, and still it's there. I remember Mom's voice as she placed this picture in the scrapbook.

"A dove. A symbol of the Holy Spirit."

"What do you think it means?"

"It doesn't have to mean anything, but I like that it's in our picture. I like that it reminds me of God's Spirit—His promise to us that we'll never be alone."

I place my phone alongside the scrapbook to compare the images. I zoom in a bit on my phone and shake my head in amazement. Every curve, every line and darkening gray that makes the cloud look to have obvious wings, is identical. The only thing different is the slight coloring—West Quoddy's cloud being bright and white in the middle of the day, and the Bass Head cloud taking on a pinkish-purple hue in the light of the setting sun.

I think there's something there for you.

Is this what Mom had been talking about? Is this what God or some crazy sense of intuition had insinuated when she made the video for me?

And why? What did it mean? I never believed Mom was turned into some heavenly angelic being that watched over me night and day, mostly because she would have scoffed at the thought herself. But I can't deny that something about the cloud fills me with hope. At the very least, that God would form this memorable image for a second time in my lifetime, just for me, feels like a promise. A promise that He cares. That He's still here, guiding me.

My gaze falls to Zack, smiling at me from my phone. If only that sweet symbol meant Zack could be included.

A soft knock sounds at the door, and I jump.

"Scout, it's me."

Zack.

I look down at the picture, the fierce need to guard my heart swelling within me. But Mom's voice comes to me again.

Never be afraid of loving, Scout. It's the bravest thing you can do.

Even in the hurt, Mom?

There's no answer, just the picture of us smiling in front of West Quoddy. Would I trade all those moments, all those years with my mother, if it saved me the pain of going through her sickness and death?

I know the answer in a moment. Legs heavy, I drag myself to my feet.

Chapter Forty

The light shines in the darkness,
and the darkness has not overcome it.
John 1:5

~ SCOUT SWIFT'S JOURNAL

I open the door, not at all sure it's the wisest decision. The light from the cottage living room falls on Zack's form. He practically wilts against the doorframe.

"Thank you. Thank you for answering."

I fold my arms in front of me.

"Scout, I know what you think you saw, but believe me when I tell you there was nothing happening there."

I turn around and walk back inside the house, an unspoken invitation for him to come inside. If Charlotte has her bedroom window open, there's no way she needs to hear this conversation.

"I don't know what to think, Zack. But I know what I saw."

He closes the door behind him. "That was Priscilla. She

showed up without calling, told me she missed me. We were on the threshold because I wouldn't let her inside. Yes, she tried to kiss me and yes, her showing up threw me for a loop. But not because I still have feelings for her—because her showing up is the kind of happy ending I want for my parents."

I don't know what to say to that, don't even know if I buy it.

He continues. "I told you the other night that I wanted to help make you whole, but that wasn't the entire truth."

I press my lips together, bracing myself.

"The truth is, I'm broken, too. And when I'm around you, I feel like I can be put back together again."

His words serve to thaw the rough edges around my heart. Still . . . "Zack, we can't just be each other's Band-Aids. We each have our own issues. Issues we might need to work out alone."

He steps closer. "Or maybe we help one another. Maybe we wade through it without pushing each other away."

"I'm just not sure that's how that works." I close my eyes. "I found my faith again today. It's fragile. What if it can't take any more hurt?"

He rubs the back of his neck. "We go slow. Even if it's long distance, even if you were in China and I could only see you once a year, I want to be with you, Scout."

Emotion clamps down on my throat. "I want to believe you..."

"Do it, then. Believe me."

"It's not that simple. I can't just decide to believe something I can't see. And . . . a lot changed for me these last two days."

"Like how you feel about me?"

I throw a hand into the air. "Like, I have a half-sister I don't know who's in jail. Like, I'm about to become the legal guardian to a teenager with a baby. Like, I quit my job and I'm moving. Here, Zack. Because it's where I need to be. It's where Reagan needs to be."

He blinks. "You're not leaving?"

"No."

"You're not leaving?"

"I'm not."

He bends his knees a bit so he's looking directly in my eyes. "Scout, you're not leaving?"

"No! And now I have to walk around this blasted town wondering if I'm going to run into you and Miss New York all the rest of my days!"

He's giving me a goofy smile. "You care about me."

"I said no such thing."

But he can't get rid of that dopy look on his face. "You do. You care about me."

"Zack, so help me. I'm not twelve years old anymore—"

"Scout, I'm not going to be walking around town with Miss New York. Want to know why?"

I raise an eyebrow.

"Because I sent her away and told her there was never a reason for us to see each other again. I told her I'm seeing someone else. And the only one I want to be walking around town with is you."

I press my lips together, shut my eyes. "Did you hear me, Zack? I'm going to be in charge of two minors. And even after Reagan ages out, she's going to be a part of my life. She's going to be my sister."

"Sign me up, too."

He has got to be joking.

Is he joking?

I lower myself to the chair in front of the scrapbook and my phone. "I don't trust easily and you're already on shaky footing."

He kneels in front of me, carefully sliding the scrapbook out of the way. "We've all been hurt, Scout. But I want us to heal, together. Be brave with me . . . please?"

I'm silent, weighing the options of hurt against that of love. My gaze lands on the West Quoddy picture, the white dove cloud like a promise above me and Mom. I think of the pink cloud above me and Zack in front of Bass Head.

Never be afraid of loving, Scout. It's the bravest thing you can do. I think there's something there for you.

Maybe Mom was right. Maybe I did find what I was looking for.

Zack folds my hands in his own. "I'm pretty handy at building things. But this—us—maybe it's something we can build together."

"I can't decide if that's romantic or totally corny."

He tilts his head. "Can't it be both?" He grows serious. "You're the only woman in the world I want to kiss. And it's driving me mad because we haven't yet."

My gaze drops to his lips. I could still back out. There's a lot of unknowns, a lot of what-ifs. But if I pull away now, I'd never know. Never know if I was missing out on one of the best things this world has to offer.

I close the gap, and when his lips meet mine, I grow pleasantly dizzy. We sink into each other, tasting, falling. The soft gesture turns more urgent as his hands curl around my waist. My hands come up to his arms, feeling the hard muscles beneath his T-shirt.

Oh my, I seriously might swoon. I cannot think of a single coherent thought aside from him.

It has been years since I've kissed anyone, but I know it's never been this good. It's as if he's absorbing me. I can't think about anything but the closeness of him, the subtle scent of cinnamon and spice and woodsmoke.

It's scary. It feels like falling, and I think that maybe Mom was right about this, too.

Loving is the bravest thing you can do. But it also might be the worthiest, as well.

/ Chapter Forty-One

ZACK

I pace in front of The Coffee Hound and scour the sidewalk
for my father. His office isn't far from here. It was hard
enough to call him to meet up. He should have had the
decency to show up on time.

I force a breath of coffee-scented air into my lungs as I check
my thoughts. While I can't claim I've arrived at any perfect state
of acceptance and forgiveness, I'd like to think I've come a
long way.

I have Scout to thank for that. Scout and a renewed faith I've
found alongside her.

"Zack, sorry I'm late." Dad jogs up to me, obviously winded.
"I couldn't get out of a meeting with a client." He gives me an
awkward hug.

"It's okay."

"I was glad you called." He jerks his thumb in the direction of
the coffee shop. "Coffee on me?"

I nod. We go in and order two coffees. Once they're in hand, I
take the lead to go back outside. "Can we walk to the park?" What

I have to say will be better said in open air, without an audience amid cramped walls.

"Absolutely."

We walk in silence for a minute.

"Heard you got the West Street job. Congratulations."

"I appreciate the referral."

"Well, you earned it. Brad doesn't hire anyone unless he feels good about it."

I gesture to an empty bench in front of Agamont Park. We sit, and I gaze across the clear water to Bar Island. Scout and I walked there the other night after our first official dinner date. For the thousandth time, I'm grateful she's giving me a chance. She could have written me off after seeing Priscilla nearly kiss me, but she didn't. She forgave me, agreed to see where a relationship could go.

It's made me think twice about second chances and forgiveness. One of the reasons I called Dad.

"Mom told me she's moving to Florida." He takes a sip of his coffee.

"Yeah, I think it will be good for her." I wrap my hands around the warm paper of my cup. "So, you guys talk?"

"We're trying to keep things as civil as we can. It's not practical to pretend we weren't married for thirty-five years."

For a split second, I want to spew out a cutting remark. *You sure had no trouble pretending you weren't married all that time, did you, Dad?*

I bite the inside of my cheek. Maybe this anger would always be a struggle, maybe a part of me would always be bitter about my father's actions. But adding fuel to the fire wouldn't help.

I drag in a long breath. "I've been really angry at you, Dad. And I'd be lying if I said I'm not still struggling with that. But I'm also realizing that I can't control you by being angry. You're my dad and . . ." I planned to tell him I've forgiven him, but I'm not sure that's true. "I'm trying to forgive you."

Like I said, I hadn't arrived.

Dad's Adam's apple bobs. "Thank you."

I acknowledged with Scout that I'm as broken as anyone. But together we're talking and praying. We're both realizing that our wholeness is not dependent on the people around us acting a certain way. It's dependent on what God has already done for us and the promise of what He will do in the end—restore all things.

This side of His kingdom, I can only strive to do my best to trust Him and work to make that happen, starting here, in my relationship with my dad.

"I don't want us to be strangers," Dad chokes out.

"Me neither."

"And eventually, I'd like you to meet Leslie."

I shift in my seat. "It was a big step for me to call you. I don't know if I'll be ready for that anytime soon."

He nods, hard. "I respect that. For now, maybe we could plan a round of golf sometime?"

"Yeah, I think we could do that. And maybe you can come by West Street and tell me what you think every now and then."

He beams. "I'd like that, son. I'd like that a lot."

Ours will never be a perfect relationship. But I'm coming to realize that's not what relationships are about.

They're about commitment and growth and love. And if I'm leaning toward all those things, then I guess I can't go wrong.

Chapter Forty-Two

Whatever my mom envisioned when she made those videos for me in hopes I'd reconcile with my dad, I doubt very much it looked anything like this.

~ SCOUT SWIFT'S JOURNAL

I walk into the jail with my dad as if this isn't the weirdest thing we've ever done together.

"You told her about me?" My stomach trembles as we approach the doors of the jail.

"I did." Dad acts as if I haven't already asked this question several times.

"And she's okay with meeting me."

"They wouldn't have approved your application if she wasn't."

"Oh."

He stops in front of the door. "This means a lot to me, Scout. Your being here."

A smile tips my mouth. "If Mom could see us now."

"Right?" He grows serious. "I want you to know, Ashley

hasn't been very receptive to my visits. I don't want you to expect much."

I try to put myself in the shoes of my half-sister. Her dad only makes one attempt to see her in her entire life but decides to be persistent after she lands herself in jail. Tough situation.

Dad guides me toward security, where I hand over my license. I leave behind my cell phone and purse, only a printed photograph in hand.

We walk into a large room with several white tables and two security guards. We're told where to sit. I place the picture face-down beside me on the table.

After several minutes, four women inmates in gray uniforms file into the room. I scan each one, trying not to look overeager. When my gaze lands on a woman several years older than me with brown hair pulled back in a low ponytail, I know it's her. My half-sister's features are very similar to mine, a bit harder and older, but there is no denying we are related.

My gaze flicks to my dad. I wonder how he felt when he saw her the first time, if seeing her stopped him in his tracks, cemented the reality of it all for him as it did for me in this moment.

She flops down on the chair on the other side of the table from us, places her arms on the table.

"Hi, Ashley," Dad says.

She ignores him but looks at me, blinks. "This is her?"

Dad clears his throat. "Yes, this is Scout."

"It's nice to meet you." I've been told we are not allowed to have physical contact, but I do wish I could offer my hand.

She presses her lips together, blinks fast. "How is she? My sister?"

It takes me a second to realize she must be talking about Reagan. Somewhere deep down, she does care about her.

I pass her the picture. It's one I took last week. In it, Reagan sits in one of Charlotte's porch rocking chairs, tiny Lucy tucked in her arms. She looks rested, at peace, content.

Ashley swallows and blinks. "She has a baby?" She swears. "She's too young."

"I'm watching out for them both. They're doing well."

Ashley nods, hands the picture back to me.

I don't take it. "It's yours, if you want it. Reagan told me to tell you hello."

Ashley's eyes glisten. "You think she'd ever come here?" She directs the question to my father, who looks at me.

"I think she needs a little time to adjust to becoming a mother first, but yeah, she said she wants to see you."

A single, small tear travels from her brown eyes down her cheek. "I have to go to the bathroom." She stands, looks at me. "Thank you, for this."

And then she's gone.

Ten minutes later, when Dad and I slide back into his truck, I release a long breath. "I'm not sure I'd call that a successful visit, but we did it."

"Are you kidding? That's the most she's ever talked. Usually, it's just me monologuing. I think her record was three words before today."

I sit up straighter. "Oh."

"Listen, Scout, there's no obligation for you to come again. It's not your responsibility or duty or whatever."

I place my hand on his, a warmth I haven't felt in years toward him rushing through me. "No, it's okay. I want to do this together."

He squeezes my fingers. "Okay, then."

When he puts the truck in drive, I understand that sometimes, forgiveness doesn't happen all at once. Sometimes, it's a mental assent, but other times, it's a know-it-in-your-heart-feeling. A hint of a promise that broken things can indeed be made whole.

And that's what I feel right now as my father drives us off into the sunset.

Chapter Forty-Three

Broken things can be made whole.

~ SCOUT SWIFT'S JOURNAL

Six Weeks Later

"Scout, Zack, come meet Lizzie and Asher!" Laney, beautiful in a lacy white wedding gown, waves me over alongside her and Jason. She introduces me to a petite dark-haired woman named Lizzie and her husband Asher, who sits in a wheelchair with a sleeping toddler in his arms. The small girl has a smudge of chocolate cake on her face and looks just like her mother.

I hold out my hand. "It's nice to meet you."

"Lizzie's family owns the Orchard House Bed and Breakfast."

"You guys sounded great together," Zack says, referring to the song the duo sang for Laney and Jason's first dance as man and wife.

"She carries us." Asher grins at his wife.

"I'd introduce you to the entire family, but it'd take the rest of the night. I'm actually still learning all their names." Laney slips her hand into Jason's.

Lizzie waves her off. "You go enjoy being a bride."

MC Hammer's "Can't Touch This" starts up, and we all move to the dance floor. Zack surprises me with his dance moves. We're laughing, having a great time. When "Wonderful Tonight" comes on, he pulls me close. Inside the large barn-turned-reception-hall of the Orchard House Bed and Breakfast, on the dance floor amid the other couples, the moment feels incredibly private.

"How are you doing?" he whispers into my ear.

"You mean am I worrying about Reagan and Lucy alone at the B&B?"

"That's exactly what I mean."

I laugh. "I know they're fine. It's nice to have a night out with you."

Not that we haven't done plenty of that. While Reagan is self-sufficient and Lucy sleeps surprisingly well for a newborn, a baby is still a lot of work. But there's no denying all of us have fallen desperately in love with her.

As for me, I never felt so exhausted or so incredibly content. A newfound, deep peace resides in my bones these days, and it's stemming from the time I've been praying, the time I've been practicing forgiveness, the time I've been allowing myself to be forgiven and, in doing so, regaining my humanity.

"Anyone ever tell you that you look really good in a suit?" I ask.

"No one that counted."

"Do I count?" I ask, flirting, teasing.

His fingers tighten on my waist, pulling me closer. "You count the most, Scout Swift. In case you can't tell, I'm kind of in love with you."

The wings of a hummingbird flitter in my stomach, stirring warmth from my center outward toward my limbs. "You are?"

He holds my gaze. "Like you didn't know."

I laugh. "I had a hunch, but I guess it's nice to be told."

He raises a hand to my cheek, tenderly runs his fingers down toward my jawline. "Well, I do." He dips his head and lowers his voice. "I love you for how determined and stubborn and kind you are. I love you for helping a pregnant teenager. I love you for how you fold your napkin exactly in half before placing it on your lap before breakfast. I love you because when I smell Purell now, it makes me think of you. I love you for how beautiful you are, for how Atticus loves you. Scout, I love you because when I told you that broken things could be made whole and I wanted a part in that, I wasn't just thinking about your brokenness—I was thinking about mine. You make me whole, Scout."

I reach up to kiss him. When I sink into his warmth, it feels like the final puzzle piece slips into place.

When our lips part, I snuggle closer to him. He wraps his arms tighter around me and I savor his grip.

"Oh." I lift my head off his chest a moment later. "I never asked you how it went yesterday."

"We broke ground. I feel good about the plans, the guys I hired. It'll be a lot of work, but I'm up for it. Dad came by yesterday. It was . . . good. Not easy, but good. I'm getting there with the forgiveness thing, I think."

We both had a lot of forgiving to do. And we were helping each other through it.

"What about you? How did it go yesterday?"

I shrug. "About the same. She doesn't understand why we keep coming. She's difficult, but if I lived her story, I probably would be, too." Like clockwork, Dad and I visit Ashley every two weeks. We bring her what we can—underclothes and Charlotte's treats and news of Reagan's Visitor Application, but she has yet to allow us past the tough shell she's erected.

We don't push too hard, but we do vow to keep up the visits. There's nothing we can do but show up and leave the rest to God.

In the meantime, Dad and I are talking. Really talking. He offered to pay my rent to Charlotte every three months and, sensing he truly wanted to give me this, I've let him. He and Brenda have invited me and Zack over for dinner. The biggest surprise? I actually like Brenda. Like, a lot.

And it doesn't feel like a betrayal to Mom. In fact, I feel like she would be okay with it.

Lexie, Reagan, and I have continued with writing group. Sometimes, we'll go out for ice cream or dinner with Kiran and the other women.

I've set up a bird feeder outside the cottage. Seeing them reminds me of Jesus' words about not worrying. I never enjoyed my little winged companions so much.

I've also taken out my paints again, and it's when I put brush to paper that I find it easiest to be still in God's presence . . . to be still in the storms of life, just like one of my lighthouses.

I'm finding my place here, in a way I never did in Massachusetts. I found a therapist who's helping me process my past. I'm going to church with Zack and Charlotte and Reagan, finding meaning and worth in a faith I'm beginning to call my own. I start my new part-time pharmacy tech job downtown next week. I've enrolled in fall classes at the local community college with the possible goal of becoming a social worker.

"Where to tomorrow?" Zack nuzzles my head with his chin as we dance.

We've been ticking off the lighthouses one by one, tackling one every week or two, enjoying the unrushed adventure of it all. We stopped at Curtis Island Light Overlook this morning. "I'm thinking West Quoddy if you're up for it."

He pulls back. "Didn't you already check that one off?"

"Yes. But I think I'd like to visit it with you. Share the spot where the light first touches the earth with the man I love."

His smile freezes. "Love, huh?"

I let my fingers trail along the skin at the base of his neck. "Love."

He pulls me as close as is proper on the dance floor. "I love you, Scout. I don't think I'll ever get tired of saying that, and I'm looking forward to many more adventures with you."

I snuggle into his arms, the familiar feeling of coming home overtaking me.

But it's not just Zack. It's this misfit family I'm a part of. It's finding my place in the world and with God.

It's about chasing after the light, and when I stumble, getting up and chasing it again and again. Because I'm learning that the Light is the way home.

Acknowledgments

Wow, I can't believe we're here again! As I sit down to write this, I am most grateful for you, dear reader. Thank you for continuing to seek out my books. You make this dream possible!

A huge thank you to Sandra Ardoin, Melissa Jagears, Donna Anuszczyk, Darlene Wilson, Erin Laramore, and Priscilla Nix for reading this book at different stages of its journey. You all are amazing!

Thank you to Hannah Linder for this beautiful cover and always to my supportive family, Daniel, James, and Noah.

Most of all, thank you to the Creator for giving me words and stories that long to be told. May they honor you.

Hope Beyond the Waves

Turn the page to read a sample of
Hope Beyond the Waves!

Chapter One

Osterville, Massachusetts
April, 1993

I stand rigid, arms pinned to my sides as my mother wraps me in a loose hug in Gram's foyer.

"I'm so glad we thought of this arrangement," she says.

Arrangement. As if shipping me off and hiding me away is a plan we'd come up with together.

My father kisses me on the forehead, but it's awkward. Probably a show for my grandmother. He's kissed plenty of babies on the campaign trail, after all—this is likely no different.

"Be good, Sweet Pea." He turns to my grandmother, who barely comes up to his armpits. "Keep in touch, Mom. Don't hesitate to call if..." His gaze flicks to me and he doesn't finish his sentence.

What? Does he think I'll find a cute boy in Gram's retirement village? One who will get me in bigger trouble than Bryan already has?

"Oh, we'll be perfectly fine, won't we, Emily?" Gram smiles up at me, her lips the color of the Radio Flyer wagon I had as a child.

As much as I want my parents to leave—and don't want them to leave all at the same time—I can't bring myself to answer.

My father's smile wavers. "We better hit the road. We'll talk soon."

And then they're gone.

A twisting ache beneath my breastbone catches me off guard and I whirl around and race up the stairs to my new bedroom. I hardly know my grandmother, and I refuse to let her see me emotional.

Once in my room, I watch my parents' Honda Accord grow smaller from behind the gauzy curtains.

The car stops at the end of the road, and a crazy hope they'll change their minds and come back floods me. But no. Dad spins the wheel right and Mom doesn't turn her head to look back at the house even once.

They'll drive back to our perfect suburban home in Maryland in their spotless car and have their friends over as if nothing has happened. If asked about me, a lie will roll off their tongues. (Lying is permissible only in the *direst* of circumstances, which my mother has told me countless times, this absolutely is.)

I can hear her now. *"Emily is spending the summer with her grandmother. She's long overdue for a visit."*

Maybe not a complete lie, but certainly not the whole truth.

I step away from the curtain and flop on the twin bed, covered in a hideous floral bedspread. It's uglier than the pale yellow wallpaper peeling off the walls. The scent of mothballs and Avon perfume coat the entire house. I try to imagine my father growing up in this small coastal home, but I can't.

I glance at the phone on the nightstand beside a stack of books I've brought with me. A new book called *The Giver* by Lois Lowry. *Island of the Blue Dolphins* by Scott O'Dell. *The Outsiders* by S.E. Hinton—a reading assignment for my new school. And *The Thorn Birds*. Mom didn't let me read the latter when I was a freshman but had recently made a snide remark about me and the heroine having something in common.

I'd tried not to care what that was but couldn't contain my curiosity—I bought the novel from Waldenbooks with the birthday money my great-uncle sent last week. Now, I scan the room for a picture of him, but don't see any family photographs. Not that I would recognize him, anyway. All he does is send money and cards.

I push a lock of my shoulder length, light brown hair from my eyes and reach for the phone before realizing my mistake. I've received enough lectures from Mom to earn a college credit in how-to-act-at-Gram's.

"No calls back home," Mom had said. "Your grandmother doesn't have a long-distance plan."

But Ashley.... Just to hear my best friend's voice would make all of this better. Surely I'm imagining the space between us since I told her my secret. I've always had a good imagination—too good, really. I used to imagine E.T. hid in the depths of my closet when I was in elementary school. I probably imagined Bryan actually meant those three little words he'd told me in the back seat of his Dodge Viper.

Yes, that had to be it—my imagination had gotten the better of me. Ashley's parents must have heard rumors. They'd warned my best friend to stay away, but of course Ashley was totally on my side. Best friends forever, right?

I run a finger along the chain at my neck to the pendant—half a heart with the letters *Be* and *Fri*. Ashley gave it to me the summer before high school, taking the other half of the heart for herself and promising that no matter what high school brought, we'd get through it together.

No matter what.

I scoop up the phone and dial the long-ago memorized number, praying that Ashley—and not her parents—will answer.

She would be home from school by now but her parents should be at work—a perfect time to call.

"Hello?"

Relief washes over me. "Ashley, it's me. Thank God you answered. I'm dying over here." I pause to catch a breath and roll over on my back, settling in for one of our long conversations. She'd want to know what Gram's house is like, if the neighbors have any cute teenage sons, if the beach is as beautiful as I imagined. Of course, we'd also dump on Bryan. Affirm how all boys with flashy sports cars, football letters, Homecoming King titles, and smooth words should be annihilated from the face of the earth forever.

"Emily...hey."

The phone freezes in my hand. She sounds...distant.

I swallow. "Is your Mom right there?" Was that why she was being so careful?

Ashley clears her throat. "Listen, Em. I'm going to be super busy these next few weeks with graduation and prom. And I also have to think about college...maybe we'll have time to catch up when you get back."

When I get back? But by then she'd be at college, living the dorm life, finding a new best friend to give a necklace to. I shake my head. "I—I don't understand—"

"I'm sorry, but we're in different places in life right now, you know? You've got a lot going on, and so do I. Take care of yourself, Emily."

The line goes dead, but I can't bring myself to return the phone to its cradle. My breaths come fast and heavy and Gram's walls threaten to close in around me. Is this what a panic attack feels like?

I wind my hand around the broken heart at my neck. No, it can't be true. *No matter what.* That's what kind of friends we were supposed to be. How could the one person I thought would support me to the end abandon me?

I drape my arm over my forehead and close my eyes, my breaths carrying away with themselves, taking me to a place of despair. A tear slips its way down the side of my face.

"Emily!"

I swipe at the wetness and jolt up in the bed, shoving my emotions aside. I can never let Gram know how upset I am. "Yes, Gram?"

"Come help with dinner, please."

I sniff and hang up the phone. I can't afford to wallow in self-pity. Things would get better. By the end of the summer, all would return to normal.

I sit slumped on the edge of the bed. Though I have a few fond, hazy memories of my grandmother and this house during my growing up years, once we moved to Maryland and Dad won the election shortly thereafter, our time with Gram had waned. She sent birthday and Christmas cards with money, but when Mom gave me the choice to write or call with a "thank you," I always chose a short, impersonal note over an awkward telephone call.

After a few deep breaths, I drag myself to my feet and over the threshold. I pass her room on my way to the stairs and hesitate. While Gram knows my big secret, I know next to nothing about her. She hasn't bothered to visit us much. And now, I'm supposed to be grateful she has taken me in, go along with her rules and help her move her bedroom downstairs so she doesn't have to navigate the stairs any longer. I walk in, noting the floral artwork on the opposite wall.

A pan clatters downstairs as my gaze sweeps over the room. Gram's comforter is only slightly less hideous than mine—that same yellow color as my wallpaper. There is a single bureau across from the bed, a small writing desk between two windows, and a nightstand with a Bible, a rosary, and a journal on top of it. Above the headboard is a picture too small to tastefully be placed there— a black-and-white wedding photo. I lean against the bed for a closer look.

I recognize traces of my grandmother in the youthful face of the bride. Hard to believe someone so old could've ever been that young. She is holding a huge bouquet of calla lilies and wearing a simple bridal cap with a veil that melts into the rest of her dress. My grandfather—a man who died before I was old enough to remember him—stands beside her tall and proud and handsome in a tuxedo and slicked-back hair. They are both wearing small smiles, as if they know a secret the rest of us don't.

My gaze drops to the nightstand and I slide open the drawer. A fifty-dollar bill is tucked in the side, but I pass it by for a worn, black-and-white picture of two women and one man in front of a clapboard cottage.

I pull it out. The woman on the right wears a long dress and blouse. Her face looks a bit disfigured—her nose too big. The woman on the left—about my age, maybe a little older—wears a jacket over her dress.

She looks slightly familiar, but I can't say for certain it's my grandmother. The man in the middle holds what I think is a mandolin with deformed hands. Why would Gram keep a picture of a man other than her husband in her bedside table? I flip the photo over.

Penikese, 1917

I know this name, don't I? Yes, my grandfather opened a school for troubled boys on the island off the coast of Massachusetts. Dad used that bit of positive family history in his campaign. Did my grandmother visit there when she was younger? She'd been a nurse at one time—that fact had made its way into Dad's campaign, too. Maybe the island used to be a hospital of sorts?

"Emily!"

I jump and drop the picture back in its place, closing the drawer as quietly as I can. "Coming!"

I take my time going down the stairs, acting as if I've just dragged myself out of bed. Gram stirs rice on the stove. Her gray hair is short and curly. I wonder if she wears curlers to bed. She moves around the kitchen well for being eighty...eighty-something, I'm not exactly sure how old she is.

She raises an eyebrow at my arrival. The gesture draws neat, crinkly lines on her forehead. "I would appreciate your help with dinner every night."

"Yes, ma'am," I say respectfully.

"And if you'd like a tour of my room, next time I suggest you ask me to be your guide."

I open my mouth to make an excuse...I saw what I thought was an abandoned earring on the floor or I wanted to see what sort of furniture we needed to move downstairs this summer—but the lies stop up behind my lips at the look Gram is giving me. She apparently hasn't lost an ounce of her mental clarity.

"Yes, ma'am." If I'm not careful, she might figure out a whole bunch more about me than I want her to know. "What can I help with?"

"After you wash your hands, you may cut the broccoli."

I slip my hands under the faucet with a pump of soap. How am I going to manage with Gram watching my every move for the next several months?

I take the broccoli and knife and saw off the little green florets.

"Child! You're mutilating it. Here." She takes the knife from me and demonstrates how to cut the broccoli into neat little trees. "Didn't your mother teach you how to cook?"

I snort. "You don't know my mother, do you?"

Gram smiles for the first time since she saw my father earlier this afternoon. "That's right. Anne never did have much talent in the kitchen. How did you survive all your growing up years?"

I shrug. "Our chef."

Gram makes a *tsking* sound as she shakes her head. "My son has done quite well for himself, hasn't he?" A moment's pause. "Although I suppose if he'd concentrated more on his daughter than his career...."

I plop the head of broccoli down on the cutting board. "Look."

She raises an eyebrow, as if in challenge.

I take it. I might as well let her know right off that just because I let my parents talk me into this banishment doesn't mean that I plan to slink around in shame.

"I'm sorry my parents dumped my pregnant self onto you. And I get why I'm here—I'm an embarrassment to them. An embarrassment to my school, my community. Dad's *career*. I'm a freakin' outcast. But what's done is done."

Gram's mouth turns into a hard, grim line. "Dear, I shouldn't have implied...but, I promise I won't belittle you for your mistakes. In return, I expect you to use decent language while in this house. Is that understood?"

I sigh, but say, "Yes." If she's upset over the word "freakin'," this is going to be a long summer.

"And as far as being an outcast...I'm not sure you have the slightest clue what being an outcast involves."

As if she knows. And she'd just promised not to belittle me. I glance down at the unfinished broccoli head and plunk down the knife. "I'm not hungry." I leave and stomp up the stairs to my room.

I half expect her to demand I come back and help. But my mini temper tantrum is met with silence.

Once in my room, I close the door behind me—not quite a slam, but with enough teenage angst to be sure Gram hears.

But as soon as I'm alone in my room, the fight immediately drains out of me. I stare at the phone, willing it to ring. Willing Ashley's voice to be on the other end, to say she made a mistake in severing our friendship. Heck, I'd even take a call from Mom letting me know she misses me, but she wouldn't be home yet.

My hopes are met with nothing but silence.

I am completely and utterly alone. One bad decision—a moment that couldn't have lasted more than ten minutes—has cast me from my home, my school, my friends. It threatens my chance at going to college, my hopes of being an English teacher... everything.

I think of my parents' driving away without looking back. Part of their punishment is making sure I know just how ashamed they are of me.

If only they knew I feel enough shame for all of us.

Chapter Two

To say I am surprised when Gram asks me to take her 1974 Volkswagen Golf into town for a few groceries is an understatement—I hadn't gone downstairs the night before, hadn't apologized for my behavior. I had expected a loss of privileges, not a get-out-of-the-house-free card. Not to mention that I don't have much experience driving, but I don't admit that to my grandmother. She offers me the keys and hands me a grocery list and some cash with directions on how to get to *Fancy's Market*.

After my shopping is done, I tuck the bag of groceries on the passenger seat beside me and turn left out of the store's parking lot toward the neatly-landscaped shops and postcard-perfect people adorning the sidewalk. A sign tells me to take another left to get to the library and I don't hesitate.

When I enter the old building, I breathe in the scents of musty books and secret knowledge. I tug my loose black T-shirt down and casually drape the sides of my open button-down shirt across my stomach. Soon I will be so big there will be no use hiding it.

I readjust my pocketbook over my shoulder, cross my arms, and walk into the depths of the library. The main floor is lit with tall windows and a beautiful children's room. I walk down the split staircase to peruse the fiction titles. I soon have a generous pile of books that will last at least through the following week. *Jazz* by Toni Morrison and the first three books in the *Flowers in the Attic* series by V.C. Andrews. I hesitate when I see a new book in the Nancy Drew Files series—*Dangerous Relations*. Though I haven't read Nancy Drew in years, I add the book to the pile. Unlike my real friends, fictional friends have never let me down. Ashley may have left me alone, but Nancy would always be there for me.

I approach the counter on the main floor. A boy about my age, maybe a little younger, mans the desk. His dark curly hair and thick black glasses make him look intelligent in a non-nerdy way.

"Find what you were looking for?"

I prop my books on the counter, effectively hiding my midsection. "Yes, but I don't have a card, but I'll be here for...awhile. I'm visiting my grandmother." The baby's due at the end of August. So until then, at least.

"I'll just need your address."

I give him Gram's address, and my gaze wanders to the banner above his head. Cartoon drawings of musical instruments advertise an outdoor music festival at a nearby park. My eyes catch on the drawing of a mandolin, and I think of the black-and-white picture in Gram's drawer.

"Do you have any information on Penikese? I think it's an island."

The librarian—is that what the boy is?—flicks his gaze from his computer to me. His eyes are a deep blue, clear and sharp through the lens of his glasses. "It is," he says.

I inch closer to the desk. "You know about it?"

He smirks. "Every boy around here has been threatened at one time or another with being sent to the school there. It's for delinquent boys."

The school my grandfather helped start. But that picture in my grandmother's drawer was too old to be part of the school. I study the boy. "You don't seem the type to give your parents grief."

He smiles, and I notice a faint dimple. "You'd be surprised."

"Oh, really?" But he doesn't volunteer more. "So, any good books on Penikese that I might be able to check out?"

He types something into his computer. "I'll be right back. Here." He slides a library card toward me. "Sign this."

I do. In a couple minutes, he's back, adding a book called *Castaways* to my pile. "That's all we have." He avoids my gaze, seems as if he wishes to say something, but doesn't. Instead, he begins scanning my books.

"You like working here?" With his thick glasses and knowledge of books, this boy seems the very opposite of Bryan. Was it possible to be friends—and only friends—with a boy? I'd never given it much thought. But how was I going to make it all summer without Ashley? Without someone I trusted to reassure me that I was doing the right thing?

"Yeah. I like checking out all the new books first, seeing what everyone else is reading."

"I've never met a boy librarian before."

He shrugs. "What can I say? I like books and it's a decent job." He holds up *Flowers in the Attic* and raises his eyebrow.

I try to keep a blush from climbing my neck. "I figured I'd find out what all the hype is about."

He shakes his head, but a smile tugs at one corner of his mouth. "You want a great read?" He digs beneath the desk and pulls out a white book with a black, skeletal T-Rex on the cover. "*This* is reading."

I scrunch up my nose. "I'm not much for science fiction."

He taps the book. "Movie's coming out next month. It's always best to read the book first."

"Thanks, but I think I'm already overloaded. I won't have time to read all these before they're due."

He adds *Jurassic Park* to the top of my pile. "That's my copy. Keep it as long as you want. Maybe when you're done, I'll take you to see the movie."

A sharp guard goes up inside me at the thought of anything resembling a date. This kid doesn't know me. And soon, it will be apparent that I'm not the type of girl a nice boy who works at the library will want to be seen walking around town with.

"I have a boyfriend," I blurt out, and immediately hate myself. "I mean...I did have a boyfriend."

He looks as if he might laugh. Instead, he slips a printed paper with the due dates into the copy of *Jurassic Park*. "Okay...you can still borrow the book. If you don't like it, I won't hold you to the movie. Deal?"

"Deal."

He picks up the books to place them closer to me. I notice the slight ripple of muscles beneath his T-shirt.

"Hey, I'm looking for someone to move some furniture for my grandmother. It's a paying job." At least now it is—hopefully Gram will approve. "You interested?"

He shrugs. "Sure. I have a buddy who's always looking for odd jobs. I'm sure we could manage with the two of us."

"Great. I have to pack some stuff first. But I guess I know where to find you."

He smiles, and it's a nice smile. The kind of smile you feel all the way down to your toes. Not in a romantic way, but in a way that makes you feel like everything's going to be okay.

"I guess you do."

I return his smile and gather my books. "Thanks for your help." I turn toward the doors.

"Let me know how you like the book!" he calls a little too loudly for the library.

Once in the car, I roll down the windows and breathe in the fresh spring air. A hint of salty sea swirls around me. I sink into the warmth of it all and grab an apple from the grocery bag beside me. I flip open to the first page of *Jurassic Park*.

I read the title of the Prologue: *The Bite of the Raptor* and flip it shut. I can't. Not even for Cute Library Boy.

I kick myself for not asking his name as I dig out the book on Penikese. It's written by a man named George Cadwalader. I flip through it, perking up at the sight of my grandfather's name in the introduction. He, Mr. Cadwalader, and three other men recruited a group of "well-educated social drop-outs" as teachers to experiment in the rehab of juvenile delinquents at their island school.

I turn the page, my eye catching on a quote.

Society has made them its enemies. Therefore, weak though they be, they will wage such war as they can.

— DR. FRANK PARKER WRITING IN 1905 OF THE LEPERS WHO WERE THEN QUARANTINED FOR LIFE ON PENIKESE ISLAND.

The word *lepers* draws me in.

Penikese had been a leper colony?

I remember the deformed hands of the man holding the mandolin in Gram's picture. I skim through the next few pages, searching for more information.

Could that have been Gram's connection, then? Had she been a nurse at the leper hospital all those years ago? I do a quick calculation in my head. She wouldn't have been old enough, I don't think....

Her words from the night before come back to me.

As far as being an outcast...dear, I'm not sure you have the slightest clue what being an outcast involves.

I swallow and fumble the keys of the car while jamming them into the ignition. Gram can't possibly understand what it's like to be in my shoes, but what did she mean when she said I didn't know what it was like to be an outcast?

"Did you find everything at the market?" Gram asks when I enter her house with my library books and the grocery bag.

"I think so. I made a stop at the library, too."

I put the books on the table with *Castaways* on top, in hopes she'll notice.

She doesn't disappoint. When she sees it, she picks it up and smiles wistfully. "Now what on earth made you choose this one?"

I decide not to disclose the extent of my snooping last night. "That was the school Grandpa helped start, wasn't it?"

She runs a finger over the scarlet title. "I didn't think your father talked about it."

"He doesn't. But someone mentioned it during one of his campaigns, I think."

She releases a short sigh and nods. "I see. Well, it warms my heart that you're interested in your grandfather's work, dear."

"I—I am." I grab the bag of apples out of the grocery bag and open the refrigerator door, my heart thudding. "Did Grandpa ever hear from any of the boys from the school? You know, after they left?" Had my grandfather helped the juvenile castaways find a better life? If there was hope for them, could that mean there was hope for me as well?

Gram nods. "Some. Though many of the boys didn't want to be helped. That was half the battle." She eyes me, but her gaze doesn't stay long, and I sense she is stopping herself from veering into a lecture.

I slide a bag of carrots into the vegetable drawer. "Did you know the island used to be a leper colony?" I don't look at her as I say this, but I sense her hesitation.

"I do."

I swallow before I speak. "I saw the picture you have in your nightstand last night."

She hands me a bag of oranges and I meet her ocean-blue gaze, shrouded with secrets and maybe something like hurt.

"I'm sorry for snooping," I whisper. "But could you tell me who was in that picture? Was one of the women you?"

She lowers herself to a chair. The sun from the kitchen window splashes bright rays on her plaid, button-down shirt. "Your father would not like it if I tell you."

Now I *really* want to know. "But I'd like you to tell me...."

She covers her mouth with one hand and I'm afraid she's going to cry.

"Gram, it's okay. You don't have to—"

"Her story should be told. I've thought so for a long time."

I pull out a chair and sit. "Her story?"

"Atta. My sister."

I lean forward. Gram had a sister?

"Not just her story. *Our* story. Our family story."

My forehead crinkles. "Then why wouldn't Dad want me to know about it?"

"Your father...feels social stigmas, like horrible sicknesses and" —she raises her eyebrow at my stomach—"other such dilemmas, are best left buried when you lead a public life. I've never put up much of a fight with him, but having you here, dear...well, I'm beginning to question if I should have."

"He doesn't have to know that I know. Please tell me."

Her bottom lip trembles. "If I don't, the story may very well die with me." She reaches out her hand to grasp mine. "I don't want it to die with me, Emily. I want it to live on."

I nod, quiet, unwilling to break the moment.

She continues. "It's a tough story. But I promise you, it is full of one thing very dear to my heart."

"What's that?"

"Hope."

My insides warm. Gram's words remind me of a storybook or a novel that promises a satisfying ending. Why does my father not want me to know about our family's history if it's full of hope? "Tell me, Gram. Please?"

"Perhaps a cup of tea is in order?" She gives me a small smile before she stands and heads over to the stove.

I hold my breath in anticipation.

Gram hands me a mug and an assortment of tea bags. "After our mother died, my sister was all I had. I couldn't imagine life without her. But it seemed fate had other plans."

About the Author

Heidi Chiavaroli (pronounced shev-uh-roli...sort of like *Chevrolet* and *ravioli* mushed together!) wrote her first story in third grade, titled *I'd Cross the Desert for Milk*. Years later, she revisited writing, using her two small boys' nap times to pursue what she thought at the time was a foolish dream.

Heidi's debut novel, *Freedom's Ring*, was a Carol Award winner and a Christy Award finalist, a *Romantic Times* Top Pick and a *Booklist* Top Ten Romance Debut. Her latest Carol Award-winning dual timeline novel, *The Orchard House*, is inspired by the lesser-known events in Louisa May Alcott's life and compelled her to create The Orchard House Bed and Breakfast series. Heidi makes her home in Massachusetts with her husband and two sons. Visit her online at heidichiavaroli.com